RUIN

WILLOW ASTER

To all of you who tried so hard to talk me into watching Game of Thrones...thank you.

Ruin
Kingdoms of Sin, Book 3
Copyright © 2020 by Willow Aster
ISBN 13: 978-1-7335137-4-6

Cover by: Hang Le
Photography by: Wander Aguiar
Cover Model: Andrew
Editing: Christine Estevez
Beta: Jennifer Mirabelli
Represented by: Brower Literary & Management

PREFACE

This book is a romance based entirely on fictional places. It is set in the present where there are monarchies in a world that doesn't operate quite like ours. There are no dragons or fairies, but there is lust, greed, pride, and wrath...something that exists in any world and has since the beginning of time.

Any mistakes I make in properly conveying royal practices and whatnot, I hope you will excuse and consider that in the kingdoms of Farrow, Niaps, Alidonia, and beyond, perhaps it's just the way it is.

List of Characters:

Safrin Family of Farrow:

>Neil* & Kathryn, father and mother
>Jadon, son of Neil and stepson of Kathryn
>Eden Safrin Catano, daughter, married to Luka Catano
>Ava, daughter

Catano Family of Niaps:

>Titus & Cecilia (Cece), father and mother
>Basile, brother to Cecilia
>Luka, son, married to Eden Safrin Catano
>Mara, daughter, married to Elias Lancaster

Also in Niaps:

>Brienne Jarvis, bodyguard to Eden
>Elias Lancaster, advisor to Luka, married to Mara Catano Lancaster
>Gentry Barrington, friend of Elias

Forbrush Family of Yuman:

>Victros & Anais, father and mother
>Alex, son
>Nadia, daughter

Farthing Family of Alidonia:

>Vance & Jonquil*, father and mother
>Omar, son
>Delilah, daughter
>Caulder, nephew, advisor to Vance

*deceased

PROLOGUE

Ava

I adjust the straps to my dress, feeling hot even though I'm wearing a sheer, flowy evening gown with barely any substance. Mother would be appalled to see my glowy-white cleavage sparkling in the afternoon sun. She'd also be shocked at the new tattoos I've added to the colorful sleeve on my right arm and the blue I've added to my long black hair, but she's not here.

Ahh, freedom. I grin and twirl a few times, feeling the material of my dress skimming the back of my thighs as I turn. Niaps is hot as Hades for someone used to the snow. I walk through the gate from the beach, my toes sinking into the thick grass and curling with pleasure. For all my complaints about the heat, I could get used to the constant sunshine. Even if it doesn't like me. I put a hand to my chest and smooth out the coconut sunscreen that's thicker on my collarbone.

"No one told me shoes weren't required for this wedding."

I turn and see a guy standing against the gate I just walked through. I don't know how I could've missed him — his dark eyes are drilling into me and I could swear they like what they see. God knows I like what *I* see. His hair looks like my hands have already been running through it, yanking it to my will. I bite back a smile.

"If you can't go barefoot to a beach wedding, what's the point?"

His lips pucker out with thought and my eyes track the movement. Holy hormones, he has the most kissable lips I've ever seen. He bends down and takes off his shoes, smirking, and I laugh.

"I sort of want to untuck your shirt, but your outfit seems a bit more proper than mine. You're in the wedding, yeah?" I recognize the tie from seeing Elias and Luka getting ready earlier.

He grins and untucks his shirt. It's the sexiest thing I've ever seen.

"My God, you are stunning," he says under his breath. "Colorful," he adds, his lips hitching up on either side. His eyes skate across my chest, which is as white as the purest snow and I know he wants to make an exception to his *colorful* statement, but he has enough manners to keep that to himself.

"Thank you," I whisper, feeling a moment of shyness.

Shy, I am *not,* but there's something about the way he

looks at me. Definitely something about the way his eyes on me makes me tingle from my head to my toes.

Like he's seeing something beyond the rebellious princess of Farrow, kid sister to the most beautiful Eden Catano, now queen of Niaps, and also kid sister to the most perfect, handsome Jadon Safrin, now king of Farrow.

There's no way I can succeed with siblings like them, so I don't even try anymore. I want nothing to do with the monarchy—no, thank you—and since they're so good at doing what they do—being perfect—I'll continue doing me. Some call me trouble, I like to think I'm simply not dull. I'll never have to bother with any of it as long as everything keeps running smoothly, which I have every confidence it will.

"What's your name?" I ask.

"Gentry Barrington. And yours?"

"I'm Ava."

"Ava—" he draws out, waiting for the rest.

"Just Ava."

He grins and I feel that fluttery feeling again across my chest and stomach and knees, like I could go down if he keeps smiling at me like that. I clear my throat and nod.

"Save me a dance, Just Ava."

"I'll be sure to do that." I put my hand on his arm and grin, passing him to walk inside. I need to cool off after that encounter. All I can think about is how much I already look forward to seeing him again.

I can't keep my eyes off of Gentry during Mara and Elias's wedding. It's a gorgeous wedding, but he's so distracting;

every time I look at him, he's looking at me too. The lights flicker across the beach and the sound of the waves is the most glorious backdrop. The sunshine from earlier leaves me feeling intoxi- cated and I decide to wander away from the party after I've eaten. I want to step in the water and let it cool me off. I start following a line of shells, picking them up and holding them in my dress as I walk. The water feels so good, I keep going.

"Are you avoiding our dance?" His voice is like butter melting down my back and I shiver before slowly turning around.

"Not possible," I tell him.

He grins and his eyes widen when he sees all the shells in my makeshift pocket. I carefully step out of the water and lower my dress to the sand, letting the shells fall into a chaotic heap. I dust off my hands and then curtsy in front of him.

"Oh, we're doing this here?" He laughs.

"Why not?"

He holds out his hand and I take it, feeling a thrill at the stomach drop that accompanies it. The sound of the music in the distance is muted, but we can still hear it enough to keep time. I step closer to him, until my head is against his chest, and we begin to slowly sway. I close my eyes and let myself feel everything. My hands around his neck, my ears listening to the *thump, thump, thump* of his heart, the way his hands feel on my bare shoulder and waist. I sigh and look up at him. He's looking down at me, his lips parted and eyes glimmering with the moonlight. He fits the face of the man of my dreams in that moment. The man all future men will never live up to.

His hand moves to my cheek and we stop swaying. Time stops. My lips feel drawn to his and I step on my tiptoes to chase it, just as he lowers his mouth to mine. The music fades away and all of my senses explode from *him*.

His sigh into my mouth.

His taste of peppermint and whiskey. The heady rush of his hands on me.

It takes my breath away, an all-consuming kiss where nothing else exists.

The kiss starts out soft and sweet, a tentative taste, and then it develops wings and soars. My legs weaken and he holds me tighter against him as we explore each other, until I don't know where he begins and I end.

It is an awakening. I'm aware that I will never be the same after this kiss.

And I wouldn't want to be.

CHAPTER ONE

THREE MONTHS LATER

AVA

"Surprise! Happy Birthday!" The sound of horns and the roomful of people yelling assaults my senses when I open the door.

I jump, stare at them with horror and then glee, and then laugh my head off when I see Eden skipping toward me. I love how Luka has lightened her up. I used to be the crazy one and now she has moments when she's really fun. It's nice.

She hugs me and Luka throws his arms around us too. Brienne blows a horn in my ear and I glare at her. She lifts her eyebrows and I can't hold the glare any longer.

"I don't turn eighteen for another month. What are you guys thinking?" I push back from Eden and grin at Mara and Elias.

"You've been traveling since the wedding and start school tomorrow—three months after it's started, senior year. You'll have too much to think about in a month. Let's get our fun in now." Mara pulls a face and groans. She's really grown on me. "With all of Luka's upcoming trips, we figured we better do it now while we're all together."

"*And* we wanted to surprise you," Eden adds.

"Well, thank you," I say, throwing my arm over Mara's shoulder.

She's shorter than me, but we're able to wear the same size and I eye the dress she's wearing now. She grins knowingly and shrugs my arm off, reaching for a big gift box.

"Thought you might like something like this," Mara says.

"Let's eat first, then presents," Eden says.

Mara and I both frown at her and Eden sighs.

"Okay, okay. God, one of you is enough. Two of you is like I'm being punished eternally right here on earth." Eden tries to look mad, but the smirk is trying to fight its way out.

I kiss her cheek and she waves her arm at me.

"Go on, go on, open it," she says.

I do and inside is a gorgeous dress similar to the one Mara is wearing.

"Part of my new line, and there are only four just like this one," she says, her cheeks turning the slightest tinge of pink. I've never seen Mara blush, but it's a good look on her. She doesn't have any reason to be vulnerable—her clothing line with Zsa has exploded.

"Wow. Thank you, Mara. I love it so much."

She shrugs a shoulder, but I can tell she's happy about my excitement.

"I've missed you guys. Farrow was so dull. Jadon was

gone most of the time. Mother is being obnoxious about him still…and don't even get me started on my visit to Jorga." I shudder and let out a long exhale. "This is feeling more and more like home all the time."

I don't mention that I haven't been able to stop thinking about Gentry since I left. I had to leave unexpectedly after the wedding. Mother insisted I accompany her on a trip to visit one of our relatives, a sick aunt that I'd never even met before our trip. I think Mother is lonely without Eden, but instead of coming here for frequent visits, she badgers Jadon about what an awful job he's doing with the kingdom.

He's not doing an awful job. He's exactly what Farrow needs; she's just always been too hard on him.

But Gentry…he never strayed from my thoughts. Some- times he was the only light during the monotonous days. I wish I'd found out more about him. We kissed and kissed and then realized we'd been away from the wedding too long. Gentry needed to get back to Elias and I helped Eden decorate Mara and Elias's car before they left for their honeymoon. When I got back to the beach, he was gone. I never told anyone about our kiss, not even Eden. Mother showed up the night after the wedding and we left the morning after that. I want to ask Elias about him, but everyone is excited to have me back and asking me tons of questions.

"I don't want to talk about the trip. It was painful. Trust me, you don't want to hear about it either. You know I want to travel the world, but Jorga is a place I can do without ever visiting again. It's flat and humid and the people there are bitter."

"Bitter?" Luka asks.

"Yes, like they know they need to get out of there but can't."

"That does sound painful," he says. "But wouldn't you rather be there than going back to school? A new school at that?"

"I can't wait. It's my senior year—I've already missed way more than I should've. Miss Dianthus and I butted heads over everything she tried to teach me—trust me, I cannot wait to get to school. And I want to learn to surf... I'm with you guys. What could be better?"

If Gentry were here too, I think, but I just smile at them and open the rest of the presents. We eat after that and I duck out of the party early to try to get back on Niaps time. I wish I could've been here at least a few weeks before school to adjust, but it just didn't work out. I toss and turn and finally fall asleep to the thought of Gentry's lips on mine.

It makes Eden a nervous wreck, but I promise her for the dozenth time that I'll be careful as I put on my helmet and hop on my scooter, backpack in place.

The high school looks more like an old convent than a high school. I love old architecture and this is prime stuff. I whistle as I park my bike and take in the stone buildings built into the cliff overlooking the beach.

"Only in Niaps," I say, shaking my head.

A girl turns to look at me and hurriedly turns away when she sees the tattoos on my arm.

"I don't bite," I say just loud enough for her to hear.

Her cheeks get pink and she walks faster to get away

from me. I laugh, I can't help it. I remember Mara being surprised I had tattoos already, but at home, it's not that unusual for someone my age to have them. The full sleeve is not common, and I wish now that I'd worn my shortest black leather skirt to show off the flowers on my leg. I'll show those off another day.

I walk down the hall and find my locker, dumping my backpack inside and getting out the books I'll need for the next three classes. I'm walking into my sociology class just as the bell is ringing. The door is closing and I grab it before it closes all the way. The person on the other side stops pushing the door and I step inside.

"Ava?"

His voice stops me and I look up, feeling that rush that comes with being near him.

"Gentry! What are you—" I put my hand on his arm and squeeze, my teeth hurting from smiling so wide.

He steps back and the smile he gives me is forced. "Miss Safrin, come in. Class is just getting started."

I look at him and then past him to the rest of the class sitting and watching our whole exchange. My heart catapults to the ground, the ceiling, and back to the ground again, when I glance at the board behind him and see *MR. BARRINGTON* written in large block letters.

His face is pale when I look at him again and I move numbly to the empty desk, nearly tripping over someone's backpack.

Shit, shit, shit, shit, shit.

The guy I've been obsessing over for months is my *teacher*.

And by the sick look on his face, he wants nothing to do with me.

CHAPTER TWO

AVA

The fifty-minute class is excruciating. I want him to look at me, to see even the tiniest bit of acknowledgment that I didn't dream up our whole encounter on the beach. That he felt even a fraction of what I felt that night...

But he does everything possible to avoid looking at me. After his introduction, he talks about what he'll be covering in the class.

The guy in front of me turns around and his eyes widen as he takes a long look. "Helloooo," he whispers. His brow creases as he checks me out and then makes a sound like fire sizzling. "Hot."

I groan. "Original. Turn around."

Gentry clears his throat and I realize he's right here, standing near my desk. The guy in front of me turns to face forward again and Gentry moves away from us. I feel the loss of his attention and wish he'd come back.

I sit there and watch the way his mouth seductively spills out words that I can't seem to concentrate on because all I can think about is the way he made my heart pound with that same mouth. He looks even better than I remembered, if that's possible. I had built him up to be quite a god by the time I'd been out of Niaps for a month, but is he ever living up to the hype. His lesson starts out tentatively, as if he's somewhat nervous, but it's endearing, and by the end of the class, he's found his stride. The result is so damn enticing, I don't know what I'll do if I can't kiss him again. Today. I had to have imagined that expression on his face earlier.

By the time the bell rings, I can't take it anymore. I wait until the class empties out and when I walk up to his desk, I hold onto the edge to avoid reaching out for him. His eyes take in my hand and then slowly travel up to my cheek. I will him to fully look at me, but he seems stuck. He swallows hard and leans back in his chair.

"Hi," I say softly.

"Hello." His voice is so formal he doesn't even sound like the same guy he did a minute ago.

My heart picks up a few beats with nerves and anticipation.

"It's good to see you," I try again.

His chin lifts and he still hasn't looked me in the eye. "The bell is going to ring in about two—"

"Did you know?" I ask. My voice sounds shaky and I turn to the side and clear my throat.

"Did I know what?"

"That you were going to be my teacher?" I don't mean now, I mean that day…on the beach. Somehow I think he'll know what I'm asking.

He stands up and turns his back to me, which makes me angry. "No, I didn't. I had no idea you were…a child."

My head rolls back, my eyes to the ceiling. I'll never let

him know his words hurt me, but they do. They sting. "You and I both know I'm not a child."

"You're a child in comparison to me, Ava. I would have never—" he starts and I see red.

I have thought of practically nothing but this guy...this man—God, how old is he anyway? He looks way younger than Elias or Luka. He can't be that much older than me. And now he wants to act like that night meant nothing?

"I never would have either had I known you're an old man," I lie.

A laugh sputters out of him. "I'm hardly old, but I am too old for *you*."

This isn't going how I wanted this to go at all. I hate how dismissive he seems. "I'll try to get out of this class so we don't have to see one another."

"That's hardly necessary. I'm sure we can manage this. It's only one class, right?" He turns to look at me and crosses his arms over his chest. I take in the way his long sleeve shirt tightens and remember the way his biceps felt under my fingers. I take a deep breath and nod.

"It was months ago. A lot has changed since then anyway." I shrug and look at him as if he's nothing.

His jaw ticks and he stares at me. Finally. "Right. Well, I better get ready for the next class. Take care, Ava."

"You too, Gentry."

"You should probably call me Mr. Barrington here."

I squeeze my books against my chest and try to calm down before speaking. "*Right*. Mr. Barrington."

I fight not to roll my eyes and manage to wait until I've turned around, so he doesn't think I'm as childish as I apparently am. I walk to the door and turn to look at him one more time. He's watching me, but when I turn, he drops his arms and faces the board. I want to go kickbox all of the anger out of my system, but I've only got one class behind me. It's going to be a long road if I have to see Gentry—Mr. Barrington—every day.

I keep my head down most of the day. I know I should be trying to make friends, but I'm shook, okay? I'm trying to make sense of what's happening here. I've done nothing but dream about the day I could get back to Niaps to see Gentry and now that I'm here, I find out he's my fucking teacher. Great, just fucking great.

I hear Eden and my mother cleaning up my language even in my head and I angrily slam my locker shut. I came to Niaps to avoid being the perfect little princess of Farrow. I'm so not that and will never be, but I still manage to have their voices chirping over my shoulder when I feel like throwing all caution to the wind. As it is now, when I'd love nothing more than to skip this day and run to the beach.

"What's up, hottie?"

I look up, already annoyed, and it's the guy from my first class.

"Name's Ava, learn it. Hottie doesn't work for me."

He frowns and laughs at the same time. "Uptight. I can work with that. I'm Toph. You're new around here?"

As annoying as he is, he seems harmless and I could use a friend. He's cute in an obnoxious boy band kind of way. Not my type whatsoever, but hell, my type seems to be older men who are off-limits, so who am I to judge?

"Yeah. My sister lives here, so I've been in and out, but yeah, here I am, senior year, woohoo," I say dryly.

He grins and his blue eyes light up. "Come on, I'll introduce you to everyone at lunch."

I bite my lip, holding back. I'm a loner through and through. I'm not sure I want to meet a crew of people. But he motions for me to follow and I do.

We grab our lunch of spaghetti—it looks better than I expected school spaghetti to look—and my eyes scan the cafeteria for Gentry. I stop walking when I see him getting a drink, but then he turns around and sees me staring.

"You coming?" Toph calls.

Gentry looks at Toph and back at me, then turns abruptly and walks out of the cafeteria. I wonder where he goes to eat lunch.

Toph nudges me and I follow him to the table. A slew of introductions are made.

Linney beams at me, Jemima waves, Malcolm is across from Jemima and he says hello, and Jacque is next to Linney and also grinning. They all stare at me expectantly and I lift a hand.

"Hey," I mumble.

"You're the queen's sister, right?" "What do you think of Niaps?"

"What made you come here for your senior year?"

The questions are rapid-fire and I finally hold up a hand. "Whoa." I laugh and sit down next to Malcolm. Toph sits on the other side of me. "Yes, I'm Eden's sister and I like Niaps. I needed something other than snow in my life and love to travel, so why not?"

"So bold," Linney says, again with the massive smile.

I find myself smiling back. "You only live once, right?"

I look around for Gentry again, hoping he'll come back through so I can get another glimpse, but he doesn't. I try to keep up with the conversation at the table, even though my brain is hyper-focused on Gentry. I need to talk to him away from school. It's too weird here, too taboo, but maybe he'll be different somewhere neutral.

I just can't let go of him that fast.

He made me feel wanted, safe, beautiful...special. And I could swear he felt all of it too.

At the very least, I need to know if he just kisses every girl he comes across and makes them feel like they've rocked his world.

It was just a kiss, I remind myself. A life-changing kiss.

CHAPTER THREE

GENTRY

It takes willpower I didn't know I possessed not to curse like a sailor when Ava Safrin walks out of the classroom. I've been trying to clean up my mouth since I got here, with Elias constantly reminding me my potty mouth won't work as a teacher.

It's fucking hard.

How I didn't put it together when I saw Ava at Elias's wedding baffles me, that she was the younger sister of Eden Catano, the lovely new queen of Niaps. I was utterly charmed by her; the intoxicating eyes lured me in first, her velvety long black hair with the blue threaded throughout only making her eyes more beautiful. Her sweet, tight little body with the full breasts and pale, pale skin except for the explosion of color on her right arm and left leg. I wanted to explore her tattoos up close and personal, preferably in my bed as the sunlight lit her up.

I pace in the class, willing myself to calm down and

berating myself for being the sick pervert that I am. I've never been attracted to a seventeen-year-old girl before. Never. In fact, in the past, I've gone out with girls who were older than me, so I did *not* see that fuckery coming. But no, it's just *her*; she's captivating. And I might not have known how young she was when I met her, but I don't have that excuse now.

I'm just glad I got out of there before having sex with her the night of the wedding. Because the way I felt that night, her lips on mine, that immediate connection I haven't had with anyone...I could have easily let myself get lost in her. Fate stepped in and we went our separate ways due to the obligations of the wedding, but I didn't stop thinking about her.

It was a week after the wedding when I got the nerve to ask Elias about the guest at his wedding that he let me know in no uncertain terms to stay the fuck away from Ava.

"Back up. You're talking about Eden's sister, right?" he asked.

"About this tall, black hair, a voice like an angel?"

He turned up his nose and I got a sick feeling in my chest.

"She's too young, man. You can't go there."

I put my hands on my hips and tried to think through every interaction with her that day. Not once did I think she was too young. The tattoos alone scream maturity, but her *eyes*; despite her quick wit, her eyes have depth, like she's been through some rough times and still manages to find the light side.

"I thought she was my age, maybe a year or two younger."

"Seventeen."

No. I had to sit down. Finally, I whistled a long, painful whistle that sounded like an eagle dying. Didn't make me feel one fuckwit better.

"She's out of town but supposed to come back to finish out her senior year here."

"What have I done to deserve this fresh hell?"

He laughed and rubbed his hand over his face. "Stay away from her. Got me? That's Luka's sister-in-law. You don't want him on your bad side."

"How did I miss that?"

"Something tells me you weren't thinking with your head that day, not the right one anyway." He walked over and got in my face, still laughing. "Snap out of it. Go find someone else to occupy your mind. Right away."

I groaned. "I need this job. I won't screw it up."

He studied me closer, his eyes narrowing in a way that I didn't like. "Nothing happened, right? You guys didn't—"

"No," I rushed to get out, even though I could still feel the way her body pressed against mine and could see the way her lips were parted and shiny when we broke away from each other. "Nothing happened."

Except everything.

I've tried my best to push her out of my mind since finding out her age. It hasn't been easy. And when school started and there was no sign of Ava the first week, the first month, two, three months later, I started breathing a helluva lot easier...even though I haven't forgotten about her.

Yesterday after classes, I got word that we had a new student coming in and didn't even consider it being Ava. I thought I was in the clear. When I looked over the attendee list this morning, I realized I was screwed.

I'll have to live with seeing her every damn day in my first-hour class.

I am so fucked.

.   .   .

I make it to lunchtime in one piece and don't see Ava again. Maybe I can do this. One class each day for six months, no big deal. And then I feel the hair on the back of my neck rise. I look up and she's staring at me from across the room. She's with that kid who was hitting on her earlier. *Fuck me.* I get out of there and drive to the beach for the next half hour, not bothering to eat my lunch.

When I make it back to school with ten minutes to spare, Phoebe and Lindsey, two of the teachers who have been very welcoming, are standing outside my door.

"We missed you at lunch," Phoebe says.

She's the more outspoken of the two. A friendly girl with an easy smile, she's been helpful in all things school-related since we met. She'd like to be helpful in other ways too—the best way I know to describe her expression when I catch her checking me out is *hungry...like a wolf*—but I've managed to keep her at a distance.

Lindsey looks young enough to be one of the students, dark-haired and shy. I've seen firsthand how her calm demeanor resonates with the students. I don't catch any desperate vibes rolling off of her; so I'd prefer to hang out with her than Phoebe any day. Now, for instance, Phoebe is tapping her foot anxiously, waiting for —who knows what — while Lindsey just smiles and holds up a bag of cookies, dangling them in front of my face. She made them the first week of school and I was an instant fan. My eyes widen and I snatch the bag.

"For me?" I ask as she's already nodding. "Thank you." I pull one out and immediately eat it, groaning. "I needed this."

"Where'd you go?" Phoebe asks, foot tapping faster.

"I took a little drive. Needed to get out of here for a bit." "You missed the beach carnival meeting," she says with no small amount of agitation and I curse under my breath. "I'm so sorry. Dammit. Did Everst say anything?"

"He asked where you were and I told him you had to take care of a family emergency during lunch," Lindsey says, grinning.

I smile back and shake the bag of cookies. "I owe you double. Can one of you screenshot your notes for me? I'll do my best to catch up."

Phoebe grits her teeth at Lindsey and nods. Lindsey fiddles with her phone and in seconds, my phone dings with the notes from her.

"Three and 0. Stop now before I owe you my life."

I hold up my hand to them and enter the classroom, thankful for another distraction. Planning the carnival will keep me busy. Hopefully too busy to think about one certain student.

By the time I get home from work that night, I've calmed down. I don't know what I'm so worked up over—it's not like I even know Ava. So we had a connection one night at a wedding. We had chemistry, big deal.

I've been too busy moving to Niaps, working on my little house overlooking the beach, and getting settled into my job…I haven't had time to meet many new people. I've seen Elias occasionally and he tells me I need to get laid every time I see him, and he's right, I do. Seeing Ava confirms that. It's time I figure out how to put all thoughts of her out of my head—something I should've done the minute I knew how old she was.

My phone rings and I check it before answering. Dad. I pick up on the second ring.

"Hey, how are you?"

"I'm good, son." His rattling cough gives away his lie. "Just checking on you."

I pause. He sounds like he has more to say, but the line is quiet. "Nothing too crazy going on here. Other than wrangling kids all day, that's about all the excitement I've had."

He chuckles. "You need to get out more."

"So you and Elias keep telling me."

"Listen, I hate to ask—I know you're busy there—but do you think you could make it home this weekend? There's something I'd like to talk to you about."

My breath quickens and I rub my hand over my face. "You sure you're okay? The cancer isn't back, is it?"

"No, no." He coughs again.

"Dad…have you been to the doctor lately?"

"Yes, and I'm fine," he says quietly. "I just really need to see you—"

"Of course I'll come." It's a five-hour drive and I was just there two weeks ago, but my dad has never asked me for anything. "I need to see you too. It'll be nice to be home."

"Great." He sounds a little better already and the guilt that I'm all these miles away when he needs me hits hard. "I'm sure I won't see your mom for days while she's going crazy in the kitchen for you, but it's worth it."

We laugh, but then he sighs into the phone.

"What's going on?" I ask him. "You don't sound like yourself."

"Didn't sleep much, I guess. I'm sorry I need to run, Gentry. Uncle Ryle and Aunt Harrah are here and getting antsy for supper. I'll see you on Saturday, yes? Let us know when you're getting close."

"I will. Love you, Dad."

"I love you too, son."

I hang up and start grading papers, hoping I can get ahead enough this week that a trip home won't set me back too far. A weekend far from Ava might be exactly what I need.

CHAPTER FOUR

AVA

When I get home from school that afternoon, Eden and Brienne are waiting for me.

"How was your—" Eden starts.

"Good. Met some people, decent classes, lots of home-work already." My response is brisk and she tilts her head, studying me closely. I motion to my room. "I'll get started now so I can be done by the time we eat."

"Okay, do you need—"

I cut her off again. "I'm good. I just need to get busy." "Okay," her voice trails off. Right before I turn to go down the hall to my bedroom, she calls, "You'll have to do better at giving details than that...I'll give you a pass because it's your first day."

I can hear the laughter in her voice, but I know she means it too.

"Okay, Mother!" I yell back.

She groans and I roll my eyes, laughing. It's best I don't

say anything about Gentry being my teacher. It's best I forget it myself. As much as I love Eden and being here with her, it feels really good to not have my entire life splayed wide open for everyone to see. Part of why I was so desperate to get out of Farrow wasn't because I don't love my home—I do—but my every move was watched and dissected and judged. The paparazzi have had so much fun making up stories about the youngest princess of Farrow. I'm considered the wild one in the family because of how I look and when my mother found out I'd had sex with our new driver, Scon, after Father passed away, she believed I truly was the wild one. I didn't bother telling her that was the first and only time I've had sex, and while it wasn't the worst experience I've ever had, it certainly wasn't memorable. Mother was eager to send me to Eden for rehabilitation and I was ready for a change in scenery... freedom, and a judge-free zone. I don't want to give Eden material to judge me with, but I'm so curious about Gentry that I almost asked her a ton of questions about him when she asked about my day. That would've been such a mistake.

Jadon texts when I get to my room. My brother is the best person in the world and he's what I miss most about home.

Jadon: Did you raise hell today? Show them who's boss?

I grin. **It's like you don't know me at all!**

Jadon: Ha. Miss you. My sparring skills are weakening without you. Both with the sword and conversation.

Mine aren't. Brienne is a worthy adversary. Bet I win next time we spar. ;) And I'm just a phone call away

for the other sparring. Can't let you lose your edge in negotiations… (I miss you too.)

Jadon: My edge is sharper than ever, don't you worry. Love you, little one. Let's chat tomorrow face-to-face.

I exhale deeply, slightly relieved that he didn't want to Facetime today. He knows me too well, and I fear he'd see right through me. I try to remember if he was around Gentry much for the wedding and imagine he probably was for the bachelor party and maybe even before the wedding. He's a good judge of character; I wonder what he thought of him.

As soon as I've had the thought, I wipe it clean. Nope, not going there with Gentry.

Excuse me, *Mr. Barrington.*

I'd like to say the next day I pay no attention to my appearance and just crawl out of bed without a thought to how I'll look to Gentry, but I'd be lying through my teeth. I wake up earlier than ever and quickly give up on going back to sleep. The sun is shining brightly through my windows, as if poking fun at my foul mood. I shower and dry my hair, straightening it with precision. I spend more time on my makeup than usual and also waste a lot of time flipping the hangers…unable to settle on what to wear. What makes me look my best? What will make him take notice? What makes me look more mature?

UGH.

Annoyed with myself and the way my brain keeps returning to *him* without my permission, I purposely put on my ratty jeans and a white fitted T-shirt. Plain. Well...as plain as I can be with my tattoos peeking out like a kaleidoscope of color. I glare at my reflection and toss my leather jacket over my backpack, sitting down to slip into my boots. They make me at least four inches taller. You won't catch me dead in heels, but give me a good pair of boots any day, even in the summer, and I feel a little more invincible.

I pull into the parking lot and take off my helmet, giving my hair a good shake. I take off my jacket and stuff it in my bag, feeling the weight of everyone watching. I should be used to it by now, but I don't think I will ever enjoy knowing how much attention comes with being a princess. The very term *princess* drives me mad. I love my family, but I hate my title. I'd give anything to be free of it, free of all the madness. I should be glad about the relative freedom I have in Niaps, but I know if I go too far with my liberties even here, thousands of miles from home, it will all be recorded and exposed before the world.

One day, maybe, I can travel the world and find a quiet place where no one cares about where I come from. My name won't matter. I look up and see everyone watching as I walk toward the school, their conversations stopping and then starting back up as they now discuss something about me...I can tell by the way their eyes dart back to me every few seconds as their hands get more expressive. Some even point. I sigh and push my hair off my shoulder, hoping I look fearless. Something I don't feel inside.

"Hey, Ava." Toph falls into step next to me, and he stares at my tattoos with awe. "Wow, speechless," he says, pointing to my arm that's covered. "Did it hurt?"

I'd be rich if I got paid every time I had to answer that question. "Yeah, but I didn't mind it. You get used to it."

"You are one badass, aren't you?" Toph smiles at me and he's trying so hard to be cool that it makes me smile back.

He's cute in a sweet puppy, adorable kind of way. I wish he were my type. By the way most girls stare longingly at him and then shoot a glare at me as we walk to our lockers, I can tell just about anyone would trade places with me right now.

More attention I don't need.

I shut my locker and am heading to my dreaded first class as Toph struggles to catch up with me.

"Hey, wait up. What's your hurry?"

"I was late yesterday. Don't want to get off to a bad start with Mr. Barrington."

"Nah, he's cool. He's the favorite around here. New and chill, a lot less uptight than the others."

I like hearing that about him and feel my heartbeat picking up as we get closer to the class. He's in there already, sitting at his desk, and when we walk in, he takes a look at me and then Toph next to me and smiles at him, not acknowledging me at all.

So that's how it's going to be.

I feel my face flush with anger and turn so he can't see, letting my hair fall like a shield as I sit down. I take out my notebook and device, preferring to write rather than type, and don't look up again until class starts. Even then, I keep my eyes on my paper, only looking up when he writes some- thing on the board.

Two can play this game.

CHAPTER FIVE

AVA

I leave class the second the bell rings, ignoring Toph when he calls after me in the hall. He's far enough behind that I hope he thinks I can't hear him. I'm not a mean person, but I don't think he's the friend I need at this school. I don't know what I need…I'm starting to wish I hadn't done this. Maybe I should just stick with the tutors I've had in the past and get started on all the traveling I want to do.

"Ava."

I stop in mid-unraveling and turn. Gentry stands there, looking slightly out of breath.

"You forgot something," he says. He holds a drawing I did while listening to his lecture. "Did you draw this?"

I nod. "I like to draw while I'm listening. It helps me focus better."

"It's beautiful. Reminds me of your tattoos."

I press my lips together and try to work up the effort to smile. It doesn't come. I'm too nervous, too disappointed, still too shaken that he's my teacher. And he wasn't the nicest yesterday. Still, the compliment sings in my veins.

"I designed my tattoos," I say quietly. "Keep it," I add, motioning to the paper.

"You have…a gift," he finishes, swallowing hard. His eyes flicker over my arm and are all lit up when he looks back at me.

This time a tiny smile creeps out. "No, you keep it. I'll draw another in the next class."

His jaw ticks and his expression changes, he looks like he ate something bad. "Pay attention in class, Ava. You're already coming in late to the year. You'll have to work just as hard as everyone else…the princess thing won't work here."

I look at him incredulously and he turns around and stalks off before I've fully processed what he's said. My skin feels heated and I'd like to go hit something, but I turn and go the opposite direction. I thought we could at least be friendly with one another, but what a *jackass*.

I sit by Jemima and Linney during lunch, the rest of the group wandering over as they get their food. Yesterday I thought Toph seemed to be the most outgoing, but Jacque and Malcolm are more comfortable today and Jacque scoots in next to me, earning a scowl from Toph. Jacque lifts an eyebrow and shrugs, then turns to grin at me.

"He thinks he can hog you just because he saw you first," he says. "We don't have a class together, so I think I should be able to sit by you at lunch."

"Not a property," I say dryly.

He lifts both hands and shakes his head, his perfect white teeth showing. He's pretty cute. Still not my type. Gentry's face comes to mind and I look around the room to see if he's eating in here today. My shoulders tense up, but it doesn't last long because of Toph's and Jacque's harmless arguing.

"Hear that? 'Not a property,' she said." Toph smirks. "*Slam*."

I roll my eyes and groan. "Come on, let's not start the drama before we even know one another. I'm only here for the rest of the school year and then I'll be on my way. There's no need to get too attached to me. Let's all be friends and when I come to visit my sister in the future, maybe we can all get together for dinner or something... you know...if we even end up getting along when all is said and done. Sound good?"

"Told you she was badass," Toph says proudly.

I roll my eyes again and turn to the girls who have been following the conversation. They don't seem upset by Toph and Jacque, which makes me breathe easier. Maybe this whole friendship thing will work out after all.

I'm turning to ask Jemima about her classes when I see Gentry out of the corner of my eye. I want to resist the urge to turn and follow him with my eyes, but I can't. I look and he's staring at me. Two girls are by him. One might be a student, I'm not sure, but the other looks like maybe she's a teacher. She's pretty and she's talking animatedly, even reaching out to touch his arm. I look at him again and he's looking at her now, the three of them walking toward a table at the back of the room.

I wonder what kind of women he dates, if the blond is someone he's interested in...I tug on my hair and remember the way he had his hands in it, he said it was beautiful...that I was beautiful...

"Ava?" Jemima nudges my arm and waves a hand in front of my eyes. "What do you think?"

"About?" I ask, dazed.

She giggles. "Want to go to Fran's after school today?"

"Fran's?"

"Wow, you really spaced out there. Coffee shop on the white sands?"

"Oh, sure." I clear my throat and take a few bites of pasta. It's better than it looks. "Sounds good."

I turn and look over my shoulder at Gentry. I need to do whatever it takes to get my mind off of him.

I park my scooter in front of Fran's and walk in with Jemima and Linney. We've just gotten our drinks and spread our tablets out on the table on the patio.

"You know the guys are going to wear you down until you go out with one of them," Linney says.

Jemima nods and looks down at her drink. She doesn't seem jealous...more resigned.

"Don't you like one of them?" I look at both and Linney shakes her head, but Jemima flushes. "I knew it," I say, grinning at her. "Which one?" I have my suspicions.

Her cheeks get even brighter. "Malcolm."

"Oh." I would've thought Jacque. Hmm.

"But he doesn't know I'm alive. And I'm okay with that...it's just a crush." She waves her hand like it's no big deal. I want to ask more about it, but the boys walk up and the conversation is over.

Malcolm sits between Linney and me and I hope with everything in me that he doesn't start flirting with me too.

I gradually loosen up the longer we sit there. Someone is chatting at all times, but we manage to get homework done too. The coffee is decent and I decide I like this group. I've vacillated a dozen times throughout the day, wondering what to do about Gentry, should I stay or should

I go…but as I'm sitting there feeling the sun against my skin and laughing at something ridiculous Toph says about my sexy white shoulders, I realize I could learn to love it here.

The point is drilled home when I get to the Catano mansion, now my sister's home, which is just so weird, and literally run into her when I head to my bedroom.

"Hey, how was it today? You went out with friends?" She looks excited and I know she wants it to work out for me here even more than I do.

"Much better than yesterday." She reaches over for a hug and I groan, falling into our default teasing mode where she chases my love. "It doesn't call for a hug."

"Everything calls for a hug," she says, laughing. "And God, stop growing already. You're supposed to stay shorter than me."

"Never fear, it's just the boots."

"I wish we were the same size so bad." She checks out my boots and I step back, shaking my head.

"These boots are not fit for a queen."

"Speak for yourself." She winks. "Dinner's ready in an hour. We've got company tonight."

"Ugh. Can I skip? I've reached my peopling quota for the day."

"How about you're free to go as soon as you're done eating…but hang out long enough to eat."

"Fine," I say it with attitude, but she knows I don't mean it.

I take my shower before dinner, still hot from sitting outside for so long. My hair is airing dry into soft waves and I don't bother putting makeup back on, but I wear a nice dress so I don't embarrass Eden. At home, my mother would've had to deal with whatever I decided to wear, embarrassment be damned, but I want Eden to know how hard I'm trying. I want her to be proud of me, to be glad I'm here.

I wouldn't have bothered if I knew who was coming... Or maybe I would've tried harder.

A lot harder.

CHAPTER SIX

GENTRY

"You're still meeting us at the Catano mansion at 7, right?" Elias asks. "Get ready for a feast."

"I...I totally forgot. We talked about that, what—a month ago? I'm so sorry, man." How the fuck could I have forgotten dinner with Elias's other best friend, the *king* of fucking Niaps? I lean my head on my hand and my elbow slips off of my desk, making me drop the phone. *Fuck me and my fucking life.*

"Don't be sorry, just show up. Don't be late. Dinner starts on time. Best be five minutes early even."

I groan. "Can't I get out of it? I have a shitload of papers to grade."

"Nope, it's time you and Luka get to know each other better...come on. I've been trying to make this happen for months. You can bail over grading papers, old man. What has happened to you?"

Ava Safrin has happened to me, I think, but manage to keep to myself. What if she's there? I feel like my feelings are transparent for the whole world to see. It's hard enough to hide it when I'm at school and she comes in looking like sin in living color. Elias knows me so well. He knows I was looking for Ava...he probably forgot about it or he wouldn't be pressing for this dinner so much.

"I need to shower. I'll see you there," I say, my mood shot to hell.

I hang up and pound it out, not once but twice in the shower. No, I don't think of her as I do so. I don't. Not even once. Beyond the feeling of her hair in my fist and her mouth on mine. But nothing else, I swear.

It helps minimally, but I'm still on edge as I pull into the driveway.

I'm going straight to hell.

Her eyes speak of truth hidden under layers of a well-groomed disguise. I wonder how long she's been wearing a mask of indifference. With me that first night, she was open and carefree; since then, I've wondered if I imagined it all. But tonight...without her usual eye makeup that makes her look unstoppable and as if she can take on the whole world and still be standing, her fresh face shows the vulnerability she works so hard to conceal. I find her completely enthralling. Every way I've seen her has lured me under the water even deeper.

If she is the fire, let me burn.

"You're staring," she whispers as she walks past me, prim in her sweet dress.

Her smirk is self-assured. I'm caught and she knows it. My mouth closes and I look around the room in an attempt to gauge how much of myself I've given away. Everyone is in conversation and oblivious. Save for one woman, the tall one who guards Eden. She looks at me with narrowed eyes and I take a deep breath and smile at her. She doesn't return it.

Elias comes over and pounds my back, giving me the bro handshake. "You okay, man? Totally forgot about the whole—" he shifts his eyes to Ava and then back to me.

Subtle.

I grit my teeth and shake his hand harder than necessary. He's a big guy, strong, wins fights and all that shit, but I could take him if I had to and right now, I feel like punching someone. He sees the look in my eyes and grins.

"Should we go out back and work out some aggression?" he teases.

"You need a swift kick in the nuts," I tell him. Mara walks up and he puts his arm around her, looking at her like she owns his world.

"Oh, what have I missed?" Mara says, grinning between the two of us. "This sounds way more exciting than the fabric samples we were discussing." She puts her hand around her mouth, unnecessarily I might add, and yells, "Girls, there's talk of a nut-kicking over here!"

My eyes widen and I laugh in spite of my foul mood. Eden and Luka wander over and I just point to Elias to let him try and explain his way out of that one. The asshole feigns ignorance and fortunately, Luka's stomach growls at just the right moment.

"Let's eat," he says, waving everyone to the table.

Food is brought out, platter after platter, but I can't seem to focus on it. Ava takes the seat next to mine and Brienne sits on the other side. It's like the angel on one side and the devil on the other, and I'm not sure which would apply in this situation.

Elias is across from us and he's very aware of how uncomfortable I am. Any thoughts of punching his pretty-boy face go out the window when he works so hard to keep conversation going between the two of us and Luka. I don't say a word to Ava or Brienne and I can feel Brienne's tension easing and Ava's building as the night goes on. Brienne and Eden talk easily, with Mara chiming in now and then, but Ava starts attacking her food with a little more aggression every minute. It would be comical if I didn't feel the exact same way. She forks her asparagus like she wants to murder it. She'd probably rather murder me.

Same here, love. Same.

I was a jerk to her and wouldn't blame her if she never wanted to see me again.

When a piece of meat goes flying after a particularly forceful stab, she sighs and pushes back from the table, ready to bolt.

"Going somewhere?" I ask softly.

"Homework. My sociology teacher is a real bitch."

I choke back a laugh and pick up my wine to drown it along with my sorrows.

"Night, everyone," she says, lifting her hand to wave. "Sorry to cut the evening short, but I need to get to my homework and go call Toph back." She points at Eden. "That hot guy I told you about."

Eden narrows her eyes and then nods. "Come back for dessert," she says.

I miss her being next to me, but it's a lot easier to get through the night. By the time dessert is served and I've enjoyed a rare night out, I'm feeling like I can do this. I can be around Ava and function. It might be awkward the first few times I see her because of knowing the way her body feels crushed against mine…that kiss. I press my fingers to my temples and squeeze. It's going to take time.

I'm almost to my car when she steps out of the shadows.

"Ava," I say, taking a step back.

"You don't have to sound so defensive. I just wanted a moment of real conversation, so I don't hate you."

"Hate me?" I put a hand on my chest and look anywhere but at her, but damn. "That hurts."

"Yeah? Well, it hurts when you avoid me too, when you won't look at me, when you won't even acknowledge that I'm in the room. *That* hurts. It also hurts when I realize you were only acting sweet the day we met and really only wanted to get in my pants…"

I grip the side of my car and take a moment before responding. It's hard to pretend to be something I'm not, but it's better than letting her see how much she affects me.

"We had a bit of fun, Ava. If I'd wanted in your pants, that's what would've happened. If you'll recall, it *didn't*, and I haven't even spoken to you in all these months."

The quick intake of her breath is like a slam into my heart. I don't want to hurt her, but this has to stop. This charged feeling I get whenever we're in the same space…it just can't happen.

"How does it change from one moment to the next? Or from a few months ago where it felt like we could talk about anything…I think we *would've* slept together had it not been for the reception…to now where the simple fact that I'm younger than you thought makes you treat me like a stranger? I don't get it. I'm the same person I was then.

So it must be you who was putting on that whole act at the wedding. Is *this* who you really are?"

"Look, Ava. I don't want to hurt you. I...I had a good time with you at the wedding. And I still think just as highly of you tonight as I did then, but everything did change when I realized you're my student. You're just too young. It's not right."

"I'll be eighteen in a month," she says with her hands on her hips. "Is it going to change overnight again then too?"

I wipe off the sweat that's formed along my brows. She's at least going to be legal soon. Makes me feel a little less pervy.

"No, it won't," I say.

Her shoulders lift higher, like she's placed armor on and is ready to come out fighting. "Okay," she nods, "I thought it might change things, but I can see you're going to live to regret me."

She steps closer to me and my breath hitches in fear and anticipation. I can't believe I'm fearful of a seventeen-year-old girl, but she has the prowess of a woman, and that's not just me wishing it. She moves until my back is against my car and her chest is against mine.

"What are you doing, Ava? You need to go inside."

"I will. Just tell me, aren't you tired of always doing what's expected of you? I am. What is a month in the big picture of time? What is a job if you are not happy in other parts of your life? I've been watching you at school and maybe it's just when I'm nearby, but you're serious all the time. Even tonight, it took you forever to relax and be the guy I spent time with that night. What are you afraid of?"

"A lot," I admit. "I'm afraid of losing a great job that I

am happy with, and I'm afraid of tearing down my integrity with one night of recklessness with you."

She leans up on her tiptoes and kisses my cheek and I hold my breath until she's back on solid ground. And far enough away that I can't move one inch and kiss her like a demon unleashed.

She looks at me for a few excruciating moments before speaking. When she does, she clasps her hands in front of her and looks younger than she has so far. "I know you're feeling what I am." She shrugs. "And maybe you're not as frustrated as I am with living my life under everyone else's rules. But thank you for setting me straight. It helps me. I can respect that. And I will do my best to keep my distance." She takes a step back and I take a deep breath. "But Gentry?"

"Yes?"

"If you ever decide to bring back the guy you were at the wedding and need to explore the reckless side, I'm here." Her eyes take on a steely glint and I'm a goner. "And if I see *that* guy again when I'm eighteen…I won't go easy on you."

I choke out a laugh and rub my fingers into my eyes. "God, Ava. You're going to bring me to my knees, aren't you?"

"I hope to, Mr. Barrington."

I'm so screwed.

CHAPTER SEVEN

AVA

Hearing Gentry say he's not willing to risk his integrity for a reckless night with me…it changes something in me. He tried a little too hard to make that night seem like nothing, but everything in his eyes, the way he clenched his hands into fists when I kissed his cheek—it said all I needed to know. He's struggling with this as much as I am.

It's validating.

I go to bed and sleep like a log. I don't bother getting glammed up for school; I don't need to make it harder on him. *Not yet.* I let him know I'm here, available and willing; I don't need to kill the poor guy. My rotten streak doesn't go *that* deep.

With all the extra time not spent on primping, I have time to go by a new coffee shop I've been wanting to try. The Coffee Library…the name wins me over right away. I'd like to try every single coffee shop in Niaps, because that's the kind of love I have for coffee. Equal opportunity. Gotta give all the beans a chance. I pull my scooter up to the front and step off, backpack already in place. As always, a guard is in close proximity, but I barely notice him anymore. The shop is cute; it's different than most I've seen here so far. Most are decorated with a tropical beach theme or a simple aesthetic with a lot of white. This place reminds me of my favorite coffee shop in Farrow, with dark wood and books everywhere. There are little lanterns on each table and the whole effect is cozy and welcoming. I get a sudden pang for home and Jadon and wish it weren't so far away. I don't miss the attention I get there, but the thought of Jadon having to rule the country and tolerate Mother without me fills me with guilt.

"Is no place safe?"

I jump when I hear his voice and he makes a derisive sound with his mouth. I turn around and Gentry is behind me in line. I frown at him and he presses his lips together.

"Are you deep in thought or just needing caffeine really bad?" he asks when I don't say anything.

"Both. What—you think I followed you here? I was here first." I put my hand on my hip but get lost in his brown eyes for a moment. They look dark from far away, but close up, there are swirls of gold and green in there, and lighter shades of brown that give dimension. Beautiful. I ball my hand into a fist to remember what a jerk he's being.

"I come here all the time...I've never seen you here... until I tell you to back off."

"Is that what you were telling me?" My anger goes up another notch. "Wow. Egotistical much?" I hold up my hand when he starts to speak. "You know, I can't have this conversation without coffee, so..."

"Well, by all means, let's get you caffeinated." We both step up as the line gets shorter.

"This is my first time here. It reminds me of home." My

voice cracks and I hurry to look away but not before I see his regret.

"Is that a bad thing?" he asks quietly.

"No, it's good. Very good. I think it would be my favorite place, even if the coffee is terrible…if it weren't for the jerk teacher who also likes the place." I get some satis- faction with the way he flinches. "I had my first pang of homesickness when I walked in—I haven't really missed Farrow yet. I miss my brother and the feeling of being toasty warm in a dimly lit room like this, with plush chairs like that velvet one over there, and the books all around. The beach is enchanting and I've loved the endless feel of summer, but sometimes I miss the dark."

He swallows hard and nods. "I can understand that. I imagine where I grew up to be somewhere between the two places. We have the four seasons, and I'm drawn to this place for the same reasons. They do have excellent coffee, by the way." He clears his throat and lowers his head, his voice so low, I can barely hear it. "I don't own the place and I won't give you a hard time when I see you here again."

He motions behind me that it's my turn and I move up and place my order. I get a scone and that makes me nostalgic too. I wait another minute for my coffee and Gentry stands next to me waiting for his.

"I'm sorry," he says.

I nod and stare ahead, not trusting myself to speak. I wish we were capable of being friends at the very least.

Our coffee is done at the same time and the barista sets both to-go cups on the counter. We reach out to grab our cups and our hands touch. That zing is there, making my blood pump faster. I can feel my face heating and don't dare look at him.

"Ava! Gentry!" she calls out.

*That has a nice ring to it...*the thought is in and out of my head before I can blink. I glance at Gentry and it's like he can read my thoughts, his frown growing as I stare at him. His jaw ticks again, that little telltale quirk that he's troubled, and he sighs.

I think I hear him cursing too, but I can't be sure. He holds his cup up and turns, walking toward the door.

Toph is extra chatty in Gentry's class and I can tell it's annoying Gentry when he stops in mid-sentence and stares Toph down.

Toph is in the middle of describing the perfect wave and how we're supposed to get more between five and seven tonight.

"You've gotta come out. It's the night for it. Tomorrow night will be too, but today's a little better. The conditions are perfect." He grins, turned sideways in his seat, facing me. He doesn't even realize that Gentry stopped talking a minute ago.

My eyes widen and I point to the front of the room, and his head tilts, but he just leans in more and whispers that he'll bring a board for me if I say yes.

I make what I think is an obvious gesture for him to stop talking, but it takes Gentry—*Mr. Barrington*—standing at his desk and clearing his throat before he looks up and stops talking. I put my fist over my mouth to keep myself from laughing, but it's hard. Toph grins up at Gentry and does not get the same response. Some of the guys behind me start laughing and Gentry holds up his hand and they go silent.

"I know there's a lot to get to know about our new

student, Toph, but can you do me a favor and curb it while you're in my class?"

Toph's brows go sky-high and he presses his lips together, looking like he could either laugh or run out of the room. "Yes, sir."

Gentry nods. "Thank you. And while you're at it, face forward so you're not tempted to distract Ms. Safrin again." He turns and stalks to the front of the room and continues his lecture without stopping. I want to be mad, but *damn. That was so hot.* Toph gives me a look when Gentry's back is turned and I hold up a hand for him to look ahead, too afraid I'm going to lose it.

When the bell rings and I pass Gentry's desk, I make eye contact with him and his eyes are stony.

I don't get in the water that afternoon, but I hang out to watch the guys surf. I adjust my bikini straps, wondering if I should try getting out there today. The next wave that comes in makes my decision. Nope, not today.

"Don't you surf too?" I ask Linney and Jemima.

"Yeah, I love it, but I'm not very good and these waves are too high for me. Toph's idea of perfect waves means it's twice the risk. Count me out for that. I like an easy ride in," Jemima says.

"Same," Linney adds.

"I'll pick a day to learn when it's a little more mellow." I meticulously rub sunscreen all over. My sister and

Brienne have reminded me daily about the sunscreen, but I'd be on it even if they didn't. Our Farrow skin is just begging to be burned to a crisp here.

"Oh my God! Is that Mr. Barrington?" Linney puts her hand over her open mouth and squeals. "*It is!* Look! He is so hot!"

I sit up straighter and look out into the water where the guys are, but then I see Gentry. He's closer to us than they are, and he looks like a sun god riding the wave all the way in. He's ripped and makes every boy out there look just that —like boys and not men. I noticed even next to Luka and Elias the other night, who stand out in any crowd, Gentry stood just a little bit taller, a little more muscled in his chest and arms, his lips and eyes a little fuller and more mysterious...oh not just a little...he's hotter than anyone I've ever seen in my life. There's nothing little about him, that I know for a fact.

I lick my lips and imagine him pressed against me again.

I can tell the moment he spots me, his initial reaction warming my chest with the way he lights up...before

schooling his face into a tight frown.

What have I done now?

He walks closer and stops in front of me. I don't know if he even sees the other girls lying on beach towels next to me. I'm sitting up, so maybe he doesn't realize we're together. Jemima squeals when a beach ball hits her and Linney yells at the guy who threw the ball.

"What are you doing here?" he says, hands on his hips. "Don't follow me, Ava. Come on, don't do this." His voice is low enough that it's possible the girls don't hear him, especially with being distracted. He said it through gritted teeth, so I can only hope they didn't hear.

My grin drops and I scowl up at him. The hurt churns in my chest, but I hold onto the anger instead. I point to the girls next to me and then look around him, out to the water where the guys are just coming in.

"Watching them. Or I was until you blocked the view."

I hear one of the girls gasp.

"Not that we mind you there," Jemima says, her voice lowered to what she must think is sexy.

He flushes and turns around to see who I'm pointing to, looking like he's been punched when he sees the three good- looking guys walking toward us. He gives me a sheepish look and turns to face the guys.

"Didn't see you out there," he says.

"Didn't know you liked to surf, Mr. Barrington," Malcolm says. "You out here often?"

"I like to hit a few different beaches along here," he says cryptically. "Heard the waves were going to be good today, so here I am." He smiles at them and for a moment I wish it were that easy between the two of us.

"Oh, when you were eavesdropping on us in class?" I can't help myself but then regret it when his face falls and he looks embarrassed.

Is it really going to turn into awkwardness every time we run into each other?

His eyes meet mine and his smile is forced. He looks like he wants a hole to suddenly appear so he could fall in it.

"Actually, I heard about it when I was out here yesterday, but..." He gives me a sheepish grin and I feel my anger cracking a bit.

"Have a good day, Mr. Barrington." I pick up my book and lie back, opening it up and ignoring him.

"Have fun," he says. "See you guys tomorrow."

Everyone else tells him bye and I look at my book until I'm sure he's long gone. Only then does my heart stop pounding out of my chest. I make an excuse to get out of there quickly and drive home, the day ruined by another misunderstanding.

CHAPTER EIGHT

AVA

It's hard since I can't avoid seeing him at all, but I manage to stay out of Gentry's way for the rest of the week. I don't trust myself to not give away my feelings to everyone in class and realizing that he keeps assuming the worst of me... I don't like it.

Regardless of my age, I'm not a child.

By Friday, I can tell the coolness I'm showing is getting to him. He doesn't like it and I don't care. I haven't been playing games with him and I'm not going to start, but I *am* angry. He calls on me more in class. His eyes linger on me when I come into the room. His expression is apologetic, but I don't even need an apology. I want to be understood; that's what attracted me to him in the first place. I've lived my whole life in a bubble, constantly speculated about. Never quite as proper as Eden, never as kind as Jadon, never as pretty as either one...although I think it's safe to say I'm out of the ugly phase now.

I thought Gentry was different, and to know he'd get that angry even if I *did* follow him somewhere, it's a slap in the face. *I don't need to get too invested here anyway*, I remind myself. I'm only here for six months and then I'll take off to see the world. Getting attached to anyone isn't a good idea.

"You left too early the other day," Toph whispers. "Come out with us today and get in the water."

I shake my head, eyes narrowing on him to stop talking because Gentry is watching us. "I need to get home, sorry," I tell him.

Toph says something else and I put my finger on my lips and focus on my notebook.

The bell rings and I gather my things as Toph shuffles next to me. I'm almost to the door when Gentry stops me.

"Ava, can I see you for a moment?" I look at Toph and shrug, waving.

"I'm sorry if I got you in trouble," Toph whispers.

"I can handle it," I whisper back.

The rest of the class exits and I stand to the side of the door. He motions for me to step closer to his desk and I do, but only one tiny step.

He sighs and walks to the door, shutting it behind him.

"I owe you an apology for what happened at the beach," he says.

"Yes, you do."

He looks taken aback at first and then nods. "I shouldn't have spoken so harshly...I shouldn't have assumed you were following me. I don't know what I was thinking." His dark eyes look bottomless as he stares at me, his mouth pinched shut. He runs his hands through his hair and his eyes pierce through me. I shift from one foot to another, a little shaken by the way he's looking at me. "I do know what I was thinking. It's just wrong." He takes a deep breath. "I wanted you to be there for me. I liked thinking you were watching me… until I realized all over again the risk." He turns away from me and sits down, staring down at his desk. "I'm the adult here and I'll start behaving like one. Again, I apologize."

I tap his desk and he looks up at me. "Stop treating me like a child. I accept your apology. If we ever run into each other again, you can just keep walking. You owe me nothing." His face falls and he reaches out, his fingers on mine. I pull my hand back and he closes his eyes. "That's the last thing I feel…that I owe you nothing. The problem is…"

He looks pained and I want to reach out and put my hand under his again.

"What?" I ask. "What were you going to say?"

"The problem is that I want to give you everything. So we're at an impasse."

As much as every cell in my body flickers to life with his words, I know it doesn't change anything. I lick my lips, suddenly dry and wanting to prolong this moment. His eyes shutter and he's back in his safe shell.

"I better get to class," my voice sounds hollow. "Have a good weekend."

"You too."

I walk out of the room, feeling like I've aged ten years since starting school. So much for living it up my senior year. I was never really that person anyway—why did I think coming here would change that? I've always been an old soul in a young vessel.

When I get home, Jadon calls.

"What are you doing?" he asks.

"Oh, just getting ready to tackle homework. What are you doing?"

"I wanted to warn you that Mother is on a rampage about getting you home."

"What? Why?" I stand up and start pacing across the room.

"I think she's bored and isn't happy with the way I'm refusing to bend to her will." He laughs and I grin.

"It's about time you stand up to her. You've let her be cruel to you for far too long."

"Yeah, well, it helped distract her from you at times, didn't it?" he says softly.

"Jadon," I whisper. "I should've known you were taking it half of the time for my sake."

"And happily...but I've had to put my foot down recently. She's been sticking her nose where it doesn't belong and I might've told her to go visit you and Eden."

"Ugh. I'm too busy with school."

"I know, and I'm sorry...for what it's worth, I don't think she listened. She started talking about you coming home and I gave up trying to get through to her. Just thought I better warn you."

"Thanks." The sarcasm is thick in my tone and he laughs again.

"I deserve that," he says.

"I've been missing home this week. Maybe it's not the worst idea ever."

"What? What have you done with my sister? You wanted to get as far from Farrow as you could."

"I wanted to get away from all the eyes. And that has been nice. But eyes are everywhere and Niaps isn't private either. It's better than home, where everyone thinks they know everything about me."

"Are you okay, Ava? You sound down."

"I'm just disappointed in people. I'd made a friend and turns out that person is not what I'd hoped."

"I'm sorry to hear that. Do you think they're worth another chance?"

"Since I'm only here for a little while...they're a surface choice, but not a solid choice."

"Hmm, I'll have to try to make sense of that later. Mother is knocking on my door."

I laugh. "It was very deep, so it'll take you a while to get it."

"Shut up."

"Love you, Jadon."

"I love you too."

Mother calls later that night and she doesn't mention coming for a visit or me coming home. She talks about how Jadon is ruining Farrow, systematically tearing down all the barriers our father built. My mother is a smart woman and I try to talk sense into her, but when it comes to Jadon, she can't see past her prejudices against him for not being her biological son.

The next morning I sleep in and when I make my way to the dining room to get breakfast, I hear voices in Luka's office. The door is just barely open and probably shouldn't be, but when I hear someone say, "Gentry Barrington," I stop and walk closer to the door.

"I don't know much about him. He's a friend of Elias's," Luka says. "I met him at the wedding and he's been over a few times since."

"You of all people know how this could turn everything upside down," the other man says.

He doesn't sound familiar, and I try to get even closer to the door without making noise, but I hear steps behind me and turn.

"You're up early for a weekend," Brienne says. "Have you eaten yet?"

"No, I was just going that way," I tell her, hoping she doesn't see how flushed I am.

"Come keep me company," she says.

I walk with her to the dining room, but I can't focus on anything but trying to see who will walk down the hall, out of Luka's office.

I hope Gentry is okay. I wonder what's going on. The reminder that I know so little about him feels strange.

I can't shake the unease I feel the rest of the day. I never see who was in Luka's office and it's probably a good thing I don't have Gentry's number, or I would be tempted to text him and get to the bottom of what I heard. But no, it's best that I forget he exists.

His words—he wants to *give me everything*—I go to sleep and wake up hearing him say it.

CHAPTER NINE

GENTRY

I've felt like someone's been watching me all week. No one has appeared outside my house looking suspicious or anything like that. It's just been a weird feeling that has me looking over my shoulder at all times. When I saw Ava at the beach staring at me with those luminous eyes of hers, I thought it was her. She must have been the eyes I've been feeling on me.

Instead of acting like a rational person, I blew up at her and even my apology doesn't feel like it made much headway. I hate that I hurt her feelings or made her feel like a child.

A child is the last thing I think of when I think of Ava Safrin. It would help if I did.

I was reminded of it again this week at lunch with Phoebe and Lindsey. They talked about nail colors for at least twenty minutes yesterday. I felt like I was at a table with my students and then realized the thought of Ava spending *twenty minutes* on anything so trivial is just something I could not see happening. I like nice hands as much as the next guy, I guess? But my brain went numb. There's a weird competitive vibe I'm catching between Phoebe and Lindsey now too, and I can't help but compare it to the nonchalance Ava carries that seems so much more elegant and refined.

I grin. I wonder what she'd say to me calling her elegant and refined. The way she dresses and all the tattoos seem like she's going for more of an edge, but the way she carries herself is pure class.

I've had hours to think about her this morning on my drive home. I almost called my dad again to see if this was really what he wanted for this weekend because I'm beat with the stress of the week, but he asks for so little, I couldn't let him down.

This will be good for me anyway, the time away. I can use the distance. If I'm dreaming up people following me and watching me, I'm clearly becoming paranoid. Shame can do that to a person, I guess.

It's time to nip this fascination with Ava in the bud. I'll enjoy the weekend and when I get home, maybe I can find a nice girl to go out with…someone to distract me. It'd be nice if it worked. Thoughts of Ava are driving me crazy.

I give the door a quick knock and walk in. "I'm home!" I call out when no one is in the entryway. I set my keys on the side table and walk back to the kitchen.

My mom jumps when I come up behind her and put my hands on her waist. "Gentry!" she squeals. "You nearly gave me a heart attack!"

I laugh and give her a huge hug. "I yelled when I came in. After that, you were fair game for scaring."

"Seems like you're never going to outgrow loving to scare me to death."

"Nope." I grin. "Where's Dad?"

She frowns. "Didn't he tell you?" She turns and goes back to loading the dishwasher.

I sit down on the barstool across from her. "Tell me what?"

"He had to go out of town."

"What?" I groan. "Seriously? The whole reason I came this weekend was because he insisted I be here. 'Something important,' he said."

She bites the inside of her cheek and keeps her head lowered. Something's not adding up.

"What's going on?" I ask. "Not that I don't love every chance to see you, but it's been crazy at work and you and Dad are both acting weird."

She laughs nervously and shakes her head. "Not the first time you've told us that."

"Is he sick again?" My heart pounds as I ask, but I have to know. I'm not sure he'd tell me the truth, but she will.

"No! He's not sick, I swear it." Her eyes wide, she looks at me fully now, and I see the truth in her eyes.

A long whoosh of air leaves me and I grip the counter. "Thank God. He said he wasn't, but..."

"I'm sorry you came all this way expecting to see Dad, but I'm sure happy to see you. How long are you staying?"

"I'll stay overnight, leave around noon tomorrow probably."

She grins. "We can go swim in the springs and then come back and watch our favorite movies."

I try not to look as frustrated as I feel. It's always great to be here. I miss my parents and love hanging out with them whenever I can...but I'm still feeling the urgency of finishing that conversation with my dad. I don't know what's going on with him, but it's making me uneasy.

"Sounds good. I'll take my stuff up to my room and I'm yours for the rest of the day."

She steps up and puts her hand on my cheek. "So glad you're home, son." When she says it, her eyes fill with tears and she hurries away, leaving the room.

Okay, now I'm really worried.

My trip home is relaxing and uneventful. We do exactly what my mom wants and it's nice to have the time with just her. For so long, everything revolved around my dad's sickness. We became used to only talking about him, caring for him, worrying about him...that I haven't even realized how long it's been since we've had a normal conversation about things unrelated to my dad.

She wants to know all about Niaps and the school as we swim in the springs closest to our house. There's a slight chill in the air, but the springs keep us warm.

"You need to come visit. When are you and Dad coming to stay for a while? I have the room. And you'd love Niaps. It's beautiful. You'd love the waves."

"I've always wanted to go there. Your father and I have talked about coming sometime in the summer, but maybe we'll have to come sooner! See what it's like before—" She stops in mid-sentence and dunks under the water.

"Before what?" I ask when she comes out of the water. "What?" she asks.

I sigh. She's been doing this all day, about to say something and stopping herself. Whatever is going on, she's not going to be the one to spill.

The next morning, I call Dad after breakfast. He doesn't answer, but I thought I'd try. He owes me an explanation and I was hoping I'd get one before I left. I'd prefer it if he'd show up and tell me in person, but Mom says she's not expecting him until the middle of the week. It's just not like him, none of this.

As I head upstairs to pack up my bag, I pass my dad's office and pause. His door is closed and I've never made a habit of going in there when I know he isn't there…but I want to see if there's anything in here that will set my mind at ease. I open the door and step inside, closing it quietly behind me. His desk is its typical state of tornado, the only place Mom allows him to be messy. I step behind his desk and sit down in his chair, memorizing where everything is placed so I can put it all back how I found it.

The first paper I pick up is about the water testing he recently had done; looks like everything is fine there. A book with several dog-eared pages. His calendar isn't on the desk, but I lift the stack of pages to be sure it's not tucked underneath. He probably has that with him. A thick piece of paper slips out from the others and it stands out because of the gold foil at the top.

I set it on top of the stack of papers and catalog underneath and read as fast as I can. It feels oddly informal for the swanky paper it's on.

We will proceed with a lawsuit if you keep pressing this matter.

Please don't let it go in that direction. Too much is at stake.

I stare at it for a long time and then look to see if anything else will tell me what this letter means. I hear Mom calling me from the kitchen and carefully tuck the page under the others.

Before I step into the hall, I make sure she's not close. "Coming, Mom," I call. "Just have to grab my things."

I run upstairs and throw everything together, jogging down the stairs. Mom follows me to the car.

"Tell Dad to call me as soon as he can, okay?"

"I will. I hope you don't feel that this was a wasted trip…"

"Seeing you is never a wasted trip," I tell her, and I mean it. My dad being sick reminded me of how short life can be, how infallible parents really are. "Love you. I enjoyed our time together. Come see me in Niaps." I hug her and kiss her on the cheek.

"I will. Hopefully soon." Her eyes fill with tears again, but that's always normal when I leave, so it doesn't concern me too much.

As I pull away, she stands and waves. I look in the rearview mirror and see her standing there, that unease building in my chest.

Something's wrong.

I nearly turn around and go back, but I know I'll get nothing out of her. I tried again last night and it was hopeless. I'll just keep trying my dad until I get him, and I'll come back if I have to.

Duty calls. This job…it seemed important before I started. Exciting…what I wanted to do with my life, all that. And I do love it; I think it's what I'm supposed to do, my gift.

But I feel too divided.

Home, my family, Ava…

It's strange how just when I felt I was getting my life together, fulfilling the timeline I'd set in place for myself—job, house, ready to find someone to share my life with—it feels as if everything is about to fall apart.

CHAPTER TEN

AVA

Two weeks down at school, and I think maybe I'm finally getting into the groove. When I'm not at the beach with the group, we've been hanging out at Fran's a lot after school, my grades are going well, things are good at home with Eden and Luka, and I'm steering clear of Gentry. So yeah. I miss Jadon, but that's really the only downer about being in Niaps…besides avoiding Gentry. Huge downer.

I stop by The Coffee Library. I haven't been back since seeing Gentry the last time. I've wanted to, but I didn't want him to jump down my throat again. Several mornings I've tried other places, but I don't like any as much as this one.

He doesn't own the place.

I open the door to the shop and look around. No sign of him. I relax and get in line.

My stomach tumbles over itself when he says, "Thought you were avoiding me."

I turn around. "You thought right."

I expect a smirk or something, but he looks completely

serious. "You don't have to do that, Ava. We'll run into each other occasionally. I want you to feel completely at home in Niaps."

"Do you feel at home here?" I regret asking it immediately.

I'm not supposed to be asking my teacher any personal questions, or getting to know him better, or falling for him any more than I already have.

He seems surprised by my question. "No one has asked me that," he says. "I like it here, could love it even...but it doesn't feel like home yet, no."

"You must miss your family."

He nods, but something flickers across his eyes and he shifts uneasily.

"Are you okay?" I ask.

I think about the conversation I overheard in Luka's office (for the hundredth time) and wonder (also for the hundredth time) what I should do about it. I wish I knew what that was all about, and I've nearly talked to both Luka and Gentry about it...but I'd hoped I'd find out more before sticking my nose even further where it doesn't belong.

It takes effort not to reach out and touch his arm. I don't; in fact, I take a step backward.

He reaches out and grabs my arms before I bump into the lady in front of me. My breath hitches in my chest and we stare at each other for a few long moments before he drops his hands.

"Thanks," I whisper.

His mouth is set in a firm line and I realize he hasn't smiled this entire conversation.

"Am I the one making you so miserable or are you just not having a good week?" I ask. I can't seem to stop caring.

"What? No, you're…I'm fine…just a lot—I don't know." He hangs his head and when he looks back up, he attempts a smile. "I need to sleep. That's probably all it is. And I need to…get out more."

"If that's code for you going out and hooking up, then no, no, you don't." I try to sound like I'm teasing, and it almost works, but the way my hands shake in my pockets, I'm probably fooling myself.

His smile is even more forced this time. "You seem to be doing fine in the friend department."

The barista greets me and I turn around, giving my order. On a whim, while I'm waiting, I write my number on a napkin and hold onto it. As I'm standing there waiting for my drink, Gentry moves next to me and he looks so sad. So lonely. I don't overthink it anymore.

"You know, there's no rule saying we can't be friends. You've come to my house for dinner and everything—no big deal. Right?" I shrug and I hold out the napkin.

He takes it and looks down at it, blinking slowly. I watch as he folds it into a triangle and tucks it into his shirt pocket like a fancy handkerchief.

"Friends," he says.

"Friends," I repeat.

I feel lighter the longer I stand next to him. More like myself. More like the weight that has been resting on my chest since I found out he's my teacher is lifting. I don't need to make out with him, as much as I want to…I just want to have that easy connection we had from the first time we spoke.

I pick up my coffee and when our eyes meet this time, he looks clearer too, like just maybe he needs this as much as I do.

"Same time tomorrow?" he asks before I walk away.

I pause, surprised, and grin. "Absolutely."

That night as I get into bed, I plug my phone in and am about to turn off the sound when I get a text.

I don't recognize the number, but I know who it is as soon as I read it. The pounding in my heart skips ahead.

Sweet dreams.

I type back quickly. **You know, if you need to talk about why you're not sleeping, I'm here. Sometimes we just need someone to listen.**

I save his number in my phone as the first thing that comes to mind besides the obvious name...*Sand*. For a moment I close my eyes and remember the way he looked that night on the beach. When I look at the screen again, he's typing and then it goes away several times.

Then finally...

Sand: It's going to sound crazy. I think someone is following me. I've never seen anyone suspicious...so there's nothing to base it on. My parents are being so strange and won't explain why. And to make it even more complicated, I can't get this fucking beautiful girl with black and blue hair out of my fucking mind and I can't do a fucking thing about it.

My mouth drops. And then my thoughts spiral out of control.

Oh my God! Is he drinking?

He thinks I'm beautiful.

What if he's in trouble? Should I mention overhearing Luka and the other guy talking about him?

I eventually type back: **You think I'm beautiful? :) Sorry I got stuck on that.**

Sand: You know I think you're beautiful. I think I said you were stunning within the first few minutes of us talking.

I think you're beautiful too. If you think someone is following you, they probably are. Who do you think it is? And your parents… maybe if they know how much you're stressing about this, they'll come out with it. I take a deep breath and try to decide what to do about telling him what I heard. I should've talked to Eden about this. And I really heard so little…what good could it do?

Sand: I don't know what to respond to first. Thank you. I think. No one has ever told me I'm beautiful.

I don't say anything for a moment, because I want to say something like *I'm sure they've said hot, sexy AF and whatnot…and that would be the truth!* But I manage to keep my mouth shut.

Sand: So you don't think I'm crazy?

I never said that.

Sand: Ha

Sand: I should let you sleep. It's late.

Tomorrow's Saturday. I can sleep in. What do you usually do over the weekends?

Sand: Well, last weekend I went home and that was a bust. This weekend I'll catch up on grading papers and finalize plans for the beach carnival.

Sounds like loads of fun.

Sand: …

No really. Why don't you at least make sure to go surfing at least once?

Sand: Maybe a stop at The Coffee Library…

Was that him just chatting or is he asking me to meet him there? I sit there and stare at the words, wondering what to say that won't send him running.

Sand: Night, beautiful

Night, beautiful ;)

Sand: I think I deserve something manlier…

Night, SAF
Sand: ?
I'll let you figure it out

I change his name to SAF in my phone and go to sleep smiling. I wake up early and when I realize everyone is still sleeping, I drive over to The Coffee Library. It might've not meant anything, but in case it did...well, I didn't set my alarm or anything, so it's no big deal if he doesn't show.

He doesn't show.

I wait for an hour, sipping my coffee and trying to read a book, but I get restless and feel silly for waiting. I clean up my area and get out of there, wondering if I imagined the whole conversation last night. I open my phone and check out the messages again.

No, it's all here.

I step outside and he's there, standing by my scooter, looking forlorn.

"Gentry?" I say softly, walking toward him.

Now that he's told me how he's not sleeping, I can't believe I didn't notice the circles under his eyes sooner.

"Didn't sleep again last night?"

"Not much," he says. "I was just standing here hoping I didn't say too much last night. I saw you in there and wanted to come in, but—"

"Hey, it's okay," I finally say when he doesn't finish his sentence. "You didn't say too much. I can head out...you can have the coffee shop now."

"Would you like to see my house?" he asks.

"What?" My eyes must pop out of my skull. I did not see that coming.

"Oh, not—I didn't mean to—no, that wouldn't be a good idea, would it? I just thought...I've been working on it so much and no one has really seen it yet. I finished the tile in the bathroom this morning. I'd really like you to see it."

"Oh." I take a deep breath and study him. He's worrying me. "Sure, I'd love to see what you've done."

He smiles and my heart falls at my feet. He tells me the address. I know the beach it overlooks, so I nod.

"Do you need more coffee?" he asks, pointing to the shop.

"Always."

CHAPTER ELEVEN

AVA

I step into the florist shop just a few stores down from The Coffee Library and pick out a houseplant with oddly shaped leaves. I think he'll like it...and it's small enough for me to strap on the back of my scooter.

When I come out, his car is gone and I'm glad I didn't get caught carrying out my surprise.

I drive the few miles to his house, the last road leading up the side of a cliff, as the houses become sparse. Midway up, just above the other homes dotting a hill and over-looking the quaint shops below, I see his. It's along the bend in the road, a house jutting out by itself. There's not another in sight, only a stone cottage surrounded by endless water. The house itself is so charming, I gasp out loud. The view is incredible and must be even better on the other side of the house. I get out and take it all in.

"What do you think?" he asks and I turn around, nearly dropping the plant.

"I'm blown away." I hold out the plant and his smile is sweet when he takes it.

"Thank you. What a weird little creature," he says, eyeing the plant. "It's perfect. Come on, I'll show you inside."

The grass and trees are plush next to the house. Farsynthias line the path on either side, making the air fragrant. Right before we get to the door, there's a wooden archway covered with vines and flowers that we walk under, the sunlight trying to peek through. The door is standing open and I take in the beautiful stone floor with colorful rugs here and there and the white stone walls that are still bare. The kitchen is in the back, open shelves with only minimal dishes. It looks nothing like I expected. It could use a few cozy touches, but it's truly so beautiful. Out the back windows, the blue water sparkles beyond.

"How much of this did you do?"

"It was a mess when I bought it. I've redone the floors, painted everything…put new windows and doors in…redid the cabinets."

"I can't get over how pretty it is."

"It's tiny compared to where you're living. This whole house is the size of two bedrooms." He laughs.

"This house is a dream. I'd trade places in a heartbeat."

He smiles. "I wouldn't make it in that mansion. A king's life is not for me. Or a princess's life either, right?" He sets the plant on the table and holds his arms out wide. "This fits. Thank you again."

I return his smile and feel a little light-headed. "I can't believe I'm here," I say, laughing nervously. I shake my head at how silly I sound.

"I can't believe you are either," he says, his eyes never leaving mine.

I will remember this later when I can't get him off my mind. Or when he's back to being distant. He looks so hot I can hardly breathe.

"SAF?" he asks.

I choke back a laugh. It's like he's reading my mind. "Are you going to tell me what it means?" He motions for me to start talking.

This time I can't hold back the laugh. "I thought you'd figured it out."

"How would I figure it out?"

"It's how you look right now," I tell him, pressing my lips together.

"But only you can see that." He's smiling too, and I don't know if he realizes it, but it's as if we're gravitating toward one another.

We stare at each other for a few moments before he finally clears his throat. He motions behind him.

"This is the part I wanted to make sure you saw." He tugs on my hand and my chest constricts.

I want to see his bedroom, but I would never ask. When we get to his room, he doesn't even pause. We keep walking, through an open and organized closet, and the last room is the bathroom. He steps aside so I can go first and I put my hand over my mouth when I see it.

The floor and up the walls of the open shower is covered with mosaic tiles, and the design is the one I drew in his class, the picture I told him to keep.

"You did this?" I whisper. I turn to face him and his eyes are bright, his expression proud and expectant.

"Do you like it?"

"It's spectacular. I've never seen anything like it. How did you do this?"

"I blew up your picture and just kept arranging the color until it felt right."

I reach out and touch the tiles, marveling at how smooth they are. "It's absolutely beautiful."

"I'm glad the artist approves."

I stare up at him and watch as his jaw ticks then loosens, as if he's about to say something. More than anything, I want to take his face in my hands and kiss him the way I've wanted to since I saw him again...really, since the day we met.

He seems to realize we're just standing there staring at one another in his bathroom and he drops my hand.

"Okay, well, I bought you a pastry from the shop. Would you like some of that?"

"Yes," I say, nodding briskly. I follow him out of the bathroom and he's going so fast, I still don't get to fully see his bedroom.

He stops suddenly and I run into his back. He turns and I'm right there. His hand lands on my shoulder and I don't move. I'm afraid he'll bolt if I breathe. When I risk looking up, everything else staying steady, his eyes are closed and he's breathing heavily.

"Ava," he says, his voice raspy. "We shouldn't be alone..."

"I'm glad I saw that—thank you for showing me."

He looks at me then, his eyes on my mouth, staring at me hungrily. He nods, swallowing hard. "It wouldn't be right if I didn't show you how you inspired me."

I smile at that. "I did just a simple drawing. You created a masterpiece—"

His lips are on mine before I finish saying my next word. I kiss him back with the same urgency. My hands climb up his shoulders and into his hair, pulling him closer.

I whimper when he yanks my waist against him, straining to get as close as he can. He walks us back until I'm against the wall and it's even better than I remembered, like we know exactly what to do from the last time, but we've had months apart and missed every second.

He groans when I arch against him and I gasp when I feel how hard he is…and then he pulls away, his eyes tormented. He lifts his head up to the ceiling and puts his hands on the wall behind me. I press my hand over my lips, willing my breathing to slow down.

"I should've known I couldn't have you here. I really did just want to show you the bathroom, I swear it. I finished it early this morning and should've gone to sleep, and instead I hoped you'd be at the coffee shop. I almost talked myself out of going in and then you caught me. I thought I—"

I clamp my hand over his lips to shush him. "I know you weren't planning on this. And it's okay. I'll leave. But first, come here." I take his hand and when we go back to his bedroom, he stops. I tug on his hand. "I'm going to leave in just a few minutes. Come here."

I sit on the bed and pat next to me. "Lie down. I'll behave myself," I tease. "You are not getting this body today. Trust me." He sits on the bed and when I lie down on one side of the bed, he drops down on his. "Close your eyes," I whisper.

He closes his eyes and I lie on my side facing him, elbow propped, and my head leaning on my hand. I run my fingers across his eyebrows and trace circles across his forehead, so softly, it's barely a whisper on his skin. He takes a deep breath and I can feel him sinking into the mattress, his body heavy with fatigue.

I do it over and over, my movements getting smaller

and softer with each pass, until his breathing gets heavier and he falls asleep.

I stay there long enough that when a bird screeches outside and he still doesn't stir, I'm sure he's sleeping deeply enough that I won't wake him when I move. I get to the doorway and turn back to look at him. God, he really is perfect. I hate to leave him, but I smile as I pass his plant, and take one last glance at his view.

I'm not giving up on him. He might have guilt about kissing me, but knowing how badly he wanted it...how urgently he held me...next time the guilt will be a little less.

I smile all the way home.

CHAPTER TWELVE

GENTRY

When I wake up, I can't even remember how I got here. I slept so hard, so soundly—and it has been so long since I've done that—I feel like I'm in a stupor when I sit up.

Ava was here.

And the next thought jolts into me like a cold-water plunge.

I kissed her.

I kissed a seventeen-year-old. AGAIN.

I bury my head in my hands. How did I ever think I could bring her here and *not* do something like that? I obviously lose my mind when I'm around her.

I groan and then groan again when I think about how she felt in my arms. Her perfect little body arched into me like she was hungry for it, and she didn't even act angry with me afterward...neither for setting her down and leaving her hanging, or for making a move on her when I'm such an old man.

You're twenty-fucking-five, hardly an old man. Compared to her, you are.

"Fucking idiot," I say out loud.

I look at the clock and realize I slept the day away.

I pick up my phone, wishing I could apologize...and there's a text from her.

Ava: If you're feeling guilt, don't. Go back to sleep. You'll feel better in the morning.

How is she so much smarter than me? I turn over, clutching a pillow to my chest and close my eyes thinking of her. Sleep comes again and I welcome it.

I don't talk to her the next day, and when I pull up to the school on Monday morning and see her parking her scooter, my heart thumps in overtime. Five months and some change to go. If she's still interested in me when she's done with school and well into eighteen, even then I should leave her alone. This is what I'm telling myself over and over.

But what scares me most is that I won't be able to. I've never felt so out of control.

I don't see Phoebe next to me until she clears her throat. I look over and she's staring at me. Did she see me watching Ava? Annoyance is hopping off of her and I grit my teeth, bracing myself.

"You didn't return my emails this weekend."

The relief is shallow, but I welcome any I can get. The guilt about Ava is still weighing me down.

"I had a full weekend," I lie. "I didn't get online." That much is the truth at least. "What's up?"

"Lindsey and I were wanting to meet with you about the carnival coming up."

"I thought we covered everything in last week's meetings."

She scowls. "That was just the surface of what needs to be done."

I want to walk away, ditch her; the nagging isn't working for me, and besides, I listened to her talk for at least five hours last week. Five hours that could've been condensed to an hour and a half.

"I think we've got a good game plan if everyone does what they're supposed to do," I tell her. "Don't worry. I'm taking care of setting up everything on the beach. Lindsey won't bail on the food. I know you've got the activities under control. It'll come together."

She huffs and steps closer, talking under her breath. "I think you're avoiding me and I wish you'd just stop ignoring this pull between us."

"What?" I take a step back and put my hand on my fore- head like that will help this conversation make more sense. "Phoebe, I think maybe you've misread something. I'm not avoiding you or ignoring any pull between us—"

She smiles. "Good, because I'm ready for us to take things to the next—"

"Whoa," I hold up a hand. "Stop right there. If I've done something to make you think I'm interested, that was not my intention. At all." I emphasize the last two words and she flinches as if I've hit her.

We stare at one another in front of the building, the kids swarming past us.

She frowns, her cheeks pink with anger or embarrass-ment, I'm not sure which. "Right. Okay. Well, I don't think I

just made it up, but if that's what you're saying, I'll take your word for it."

I nod. "Please do."

Her head rears back and now it is anger for sure that I see in her eyes. *Shit.*

"It's not Lindsey, is it? Because that would be so embarrassing if I completely misread the whole situation."

"You *have* completely misread the situation. And no, I'm not interested in Lindsey either."

Her shoulders tighten and then she frowns. I don't think anything I say will make her happy at this point, so I move past her and say over my shoulder, "The crew is ready for setup on the beach at seven Friday morning. We'll be ready for everyone else by eleven. Everything should be good to go before we open at three, so I think we'll start without any hitches. Another crew has promised to tear everything down at eleven, so I think we're covered. If you think of something else that needs to be set up or torn down, we can discuss it at the meeting after school on Wednesday afternoon."

Her mouth opens and closes and she finally nods, her eyes dropping to the ground as she walks into the school.

My head drops to the ground too, as I blow out a long breath.

"I'm not the only one who thinks you're SAF," Ava says under her breath as she walks by.

"It's not nice to eavesdrop," I call after her. "And what does it mean?"

"Didn't have to. You guys were that loud," she says, smirking. "And I'll never tell…"

I groan when she keeps walking. She stops at her locker and I try not to punch a wall when I see Toph, Malcolm, and Jacque all standing nearby, practically panting with their eagerness for her to get there. They swarm around her, and I want to revise my plan about leaving her alone… when she's graduated.

Instead, I nod to all of them. "Still good for the meeting today about the carnival?" I ask them. "I need to go over a few details with you guys before the staff meeting later this week."

"We'll be there," Toph says.

I can hear Ava asking them about it as I walk away and wish I'd waited to say anything. I don't need her showing up and distracting me or the boys on Friday.

Sure enough, she shows up at the meeting for the carnival. "Hi, Ava, what are you doing here?" I smile at her, but it's a little pointed. *Please don't make this harder than it already is*, my eyes beg her.

"I wanted to help. My friends are helping." She points at the guys and grins. "I'm not great at handling food or crafts." She shrugs. It's her eyes that give away the mischief she's stirring up.

I sigh heavily and write her name under the list of helpers.

"Do you prefer to set up or tear it down?" I show her the time options and when she sees that we're meeting at six thirty Friday morning, she frowns.

She steps closer to skim the page and I smell her shampoo.

She taps on the eleven p.m. slot and grins. "Late shift."

I nod and write that down. "Show up at ten thirty."

"Yes, sir," she says under her breath.

I don't know if she means to be so seductive, but everything she says lands on my skin like gasoline catching flame. It's a struggle to get through the meeting without looking at her again. Every time I do, Toph or Jacque are fighting for her attention.

It's for the best. If she can fall for someone else, it'll be better for everyone involved. What princess ever ended up with a schoolteacher?

Later that night, I try to reach my dad again. He still hasn't returned my calls and I don't know what to think. I tackle the laundry room. It's the last room to be updated, and it's the ugliest, so anything will help, but I find myself making things more complicated with the flooring just to prolong the physical labor. Several hours pass and I still can't ignore the urge to text Ava. I give in while I'm standing at the counter eating chili out of a can. Pathetic.

Sufficient At Friends?
Ava: Lame
Sun And Fog
Ava: Cold
What do you mean by cold?
Ava: I mean you are so far off it's not even funny
Soul And Fire
Ava: Hmm, that's a teensy bit warmer, but not much
Salamanders And Frogs
Ava: Frozen
Sassy And Fresh
Ava: Thawing
Hmm. Sexy And Fresh!
Ava: o.O VERY WARM

I'm grinning so wide I should be embarrassed. **Fresh? No way.**

Ava: … Sexy?

Ava: Keep going

Sexy Ass Friend

Ava: It's weird how you can be so hot and so cold all at once. Also, this is proving just how old you really are. That the letters AF don't clue you in at all. Sad.

Sexy As FUCK! That can't be it. Is it?

I laugh out loud and then feel like an idiot when she doesn't answer right away.

Okay, now I feel dumb if it's not Sexy As Fuck because that would be very presumptuous on my part.

Ava: You're so cute when you're presumptuous.

I laugh again and rinse out the can, tossing it in the recycling generator and waiting until I hear the satisfying crunch of the can flattening. I take the phone to my room and stretch out on my bed.

I think I'm blushing.

Ava: And this is why you're SAF.

I hesitate over the keyboard a few seconds, knowing I should end this conversation right now, or ten minutes ago, but I'm eager for any scrap from her.

Ava: Still feel like you're being followed?

That douses my smile somewhat.

Actually, no. I didn't get that feeling even once today. Maybe I just needed to sleep.

Ava: You did seem like you were getting delirious on Saturday. Let me know if you ever need me to come put you to sleep again.

I let the innuendo hang in the air even though my dick springs to attention. I ignore it. *This is me ignoring it*, I think three times before palming myself.

CHAPTER THIRTEEN

AVA

It's been fun watching Gentry squirm this week. His face paled when I showed up at the carnival meeting a few days ago and I thought he was going to tell me I couldn't help, but I got on the schedule. We've texted the past three nights and I'm kind of surprised I haven't heard from him tonight.

He's been the model of propriety in class. I wish he'd look at me more, find a reason to talk to me in person, but he is determined to do the right thing.

In our text conversations, it's a different story. He's still not saying anything out of line, but he's far more relaxed and open. Every night before we say goodnight, I wish that I could ask him to be the same the next day. In person. Show me that playful side. Give me a little bit of hope that this is not my imagination.

I look at my phone and it's ten o'clock already. The carnival is tomorrow and it'll be a long day. I technically don't have to do anything until tomorrow night, but if I'm awake, I'll go see if I can help in the morning too.

I fall asleep around midnight, my texting streak with Gentry broken.

My sleep is fitful and I wake up at six. I toss and turn, trying to force myself to go back to sleep since it's a rare day to sleep in.

I wonder if Gentry will be weird today since he didn't text last night. What if he's decided we can't talk anymore? I would miss him. I look forward to our conversations all day. Maybe he finally decided to go out with someone, or maybe he took Ms. Shoman up on her offer to move things to the next level. Maybe last night he got sick of dealing with such trivial conversation going nowhere and went out and got laid.

I sit up, my stomach clenching into a tight knot.

I throw on a tank top, shorts, and a wide-brimmed hat so I won't have to be as diligent about sunscreen. I stop by the coffee shop and get my usual and what I've heard Gentry order a few times now. I make it to the school in half the time as usual since there's not the normal school traffic. Gentry and one other guy are at the beach already, unloading a van of equipment.

Gentry gives me a cautious look when he sees me and I hold up the coffee.

"Sorry, I can split this with you," I tell the other guy, offering my coffee.

"Not a coffee drinker," he mumbles.

"Yay, more for me," I say.

The guy doesn't crack a smile. Geez. It's going to be a long day if this is what we have to work with.

"Thanks, Ava," Gentry says when I hand him his coffee. "You didn't have to do that."

"I know, but I couldn't sleep and it seems like you get the bad end of this deal. You'll be here the longest of anyone, teachers included. You deserve a little extra."

He holds his coffee up to mine and we clank it in a mini *cheers*. "Thanks."

Three guys I haven't met yet show up and a couple of girls who I'm sure are here for the same reason I am—Mr. Barrington. Every time Gentry says anything, they giggle in tandem.

I knew Toph, Malcolm, and Jacque were helping tonight, so I'm not surprised when I'm the only one from our group who shows up. Gentry shows us where every table should be placed and we get to work. The sun gets hotter as the day goes on and I'm grateful for the covering we set up over each table. When sweat is pouring down my temples, I'm tempted to run cool off in the water. The guys do, and it looks so inviting. I finish the last tent and look around, setting my hat aside. Gentry is showing everyone the next steps in our assembly.

I run out to the water and wade until it's deep enough for me to dunk my hair back. I come up and enjoy the breeze filtering through my wet hair and skin. *Much better*. I take the band off my wrist and pull my hair into a massive topknot. My tank clings to my skin. I should've done that an hour ago.

When I walk up to everyone else, they turn to look at me and the guys do a double take, zeroing in on my chest.

I look down. My hot pink bra is like neon flashing, and to my horror, my nipples aren't toned down even a little bit with the padding in my bra. Gentry's eyes flash and he looks slightly dazed when his eyes meet mine. I pull my hair out of the bun and let it fall down my chest on either side, then cross my arms.

Gentry clears his throat and his voice is tight when he tells each person where to set up their assigned task. He shows me where to set up the popcorn popper and fairy floss machines last and carries one of the machines behind me.

"Are you doing this on purpose?" he asks, under his breath. He sets the machine down next to me and turns to face me, his hands on his hips.

"Doing what on purpose?"

He looks around to see if anyone is near us and his tone is biting. "I'm on a thin rope, Ava. Every time I turn around, you're there looking at me with those *fuck me* eyes and your nipples just begging to be pinched." He yanks on his hair and gives one more desperate look around us. "Is it too much to ask for you to give me a little space? Have mercy… and for god's sake, cover them." He points to my chest and then covers his mouth.

My chest caught flame the moment he said *fuck me*, but his eyes are so tormented, I take a step back instead of moving toward him like every nerve ending in my body is begging me to. I shrink into my embarrassment, wishing I could run, but I'm also sick of his back and forth.

"You're being a bit of a jerk right now. Space. Yes. If that's what you want, absolutely," I snap back, licking my lips. I'm dry; I'm not trying to make things worse, but his eyes track every movement and his mouth falls open.

"Mr. Barrington," one of the giggle girls calls. "What should I do with this shovel?"

"Put it back in the van if you're done with it," he barks.

He turns to me and practically growls. "You're right. I apologize for my confusing behavior. It's unacceptable."

I start to say something, but I am at a loss. I watch as he stalks off and finish my job as quickly as I can. I don't bother letting anyone know when I'm done. They can figure it out. I get out of there, stopping by the house to get the fine-line pens I use for tattoo drawings. A car I don't recognize is where I usually park, but that's nothing very unusual. A steady stream of people come through the Catano mansion. What's unusual is how nice the car is; Luka has some fancy-ass cars, but this one is more extravagant than what he typically goes for.

When I walk inside, Luka is just coming out of his office and a guy steps out behind him. I try not to stare, but it's hard, the guy is really good-looking. *Really. Good. Looking.* He looks familiar, but I swear I'd never forget meeting a guy who looks like him.

He grins when he sees me, his eyes warm and friendly. Luka puts his arm around my shoulder and squeezes.

"This is my sister-in-law, Ava," he tells the guy. Looking at me, he adds, "And this is Alex Forbrush."

"Forbrush—are you Nadia's brother?" I ask.

"Don't hold it against me," he says with a wink and I flush.

Luka's arm drops and he puts his hand on Alex's shoulder. "You can turn down the charm, Alex. It won't work here. You had your chance with my sister." His tone is light, but there's a bite to it when he glances back at me. "And my sister-in-law is off-limits."

"Luka!" I glare at him. "Quit being so weird." He shrugs. "She's seventeen," he tells Alex.

"God! You guys are so uptight about age in Niaps." I throw my arms up and Alex's eyes light up, crinkling at the corners. I stare at him, biting my lip. "You look so familiar."

"I'd remember you," he says, his lips turning up.

"Ava, if you'll excuse us," Luka says, sounding more agitated.

Alex laughs and lifts a shoulder at me. "The pleasure was all mine, Ava Safrin," he says.

"Off-limits," I hear Luka gruffly muttering as I leave the room.

They're all ageist dimwits around here! What would Luka do to Gentry if he found out we'd kissed? Gah. I don't want to think about it.

CHAPTER FOURTEEN

AVA

I draw by the ocean for a while, my thoughts becoming more disjointed the longer I sit staring at the waves. Drawing usually calms me, but I have a feeling my heart is too tangled up to relax. Not today.

It's hard to figure out what guys are thinking on a normal day, but add to that a guy I don't know very well, who's doing his best to act like we're just friends when we're really not, and the taboo fact that he's my teacher, and I feel like I'm striking zero every time. The only thing I know I've done right was helping him get to sleep last weekend, and some would argue *that* was so wrong of me. To be in his house, his bed, touching him. That wasn't wrong at all.

What *is* wrong is the way he treated me today. And add to that his silence last night…I worry my lips between my teeth, shredding the skin until it bleeds. I check my phone and turn on the sound, looking at the texts from Toph and Linney.

Linney: Where are you? We're at the carnival.

Toph: I thought you were coming to the carnival today. Come hang out with us.

And an hour later…

Toph: I can come pick you up if you need a ride.

I go back to the house and take a nap, feeling somewhat better when I wake up. I text Toph and Linney back.

I fell asleep, but I can come over soon. Are you still there?

Toph answers right away. **Yes. Come on! I need a partner for the rides. Hurry.**

I roll my eyes, imagining every girl longingly staring at Toph as he walks around the carnival. He hardly needs me to fill an empty spot.

I almost text Gentry and ask him if it's okay if I come—with a heavy helping of snark—but I leave it alone. I'll stay out of his way tonight when we're tearing down too.

Linney texts where they are, and when I get there, I see Jacque first. He's with a pretty black-haired girl and a girl with short black hair has her arm around Linney. Jemima and Malcolm look chummy, and I smile at the scowl Toph gives me.

"It's about time," he says into my ear. "It's like everyone is in heat and I'm just having to watch it all go down. It would be hot if I had company." He puts his arm around my shoulder and lifts his eyebrows. I fling his arm off of my shoulder and he frowns but laughs a few seconds later. "Are we gonna ride the rides or what?"

"Yes! We have a few hours until we have to meet to tear everything down. Let's do it," I say.

Jacque introduces me to Sade and she smiles shyly. "She doesn't go to our school," Jacque adds.

"Tutors," she groans. I know right away that she's more than just a pretty face when she says, "You've always been my favorite princess to watch—maybe because it's obvious you try to stay out of the limelight." Her dark skin glows when she smiles again. She's beautiful and when I look at Jacque, he seems smitten. Interesting. I like it.

"Well, thank you. You're right. The spotlight is the last thing I want. And I have a feeling we feel the same about tutors. I'm over them," I add.

"My parents are ridiculous about education. They're determined to send me to Kings Passage, but I have no desire to go there," she says. "I'd rather not be around the smartest people in the world, thank you very much."

Jacque and I laugh and the others shift restlessly. "Come on, let's get in line for the Dinjargo," Linney says.

I pause and Toph bumps into me. "I wasn't sure if I wanted to ride that one," I admit.

It's a Ferris wheel-type ride with individual cages that go upside down, especially when they're stopped at the top. We walk toward the ride and when I see it looming ahead, I stop. I hear arguing and look over to see Gentry and an older man in each other's faces. The older man is pleading, but Gentry is clearly angry. Gentry says something and then the guy points his finger at Gentry's chest, making Gentry stop talking.

"Hey, you guys go ahead," I tell them. "I don't feel so well. If I ride that one, it'll wreck me for everything else tonight."

"I can stay and wait with you," Toph says.

"No, I'd feel bad. Go ahead. I'll wait here."

He tries to convince me one more time, but I shake my head and he fake pouts but then gives up, laughing when I roll my eyes.

As soon as they're far enough away, I move closer to

Gentry and the man. I stay behind the fairy floss machine, where I can hear them better but still remain hidden.

What I hear next stops me cold.

"You had to wait until I'm at a work event to tell me I'm *not your son*? I don't even know what reality I'm living in right now." His voice breaks and he bends over, putting his hands on his thighs, breathing hard. "You ditched me when I made the trip home and now you're in my face, desperate for me to know. Why? Why now?" He stands up suddenly, eyes blazing. "Have you been following me the past couple of weeks?"

His dad reaches out to touch Gentry's arm and Gentry lifts it up so he can't. The anguish in the older man's face is unbearable, and I don't know what caused him to keep this secret all these years, but I know with everything in me that it's killing him to tell him now. Killing him to break Gentry's heart.

"I haven't been following you, but it's become urgent that I tell you about everything...I'm so sorry I didn't sooner, son, but they wouldn't—"

"When did you start speaking so cryptically, Dad? Just spit it out. Start from the beginning. The short version for now, because I don't know if you noticed this, but I have a job to do." His fingers circle around the air, motioning to the commotion around him.

"I can't here, but I'll tell you everything. The second you get done tonight, find me. I want to be the one to tell you." He looks around, as if someone is going to pop out of hiding any second.

"You've already told me the kicker. How did it feel to lie to me every day of my life? And what more could there be than this?" Gentry asks, his eyes glassy and cold.

"I should've told you the truth as soon as you were old

enough to understand it. But in all ways besides this one truth, our lives were not a lie." The man clasps his hands behind his back and bows his head.

"I wonder how I'm supposed to believe that," Gentry says.

He turns then, almost as if he can sense my eyes on him. I wonder if I can stay hidden behind the fairy floss machine, but I know the second he spots me. I start walking toward him, not stopping to overthink it.

When I reach them, I hold out my hand, "I'm Ava," I tell the man.

"I'm Hal Barrington, Gentry's…father," he says.

"Nice to meet you." We shake hands and I look at Gentry. "I'm just checking in. You said to meet here," I add. I don't know if he'll shut me down or hold onto this lifeline, and he doesn't wait long to make a choice.

"Right. If you'll follow me, I can show you where to start," he says. He nods at his dad and motions for me to follow.

We leave his dad standing there and walk to the opposite side of the carnival. The sounds of families laughing collide in the air, children shrieking with excitement when they see something else unexpected. The bells and strange clicks and beeps that go with the games lend an otherworldly feel to the desolation I sense in Gentry. He looks around him, taking it all in, and yet I know his mind must be going in a thousand directions.

"I'm assuming you heard some of that conversation. You appeared like an angel with a mission to save me."

"I did hear a few key points," I say. "Are you okay?" I turn to him and he closes his eyes.

"Please don't look at me right now," he whispers.

I nod and turn away, compassion filling my chest. "I

don't know the right thing to say right now, but I'm here. We don't have to talk about it, or we can. I can be a distraction, an ear, an ally. Just say the word."

"I've always idolized my father," he says, his voice hoarse. "There's never been a second that I doubted his love for me, never a moment when I had the thought, *hmm, I don't fit in this family*...I feel blindsided. And I can't figure out why he'd bother to tell me *now*. My parents played their part so well, my entire fucking life...why mess that up now?" His voice rises at the end and I see Ms. Shoman walk by. The pretty one who's always watching him.

She stops when she hears his last sentence and I shrink back into the booth behind me, wishing I could disappear.

"What's going on?" she snaps. "Gentry?"

He motions to me. "Discussing families. Ava is a family friend," he adds.

She turns to me and her eyes narrow. "I recognize you. You're a senior, right? I don't have any classes with you though." She leans in a little bit and then grins self-consciously. "Oh my god, you're the queen's little sister!" She pushes her hair back and stands taller; I can tell she's one of those people who will automatically see what she can get out of me, whether it's more donations for the school or gossip about my family...three, two, one...

"Do Eden and Mara really hate each other as much as they say?" she asks, looping her arm through mine.

Okay, at least it's not the money she's after first. Good to know which side she falls on. I want to push her off of me, but I'm glad she's distracted from Gentry. It also makes me more leery of her. Money could hold her in a nice holding pattern for a long time; a mind hungry for the dirt will have her looking for it everywhere she goes. There's too much dirt for someone she's already keen on staring down—Gentry.

She's dangerous.

"They're close," I tell her, smiling widely. "Just had to get to know one another…you can't believe everything you read, Ms.—"

"You can call me Phoebe." Her laugh is grating and superficial, lasting longer than it should. I cringe with practically every sound she makes and hope to God Gentry knows better than to ever date this woman.

"I need to head to the meet-up," Gentry says. "Ava, are you coming?" He motions for me to come on and I jump at the chance, waving at Phoebe over my shoulder. I stay far enough back from Gentry so it'll look like I'm struggling to keep up, anything to keep that nosy woman off of the scent for as long as possible.

When we're far enough away, Gentry turns to me and bends close so I can hear him. "You didn't have to come with me, but she's relentless. Listen, forget what you heard tonight. I'm going to. I don't know why the urgency with my dad, but I can't think about it right now. And I'd rather you not say anything to anyone about this, okay?"

"I would never," I tell him.

He shakes his head and looks over my shoulder, his lips thinning. He looks pale even in the evening light, and I grasp his arm.

"Are you sure you're okay?" I look over my shoulder to see what he's staring at and am in for my own surprise. "Alex?"

CHAPTER FIFTEEN

GENTRY

"That's who's been following me. I can feel it." I put my hand to the back of my neck and along my scruffy jaw, that unsettled feeling I've had for weeks going into overdrive.

Ava looks at me, her forehead crinkling with confusion. She turns to the guy and says, "Alex, what are you doing here?"

He glances at her and softens somewhat, but his face transforms into a stony slate when he turns back to me.

"You know him?" I ask.

"Hi, Ava. I need to speak to Mr. Barrington, if you don't mind." His comment is directed at her, but he looks at me as he says it.

What the fuck is his problem?

I turn to Ava and am firm. I want her out of here. I don't know what this guy is capable of. "Let the crew know I'll be there in fifteen. Go ahead, I'll meet you there."

She frowns. "Are you sure? I don't mind waiting." She looks at Alex, her eyes darkening when she looks at him. "Everything okay, Alex?"

He smiles at her and it seems to work, she relaxes. "Of course. Seeing you twice in a day, my lucky day."

I groan and they both turn toward me, Ava's face bright and Alex's going dark when he plants his feet apart and stares me down.

I don't back off, daring him to say one more thing to her.

Ava pauses and motions behind her. "I'll just go…"

When she's gone, Alex looks at me with a grim expression. I put my hands on my hips, trying to place where I have seen him before. Ava recognized him and he does seem familiar to me, but I can't figure it out.

"We need to talk," he says. "Your father has been sticking his nose where it doesn't belong, and I'd like it to stop."

"I don't know what you're talking about." I cross my arms and try to look my most intimidating. "Are you the reason he's so unhinged right now?"

"I'd say it's all his own doing. He's the one causing all of this—his lies about you. Did you know he's threatened to go to the press?"

My eyes narrow. "You know I'm not his son? Why would that matter to you?"

Alex's lips thin and he gets in my face. "My father doesn't deserve this kind of blackmail. He's a good man. You're not his son and no one will believe you are."

"His son…who *are* you?" I yell. "No one is blackmailing anyone. My father would never stoop to that, trust me."

Alex steps back, surprised, and then he rushes for me, grabbing me by the shoulders. "He *is* capable of it. My security team caught it all on camera. He's inexperienced, mind you, so I shouldn't have used the word *capable*…he's more like a child shouting *I did it*, proud of the attention he's getting. He's a disaster and he won't stand a chance with the people of Yuman. They'll never believe my father has kept you a lie all these years." He looks me over then, the disgust all over his face. "And you will *never* be king," he spits the words. "I can promise you that."

I have to shake my head to rattle out the crazy this man is spewing. Not one bit of it is making any sense. My head is still reeling with the first revelation of the night from my dad. The carnival atmosphere with the music from the rides and the loud chatter of the crowd is turning it into a walking nightmare.

"Did you say, king?" I ask…before I see a fist coming at my face.

"I can't believe you hit me!" I yell, jumping up and throwing out a shot of my own.

"You deserve worse than that," he spits out. "Taking my country's time and threatening ruin. I should lock you up." He goes to punch me again and I aim for his gut, knocking the wind out of him. While he's clutching his side, I knee his nuts and he bends over, cursing under his breath.

While he's quiet for once, I get in his ear. "I'm going to say this once: I don't know what you're talking about. My father just told me tonight that I'm not his son. I still haven't fully registered that one. I don't know who you fucking are and I don't fucking care, except you've made me angry doing this here and now, and at a school event, no less." Which reminds me—I look around, taking note of all the security I'd lined up. There are only two watching us and they're blocked from getting closer by four guys who must be with Alex. Hopefully the rest of security is doing a better job around the rest of the property. I sigh, looking at Alex again. He's standing up and looking at me warily.

I stare at him, not knowing what else to say. I bite the inside of my cheek and wait, clasping my hands behind me so I don't hit him again.

He opens his mouth to speak then shuts it. He puts his hand over an eye and shakes his head, looking shaken. Finally, he takes a step back and clears his throat.

"I've handled this poorly. This is not me," he says quietly. "I don't create scenes unless a woman is involved." He tries to grin and it looks like a grimace. I'd feel sorry for the guy if my nose wasn't bleeding because of him. "I let my anger take over and I apologize."

He turns to leave and I grab his arm. "Hey, wait. I want to know what this is about. You might've picked the wrong place, but I need to know what's going on. Will you meet me later? Explain yourself? Who are you?"

"There's no need," he says. "I've heard what you have to say and I will take care of cleaning up the mess your father has created. I believe you when you say you don't know what's going on." He turns around and speaks with his back to me. "But you need to tell him to stop. Yuman is a peaceful country and we like to keep things that way. Your father is starting something he can't see through and I won't let it touch *my* father."

"Wait, just tell me what my father is saying. He's claiming your father is my dad? What did you mean about king—are you…my *brother*?"

"No. It's not true." His voice rings of finality and it stops me cold. "None of it's true. Please, put a stop to your father's lies."

I'm so confused that I let him walk away. None of this makes any sense to me, but I have a job to do. It might not be the most important job in the world, I scoff to myself, like being an entitled fucking prince like this guy apparently is, but I take my commitments seriously. My life has been relatively simple, the only exception being when my dad was sick. That was the worst thing we'd ever gone through, but this feels like it could do a number on me in its own right. I pause and bend over, putting my hands on my knees and breathing out a few rattled breaths.

I might be in shock right now. In fact, I'm sure I am. My world might be falling to the crapper and I still can't get a straight answer out of anyone, so I'd say I'm in shock.

I'll deal with this clusterfuck later.

Once I'm walking toward the crew, Alex and his entourage are long gone. I pinch the bridge of my nose, wishing for ice to put on it.

Everyone is there waiting and when I step up, there's a small rush of concern when they see the blood on my face.

"I'm fine. I didn't need my large nose getting any larger, thank you very much, but here we are." I try to make light of things and it relaxes the kids. I notice my dad standing just behind them and look away quickly. I grab the clip- board from the table and start reading who needs to go where.

As the kids begin dispersing, Ava steps up and hands me a bag with ice. "For your large nose," she says, cringing when she sees it better.

"Ha-ha." I roll my eyes but take the ice. "Thanks."

"You okay?" she asks. "Did Alex do that?"

I grit my teeth and shake my head. "You guessed it. The guy's a real charmer." I want to ask what she knows about him, but we don't have time for that right now. I take a deep breath and put the ice to my nose. "Let's get to work. I need this night to be over."

"You got it." As simple as that, she heads to her assigned spot. I wish everyone were as uncomplicated as she seems.

I choke back a laugh at how "uncomplicated" she really is, reminding myself of the fact that I'm attracted to a young princess, for crying out loud. *What the hell?*

My dad walks up as soon as she's left and puts his hand on my arm, assessing my face.

"I saw Alex confront you. I'm sorry I couldn't stop him," he says.

"What is this mess you've gotten involved in, Dad? Help me out here."

"I promise I'll tell you everything. How long do you have?"

"I have to oversee everything being torn down tonight. It'll be a while." I lean in. "But I've got time to hear this. Start talking."

"I clearly can't get into all of it here, not with Alex beating you up at your first meeting. But, I'll tell you this much, Gentry...you are the rightful king to Yuman." He clenches my arm. "And if anything happens to me, you make sure you fight for it."

CHAPTER SIXTEEN

AVA

When I finish my tasks and look around to see how everyone else is doing, I pitch in with Toph's booth and we meet in the middle with the tent, his hand brushing against mine. He looks at me meaningfully and I cringe inside, knowing we're due a talk pretty soon. If he keeps looking at me with those lovesick derpy eyes, it's going to go downhill so fast with the awkward vibes.

I help him carry the last of the tents to the vans and there's a group finishing up. Gentry isn't with them and I look around, asking the closest girl if anything is left.

"I think this is it. Mr. Barrington said once all the tents are loaded, we can leave."

"Where is he, do you know?"

"It's been about twenty minutes since I saw him. Jacque is supposed to drive the van back. Maybe Mr. Barrington is back at the school already," she says, pushing up her glasses.

"Okay. Thanks." I turn and start heading toward my scooter.

"Hey, wait up," Toph calls.

I turn and smile, my shoulders tensing as he gets closer.

"Some of us are going to the diner. Will you come?" he asks.

"It's been a long day. I think I'll pass. Thanks, though."

"Aw, come on," he says, tilting his head to the side and putting his hands together like he's begging. "It'll be fun."

I just shake my head and his shoulders sag, but he grins and waves as he walks to his car. I get on my scooter and head to the school. Something tells me Gentry didn't tell many to come help finish up the jobs left. And maybe I just want to see if he's okay. I can't believe everything that happened to him tonight and he still stuck around to make sure things ran smoothly for the carnival without delegating it to someone else. Talk about dedication.

I think about Alex again and wonder what that was about. He seemed so nice with Luka; it was weird seeing him in such a different light with Gentry. I didn't like the way he looked at Gentry, and I feel bad that I didn't stay. Maybe Gentry's nose wouldn't be swollen to twice its size if I had.

Sure enough, Gentry's car is in the parking lot and I see him unloading the gear into the small outbuilding behind the school. I follow him in the building and he jumps when he turns around and sees me standing there.

"Can I help?" I ask.

His jaw ticks and he nods, not speaking.

We work silently, carrying as much as we can, and when the other van shows up, the work goes faster. Toph isn't in the group and I'm glad he didn't have another chance to ask me to hang out. I stay until the work is done and when the last person drives out, I turn to get on my scooter.

Gentry comes and stands next to me, looking lost.

"Do you need me tonight?" I ask.

His eyes drill into me, turning me into a pool of want. I will be whatever he needs me to be tonight. I know he sees it in my eyes and I feel him weighing it all over in his mind. His thoughts are at war all across his face.

"I need you to stay far, far away from me, Ava. Do you understand?" He steps closer and his teeth pull in his lower lip as his eyes take me in, feeling like a caress everywhere they land. "My restraint is gone. Please, just go."

He tilts his head back to the sky and the torment in his eyes is hellish when he looks at me again.

"Okay. I'm going. But Gentry? Text me. Okay? Let me know you're all right. Or reach out to Elias…whoever you trust. I don't want you to be alone right now."

"As usual, you're the adult in this little friendship we've got going. Thank you. I'm okay…or I will be eventually… right?" He laughs and looks so sad, it kills me.

It hurts to leave him, but I have already inserted myself into his life too much for one day. When he thinks back on this day, I don't want him to add me to the mix of chaos that he remembers. He has a heavy enough weight to carry.

It's hard when I don't hear from him. The weekend drags by; it's busy enough—I spend Saturday shopping with Eden and Brienne—but I'm conscious of every second ticking by that I don't hear something. I'm worried about him, and I'm hoping he won't shut me out now. Not when he needs me the most. Not when it feels like he'd started letting go of some of the walls he'd erected between us.

Eden gets stopped everywhere we go. The citizens of Niaps are in love with their new queen, while they eye me with suspicion. We arrive at an upscale restaurant over-looking the water that evening, a few minutes late for our reservation, and all eyes turn our way when we step inside. The staff is so ecstatic the queen is there, they surround Eden and sniff at me like I'm a dirty dishtowel.

I'm not jealous of the attention she gets; in fact, it's the very opposite. The scrutiny she gets drives me mad for her sake, because I know she doesn't love it either, but the thought of being on the receiving end is far more distressing than the lot in life I've been given. The attention I'm paid is minimal in comparison to her and it's still more than I can take. And she does seem to be coming into her own, flourishing under Luka's affection and maybe even the people of Niaps, while the very thought of having to tolerate this attention for the rest of my life is suffocating.

"I'm too colorful everywhere I go," I tell Eden when an older woman curls her lip in distaste as I walk by. "Turns out the same judging eye is alive and well in Niaps, not just Farrow."

"Sad but true," she says. "Although I find they're a little more accepting here, don't you?"

"I don't really know. I haven't been to many places besides school and coffee shops. So far neither have been bad. Maybe it's just when they see me next to you, *oh Queen of all that is good and proper*. Especially in a restau-rant like this." I snap my dinner napkin out with a flourish and lay it across my lap.

She rolls her eyes and laughs. "Always a flair for the dramatic."

I shrug. "Only when it's convenient." I pick up my menu and grin.

"Have you met any cute guys at school? Mother asks every day if I'm making sure you're not in the back seat of any cars…"

"Haven't been in a single back seat, I swear it."

I made out with my teacher against the wall in his house and it was heaven, I want to tell her, but instead I start thinking about Gentry in a back seat, how his bulking frame trying to fit over me in a car would never work. It would be a disaster. Gentry is meant for open spaces. High ceilings and his massive bed. I picture him in a field with an endless sky or on the sand with the ocean in the distance. He can't be contained and I like that about him.

"Where did you go?" Brienne asks, waving her hand in front of my eyes.

"Back seats with boys," I tell her, taking a long drink of water. "It got me hot."

"Ava!" Eden gasps, laughing and fanning her face. "I don't like to think about you and…that…"

"You're worse than Mother. Especially since I've heard you having sex." I lift a hand when she sputters. "Not that I ever want to hear it again. It was scarring. But I am a free-spirited woman with a healthy sexual appetite. I might not be as experienced as I want, but I will have sex again and it will be better than the first time. So help me, god of Niaps."

We're all laughing by the time I'm done and Eden's face is bright red. So is Brienne's. It's so fun to get them all riled up.

"Your birthday is in just…six days? Right?" Eden studies me with her brow quirked. "Friday…I know we've already had a party, but if there *are* any boys in back seats…I'd say you at least need to have him over for dinner. Let me meet this boy."

I put my hand on her arm to get her to stop talking. "Eden, trust me…there is no boy."

He is *all man*.

I smile to myself and tune out when Brienne and Eden start talking about a book they're reading.

CHAPTER SEVENTEEN

AVA

My stomach is tied up in knots by the time I get to school on Monday morning. I never heard a word from Gentry. It didn't seem right to text him when he told me to stay away, but it's killing me, not knowing what's going on with him.

I walk into class ten minutes early, looking around expectantly. No one is here yet. I sit at my third-row desk and wait. A woman comes in right after I've taken my notebook out. I look up hopefully, lifting my pen from the drawing I've started to help settle the nerves. It's a woman I don't recognize.

"Hi." She smiles nervously. "I'm Mrs. Newell, the substitute." She waits for me to tell her my name and when I do, she nods, setting her things on the desk. "Nice to meet you."

"Will Mr. Barrington be back tomorrow?"

Kids trickle in and she writes her name on the board.

"It'll be me again," she answers just as I'm about to ask again, only louder.

I sit back in my seat, shaken. I don't care what he said

about staying away, if the roles were reversed, I think he'd be checking on me by now.

I'm worried about you.

That's all I say and the anxiety ratchets up a notch, washing over me and confirming my statement. I shouldn't have agreed to anything when he was so distraught. And checking on a friend is harmless anyway, right? He said to stay far, far away. For all I know, he could be very far away right now and I am merely seeing about him. No harm, no foul.

My brain has run away with me by Thursday. Still no word from Gentry. No word at school about where he is or when he'll be back. And Mrs. Newell is a distracted joke of a teacher who can't teach sociology to save her life. She reads her device for most of the class and the way her cheeks get pink every few minutes, I'd swear she's reading erotica.

Gentry, where are you?

My birthday passes without a glitch at school. I've told no one here that it's my birthday, and fortunately, it seems Farrow hasn't spoiled my secret. At home, they post snapshots and video of me from the time I was born until whatever most recent photograph of me is out there, usually some wretched pimpley one of me before I had my growth spurt. The footage plays all day and people I don't ever recall setting eyes on in my life talk about me as if they know me.

I could get used to more birthdays in anonymity, I think, as I'm shutting my locker at the end of the day.

"Go out with us tonight?" Toph asks, falling into step beside me.

Linney and Jemima are with him and they jump in. "Come on, it'll be fun. You've been so quiet all week. You need to chill a little. Homework can wait."

I've been acting like the workload is so overwhelming, when in reality, I'm ahead in all my classes. The benefit of on-one-one teaching worked for me, I guess.

"I can't tonight, you guys. Dinner with my family. But maybe Sunday?"

"Okay, but don't bail," Jemima whines.

"I won't. Promise."

Dinner is a quiet affair. I'm grateful Eden didn't dig deeper into my school life and surprise me with any guests. It's just the family. Uncle Basile even, who I've come to consider as family. He's Luka's uncle, but from what I know of his family, Luka's closer to him than he ever was to either parent.

Luka holds up a glass of wine and we all follow suit. "Now that it's finally legal for you, little sis," he winks, "I'd like to be the first to toast to your year. We have a saying here that goes: 'Say goodbye to a passing year with gratitude and hello to the new with the expectation of even more gratitude to live.' I like the way you grab onto life with both fists already. I know you have your sights on traveling the world and I, for one, am grateful to have this time with you now. I know Eden is happier when you're here, and that's enough reason for me to want you to stay forever..." He squeezes Eden's hand and she turns her swoony eyes toward him. It would be disgusting if it weren't so sweet. "Save room for the best cake Chelsea's ever made. And drink up! You're officially an adult now and look at you, already starting it out right."

He grins and we all take a long swig of the drink. I swallow it all in one gulp and everyone turns to stare at me.

I'm saved by Chelsea, who walks in with the serving dishes piled high with food. Basile checks her out from head to toe. Ew. Love is in the air and I need to rinse my eyes with soap.

Fortunately, I haven't had to put up with the former king and queen of Niaps since moving here. Both are in prison where they belong, although I think we're all holding our breath, knowing the way the courts are regarding royalty can tip upside down at any time.

Luka is constantly on top of the appeals that come up. His parents are determined to get through to the courts of Niaps, and he continues to fight them. I hope they both rot in prison forever.

"What are you thinking right now?" Brienne laughs, her eyes widening as she looks at me.

"Just morbid thoughts, nothing worth repeating," I tell her.

But now that I've thought of the king and queen, I feel more unsettled than I did before dinner. Bad things happen in threes, right? There's the mess with Gentry finding out he's not his parents' biological son. And things have been quieter than usual with Niaps and Farrow...I need to ask Jadon about Alidonia. That's another perk of being the kid sister…it's not as urgent that I stay up on everything, and I've tried my best to actually remove myself from all of it. One day I hope to completely. I'm not cut out for this life. I want peace and anonymity. Freedom.

And Gentry. I want him too.

In whatever capacity he'll allow me.

But now that one more roadblock is out of our way— my age—I'd be lying if I didn't admit that I want all of him.

I have a feeling he's still not going to come around so easily, whether I've had a birthday or not.

We watch a movie after dinner and after everyone goes to bed, I'm restless. I wait until the house is quiet and then I leave quietly, starting my scooter once I'm at the far end of the driveway. I drive to Gentry's house. It's dark and I hope he's sleeping. That would be a gift right now.

I stay there for several minutes…until I get the odd sensation that I'm being watched. I'm sure if it's anyone, it's my guard…even though I thought I'd managed to sneak past him. No one is around from what I can tell. The air is silent and there isn't another car in sight. I start up the scooter and go back down the winding road, trying to shake the jitters that have settled into my bones. I shouldn't have done that.

The last thing I need is to drag the paparazzi to Gentry.

By Sunday, I've gotten over my paranoia about the paparazzi. Nothing has come out about me in the news here, so I shake it off and decide to see if Jemima and the crew can get together earlier than we'd talked about. I don't need another day inside my head.

I text Jemima first, then when I don't hear back right away, I do the dreaded group text. I mind them more than they do, and I groan when texts immediately chime back-to- back.

Toby: Let's hit the beach by the dunes. I can be there in 30.

Linney: I'm finishing breakfast with my parents by there. I'll beat you there :)

Jacque: It's too early. But I'm up for the challenge, L.

Malcolm: It's a good thing I like you, Ava. Once you turn these bastards on, they don't shut up. I'll be there, but shut up.

Jemima: UGH. I overslept. I look terrible. CU there.

I throw clothes over my bikini and throw my hair in a messy bun on top of my head. My bag is already by the door, my beach towel, sunscreen, and hat ready to go.

I stop at The Coffee Library before the beach, but there's no sign of Gentry. It's the one allowance I give myself, the last time I'll think of him today.

I've gotten really good at lying to myself.

Everyone but Jemima is at the beach when I arrive and they greet me like we haven't seen each other in years. I feel some of my tension draining as I run into the water and let the waves carry me out.

Toph and I body surf for a long time, and I feel like a

limp noodle after an hour of waves knocking me back and forth. Toph looks over at me and grins, inching closer.

"You getting tired?" he asks, reaching out for my hand as we float back toward the shore.

"Yeah, a good kind of tired though. I needed this." I lean my head back and float and he does the same, still holding my hand. When it registers that we're still holding hands, I let go and stand up, the water reaching my chest.

He stands up too and pulls my waist to him, leaning in to kiss me before I can stop him. I stand frozen, as he tries to deepen the kiss and then I lean my head back.

"Toph," I whisper.

He puts his hands on my cheeks and comes back in, kissing me with more determination.

I gently push him back and we stand in the water, staring at each other.

"I don't want that," I tell him. "I'm sorry, Toph…I just don't feel the same." I walk out of the water and hear him calling after me, but I don't stop.

Standing by my scooter, just past the sand, Gentry stands there watching me walk away from Toph. I can tell he saw the kiss by the look on his face.

He looks as distraught as I'd feel if I'd just seen him kissing someone else.

CHAPTER EIGHTEEN

GENTRY

Just when I think life can't get worse, the universe tries to prove me wrong. I've had everything thrown at me this week and am barely keeping my head above water. I came to the beach hoping for relief, anything to get my thoughts out of the sewer, anything to escape the chains my life will become if I give in to who I'm now supposed to be.

I'm in denial, plain and simple.

I want to be a schoolteacher. I want my parents to be the nice couple from the small mountain town who argues over board games and who become closer after cancer rather than falling apart. I want to meet a woman who knocks me senseless and makes me feel like every day is brand new. I want the two children, maybe three, and the dog...overlooking the ocean in my fixer-upper that I keep adding onto...

I don't want to be a king.

My dad tried to tell me.

And Alex tried to deny that it was the truth.

But I've done some digging of my own, and if my dad

is right, which I'd believe him over that entitled jackass of a prince any day, I am the rightful king to Yuman. My father is Victros Forbrush and my mother is a prostitute he slept with right before marrying his wife Anais.

Not only is my biological father a cheat, but he's also a liar, because he's been intent on keeping my identity a secret for going on twenty-six years. I guess my adopted father is too, but he claims he has his reasons for the secrecy, good reasons. Reasons he's not shared with me yet, but I think my brain is maxed out with this much anyway.

My mind is still reeling with this news.

Yet nothing braced me for seeing Ava kissing Toph at the beach just now.

I drive back to my place, not bothering to unload the surfboard. I go inside, slamming the door behind me, and get out the bottle of tequila.

The knocking begins after I've taken my first shot. I slam the glass down and pour another, ignoring the door. It's been a revolving door this week between my parents, Elias, and the investigator I've hired.

"Gentry, open the door. I know you're in there," Ava calls.

I finish the second shot in one gulp and pour a third. This is the first time I've turned to alcohol all week—I think I'm due a deeper spiral into the hell I'm already in.

"I want to talk about what you saw...it wasn't how it seemed." Her voice gets stronger. "Please, let me in."

She knocks again and I open the door, not bothering to school my anger.

"I don't want you here, Ava. How many ways do I have to say *go away*?"

The hurt clouds over her eyes and she steps back,

shoulders sagging. The desire to reach out and pull her into my arms is staggering.

"I just want to make sure you're okay," she says quietly.

I sigh and put my hand on the doorjamb, head bowed. "I'm sorry. Listen, I don't want to take it out on you. I don't know which way is up right now. It's best if you're not here for this."

"Let me just say this...because I saw your face...I know you care. I don't have feelings for Toph. I told him I didn't want that kiss," she says, her eyes a deep ocean that I want to dive into. "I don't want him." She steps closer. "I want you."

"You should've wanted him," I tell her. I put my hand on her waist, leaning in. "He's the one you should be falling for, not me."

"Too late," she whispers.

I groan and lean my forehead against hers, my eyes closing. She feels so damn good.

I step back and she stumbles forward, and instead of pushing her back and making her leave, I let her in.

She shuts the door behind her and pulls me against her, standing on tiptoes to wind her hands in my hair. Her lips are on mine and I feel powerless to stop her. I know I could if I really wanted to, if I didn't want this more than my next breath. My tongue collides into hers and I moan into her mouth, hitching her leg up to get her closer. She is a thunderstorm, sending streaks of lightning through her fingers and skin and tongue, and I live for every jolt.

I pick her up and carry her to my bedroom, lying her on the bed, her black and blue hair like midnight against my comforter. She bites her full lower lip and grins and I know I've lost my mind. I can't be thinking clearly to go through with this, but every part of me feels wide awake, hyperfocused. She is the clarity in my tunnel vision.

"You haven't wished me *Happy Birthday* yet," she says, leaning up to kiss me when I pause over her. "I'll forgive you this time, but next time, I deserve a song."

I brush my fingers across her cheek and kiss her nose and all around her mouth. "Happy Birthday, beautiful. You deserve way more than a song."

She kisses me then and I am lost in her. It's the first ounce of relief I've felt since my world came crashing down. The first time my brain isn't racing.

She pulls off my shirt and stares at me with wide eyes, taking me in.

I sit back on my feet and watch as she takes off her shirt.

"I can't get over how perfect you are," I tell her, reaching out to touch her neck. And in the next second, I'm laying her shirt back over her bikini top. "We can't do this, Ava."

She leans up, the shirt falling to the side. "How about you stop denying yourself and let it all go for a little while? We're not hurting anyone…we're not even breaking any rules."

"I'm sure we're breaking a thousand and one rules since you're my student."

"I'm legal, we're not on school property…hell, in Farrow, this would've been legal two years ago. We're behind the times." Her voice is husky with her wit and lust. Her tongue traces across the seam of my lips and they part, eager to let her in.

I kiss her hard, content for now to explore her mouth, to feel her body against mine—my cock is straining to get closer, but I try to rein it in, even while I'm falling apart.

I keep her shirt in place, her bare shoulders the only skin I touch. I crave more, and the way she arches into me lets me know she does too. I pull away and her full lips part, her eyes a hazy blue as she looks up at me. She leans up and gives me a long, slow kiss that wrecks me. I sink into her, still partially clothed, my body lying flush against hers and when that's too much, I kiss down her neck and down her chest, lifting the bottom of her shirt to kiss her belly button. I look up at her and she grins, knocking the shirt off of her chest and onto the floor.

I laugh and lean my forehead between her breasts, pausing to inhale her sweet scent, not wanting to forget anything about this moment. When I lift up and lick a path between her breasts and veer to the right, shifting the material to the side and blowing after I've traced a trail with my tongue, she gasps and her mouth drops when my lips close over her nipple.

She pulls my hair as I suck her rosy tip into my mouth and I lose my mind when she reaches down to put her hand between us.

She drops her hand and my lips come off of her with a pop.

"What—? I ask, turning toward the sound at the door.

CHAPTER NINETEEN

AVA

The knock on the door is like a car wreck slamming into the bed. His mouth was doing the most amazing things—he hadn't even gotten to the best part yet, but I was *all in*.

Then the pounding starts, and he looks up at me with horror, jumping up.

I dive for my clothes, putting them on as fast as I can. "My scooter is out there," I tell him frantically, looking for my shoes. "Whoever is here has seen that already."

"I'm not answering the door," he says. I toss him his shirt and he pulls it over his head.

"See who it is."

"Who could it be that would really be okay with this?" he asks, his glare drilling holes into me.

I glare back and want to cry that the magic of the afternoon is already diluted into this gross feeling of rejection.

"I'll sneak out the back anyway. Maybe they *didn't* see the scooter. It doesn't sound like they're going to leave."

He nods and I want to scream at him for agreeing. I don't want to be someone he hides. I want to stand by his side. I want him to be proud that I'm there. Or I want him to ignore the door altogether and get lost in me again.

The knocking continues and I grab his arm before he walks out of his bedroom.

"Don't push me away. Whoever it is, whatever time you have to think about things between now and when I see you again…just please don't push me away. We can deal with whatever comes." I take a deep breath and let go of his arm.

He doesn't say anything, his chest heaving with his breaths, and I know that I've lost him. He's already pulled away.

I pace my bedroom floor, checking my phone every few minutes. My thoughts scatter to all of the worst scenarios. Why won't he just let me know? It could be Principal Everst, Elias, one of his students. It could be anyone. It could be Alex again, and if that's the case, I'm worried about him. I'm worried, period.

I turn, about to go ask Eden to tell me all she knows about Alex, when a text comes. I sigh when I see that it isn't Gentry, but it's Jadon, and I'm overwhelmed with homesickness for my brother.

Jadon: You've been awfully quiet this week. What new Niapsianisms are you addicted to now that you're on the beach every day?

I wish I was at the beach every day! Not all of us can live in the Lap O Luxury as you do, O Mighty King…

Jadon: Aw, don't spoil my visions of the endless sunshine and constant beach time. I'm envious of your days outside this castle. The walls are closing in on me. I

even miss Mother right now. She's been gone for a week and I thought her silence would be a relief. Instead, it's like a tomb.

I miss you so much. I stare at the ceiling, trying to force the lump in my throat to go away. **When I'm done with school, we should go on a trip together. You deserve a vacation. Speaking of needing a vacation… everything okay with Alidonia? I don't know if I'm just in my own little bubble more than ever, or if it's actually quiet.**

Jadon: You're in a bubble, but I think it's good. Best to stay that way.

A sharp pang slices through my chest. Fear. **What do you mean? What am I missing?**

Jadon: You're safe there. That's all that matters.

You're being a dick, being obviously vague.

Jadon: I see that kingdom is not able to clean up your mouth any better than this one is. I'll see you soon, Ava. I don't want to talk about heavy things right now. I'll come see you and I can spoil our visit with all the negative if you insist.

It's a deal. When?

Jadon: Well, I did miss your birthday. I was hoping you'd be free on Friday.

This Friday?! YES. I will absolutely be free. I can't wait to see you.

Jadon: Night, little one. Sleep well. XO

Finally, right after I've turned my light off, I hear from him.

SAF: I'm sorry.

I wait for what he'll say next because he can't leave it at that, can he? What does that even mean? I'm sorry? He regrets kissing me? He feels bad that we had to stop?

And who was it? If nothing else, I thought he'd put my mind at ease about that.

When he doesn't say anything else, I come up with several responses, most of them sounding cold and bitter. Fortunately, I think before I send. I have too much dignity to respond. If he regrets what happened, he won't listen to me tonight anyway, and I'm tired of trying to convince him we should be together. His body and his mouth said something completely different than whatever regret he might be feeling now.

I try to shut my screaming thoughts off and fail miserably. I play and replay the way he gave in to his feelings today, the way time stopped when we kissed. Somewhere in the thoughts of him on top of me, his tongue sending bursts of adrenaline inside of me as he made his way down my body, I realize we never even talked about what's going on with his family. Part of me wonders if that's why he touched me at all...so he could forget.

I hit the snooze button four times before I get up, tripping over the shoes I left out. Cotton stuffs the inside of my head and chains hang over my body, the result of a discombobulated light head and heavy body. Or maybe it's the other way around, I think as I stare at myself in the mirror. I look hard and hollow.

But I'm not broken, I tell myself silently, running my fingers over my reflection. I half expect the mirror to crack as I touch it. My lies to myself bleeding out of my skin.

I didn't sleep last night. Not until this morning; the last time I looked at the clock was fifteen minutes before the alarm went off.

I shower in a daze, my limbs feeling weighted down and my head like it's stuffed with fairy floss. I don't even remember washing my hair, but when I bend over to wrap a towel around it, it feels clean. I think I did. It's raining outside, something that hasn't happened since I moved to Niaps, and at the last second, I ask Brienne if she'd drive me to school.

She looks concerned. "Are you okay?"

"I didn't sleep and it's raining. I can ask Harmi too. I just didn't see—"

"No, no. Your sister won't be up for another hour. She won't even know I'm gone. Let me speak to Harmi and I can leave within five minutes."

I nod and slump against the wall, vacantly watching the storm brewing outside. My still-damp messy bun leaves a mark on the wall I lean against and I force myself to stand up straight.

Brienne is back before I can get too comfortable there and for someone who's mostly quiet and stoic, she's unusually chatty and animated.

"Look at this rain. I didn't realize how much I missed having weather until moving here and it's the same all the time. Do you miss Farrow?"

"I miss Jadon. I do miss the dark..." I stare out the car window. "The rain *is* nice."

"Why aren't you sleeping?" She gets straight to the point.

"Relationships are complicated." I start to say more, but

I pause and then she's turning to look at me before she turns on the car.

"That's all you're going to give me?" She laughs and backs out of the parking spot, going slowly down the long driveway. When we reach the gate, she looks at me again and sighs. "Have you made good friends here? I know it was so complicated at home. I'd hoped it wouldn't be that way for you here."

"It's been great. I've made a few good friends...five or six, actually."

She makes a sound in her throat and I turn to look at her. She's staring in the rearview mirror.

"What's wrong?" I ask.

"Nothing...I think. I don't know...for a second, I thought someone was following us."

I turn and look at the cars behind us. None seem to be too close or acting bizarre.

"One of my friends has felt like that recently," I tell her. "Weird."

She shakes her head. "They turned off. I must've been imagining it. Sorry—old habits die hard, you know."

"So they say."

She pulls into the school parking lot and I turn to her before I get out. "It'll be okay," she says. "Whatever relationship issue you're having, just be honest and expect the same in return."

I nod. "That's good advice. Thanks for the ride." "Anytime. Will you need to be picked up?"

"No, I can work something out for later," I say, turning to lean in. "See you at dinner."

She waves and I walk off, feeling a little more awake than before. My nerves are on alert.

When I head inside, I get to the entrance and turn

around, looking at the parking lot behind me. I don't know if it's all that's happened with Gentry or with Brienne thinking someone was following us, but I get the strangest feeling that someone is watching.

Gentry looks as bad as I feel. There are dark circles under his eyes and he doesn't say anything when I walk in. The bell rings right after I enter, and he starts teaching right away. Usually, he has a few personal touches he'll throw in —how was our weekend, did we see the moon last night? Whatever random thing that comes to his mind—but today, he tells us the pages he wants us to click on our device and goes after it, like it's memorized.

I have to sketch to stay awake—not that he's not inter-esting—but just sitting still is enough to knock me out, so I make an elaborate drawing of flowers and eyes; it fills the whole page by the time the bell rings.

He passes out our test scores as we walk out of class and I make sure to be the last one leaving. I see Toph waiting for me and bend down to fix the lace on my boot. When I look up again, he's gone and Gentry is standing there watching me.

"It was my dad," he says, his voice low and hoarse. "I apologize for not finding a way to let you know, but he stayed until this morning. He did notice your scooter, but he won't say anything. He thinks it's mine." He drags a hand over his jawline and my heart aches with how exhausted he seems. "Are you okay? I was worried about you…after…"

"We kissed?" I look around as I whisper it, but the halls

are loud with students passing by. No one is paying atten-tion to us. Having this conversation at school isn't wise, but I'm so happy to finally be talking to him, I let caution fall to the wind. "I was worried about *you*...and fine about everything else."

When I smile at him, his eyes soften and he leans in a bit closer. "You're invading every thought I have. I think I need you to come put me to sleep again." He grins and I see the guy on the beach at the wedding again, the lighthearted guy that didn't have the world on his shoulders. "I'm walking in my sleep and losing all scruples in the process."

"I can see that. You'd never use the word scruples on a normal day."

He chuckles but then quickly sobers. "One slip and this could all be over." He slides his palms together. "I look at you and I don't care if everything else burns." His eyes gleam and he stares at my mouth like he wants to inhale me. "Talk sense into me, Ava."

"I've always loved bonfires," I whisper with a smirk.

He runs his hands through his hair and takes a step back, closing his eyes.

"This is such a bad idea," he says. "You know that, right? We just...it's not..."

I hold up my hand and shake my head. "Stop. Just stop overthinking everything. You have enough on your mind without me adding to it." I turn and walk to the door, turning around one more time to look at him. "You need to sleep. I'll help with that. *Later*."

CHAPTER TWENTY

AVA

I'm relieved when Toph acts normal at lunch. I was afraid he'd be moody, but he's sweet, if not a little quieter than usual. He makes an effort to include me in conversation and I'm so grateful, I want to hug him. Bad idea, so I don't. The others are in good moods after the weekend. Jacque can't stop talking about Sade, and finally, Malcolm throws a dinner roll at him to put an end to it. The normalcy feels nice. This is what I wanted in my senior year of high school —friends and even a guy who makes my heart pitter-patter expecting to see me later tonight.

Okay, nothing about the guy—*man*—is normal, but it still feels like maybe we're heading there.

I want that more than anything.

I look up to see him walking away from Ms. Shoman. *Phoebe.* I want to roll my eyes every time I think her name. She looks pissed and is trying to catch up to him. She must feel eyes on her because she glances across the room and sees me staring at her. Maybe it's the only time my royal blood is convenient because she schools her features into a friendly smile and stops chasing Gentry.

Good. Give the poor guy a break.

Linney gives me a ride home and we work on homework together for an hour before she leaves for dinner. I eat with the fam and head to my room early, feigning a heavier work- load than I really have. I wait until the house is quiet and then leave out the back door, cutting across the pool to where my scooter is parked.

I'm only a few blocks down the road when I see someone following. I think it's one of the Catano guards by the look of the car.

Not tonight. I don't think so. I turn down a side street and then down an alley, shutting the scooter off. I wait until I see them passing several times, searching for me. When they head in the opposite direction I want to go, I grin and take off, enjoying the night breeze against my face as I ride to Gentry's house.

His street is quiet, and the lights twinkling below are magical, skirting across the water. He has the best view in Niaps. The door opens as I'm walking on the farsynthia-lined path and I lean down to stick my nose in one. Gentry walks outside and plucks a bloom off of the stem and tucks it behind my ear.

He's not as tense as he was earlier, and I wait until he closes the door behind us to ask him about it. Before I have a chance, his hands curl around my shoulders and he wraps me in a bone-crushing hug. I close my eyes and wrap my arms around his waist, my head leaning against his chest.

Time pauses while our breathing synchronizes. I forget how tired I am when my body is against his and he seems to have the same thought, his chest rising and falling more rapidly as the tension between us begins to crackle.

When he leans back and looks at me, desire haunting his eyes, I lean up on my tiptoes and touch his nose with mine.

"I want to light the match." I practically breathe the words into his mouth, our lips are so close to touching.

His hands clench my waist and he closes the space between us, his lips whispering across mine as he says, "You already have."

His kiss is an all-consuming blaze. It's crazed, our teeth, our tongues, our lips colliding. He lifts me up, his hands landing on my backside as he carries me to the bedroom. His lips never leave mine, his tongue wreaking havoc on me as he leans over me, placing me gently on the bed.

I pull him against me and whimper when the weight of his body presses into every contour of mine. He feels like he could crush me, and I would be begging for more. I want to seep into his skin and live in there, he feels like my lifeline.

He pulls back and looks at me. "I don't think I can stay away from you, Ava."

"So, stop trying," I tell him.

He sits up, his knees shifting forward as he looks at me the way I've dreamed about, the way he can only look at me when we're alone. I pull my tank over my head and his eyes glaze over when he sees my breasts.

"You're the most exquisite thing I've ever seen," he says, his tongue peeking out to swipe his lower lip, followed by his teeth.

His shirt comes off in one tug and he reaches down and drags my pants down, my boy shorts along with them.

When his breath skates across my bare skin, the heat rushes between my legs and I gasp, every nerve ending coming to life. His fingers slide down my thighs and legs and then suddenly I'm chilled when he stands up, his pants landing on top of my shirt. I stare at him, drinking in the sight as he bends down, kissing my stomach and up to the valley between my breasts. He places his knee on the bed and then straddles me, nothing touching except his mouth on my neck. I lean into his lips and my eyes flutter closed. He teases me with his soft touches, while my body begs him for more.

"Gentry," I whisper into his skin and then I bite his shoulder when his nose tickles my neck.

It awakens something primal in him when my teeth dig in and he bucks into me, hitting that sensitive spot between my legs just right. I arch into him and he stares at me before rubbing against me again. I pull his briefs down and he doesn't stop me, leaning up long enough to get them out of the way before kissing his way down my body. When he places a kiss between my legs and then dives his tongue into me, I lean up to watch. When my eyes start to fall back in my head, I pull his head up, loving the way his lips are shining with me.

"I want you inside me when I come," I tell him.

He pulls a condom out of the drawer of the side table and slides it on, his eyes never leaving mine. I want to watch him, but I can't tear my eyes away from his. I want to know what he's thinking, but I don't want to break the spell by speaking. When he pushes just the very tip into me, I nearly fall apart with that one touch. I was so close already.

"More," I gasp.

"You feel so good." He dips further in and I spasm against him. He closes his eyes and we breathe together. "I never want this to end," he says against my mouth.

He thrusts all the way in and I adjust to the fullness, loving the way he fills me up. I can't believe this is happening, and yet, it feels like everything has been leading up to this moment, right here, right now.

I clutch his face in my hands when he starts rocking into me, a slow and steady building push and pull that ramps up the need in me. My hands are all over him. His hair, his back, his face, his thighs. I pull him into me, so it doesn't feel like there's an end or a beginning to us. I want all of him.

"Ava," he says on a long groan. "Fuck. You are meant for me." He drags out of me and then glides back in with a slow deliberateness that makes me shudder. "Do you feel that? You are my destruction and I just want *more*."

He pulses into me and I cry out, coming apart against him. I shake and clench around him as he swears and goes faster, prolonging my sweet torment.

He doesn't stop and the feeling in me builds until I'm panting harder, about to fall apart again.

"Ruin me," I tell him. "Until there's nothing left."

He groans into me and lets go, like a beast unleashed.

I hold on for dear life as he drives into me faster and faster, faster and faster, my eyes rolling back, my mouth falling open as he explodes into me.

I crash along with him, feeling like I'm a shooting star jumping from the sky into the deep blue waves. I soar and then crest along the peaks of the wave, each pulse different than the one before.

Our bodies are slick with sweat and when he gives one

last long push into me, just to squeeze out the last ounce of pleasure, my breath quickens again. He hears it and puts his hands between us, his thumb pressing the exact spot I need to detonate again.

"Ahh," I cry out.

He's there to inhale my whimpers, his kiss long and sweet. I feel wrung out when I come down from my high, my body lazy like a cat in the sun.

Gentry looks like he's ready for a marathon, his gaze dark and heated as he looks down at me. He slides out and discreetly takes care of the condom while I stretch out under his covers. He comes back and I turn to watch him, his beautiful body on display. God, I can't believe he fit; he's huge everywhere. I flush when I look at him and he notices, sucking in a breath. His dick reaches out to meet me and I lean up on my elbows, the sheet falling off my breasts.

"I'll remember the way you look right now...forever," he says, leaning over to kiss me, his fingers looping through mine. His face dives into my hair as he inhales and his nose teases my neck. "I never want you to leave my bed."

"You need to sleep, remember?" I tease. I wrap my arms around his neck and my hands tug on his hair. I lick a trail against his neck and he shivers against me, lowering his body onto mine.

This time, we move slowly, reverently...like it could be the last time we ever do this, so every moment is savored. I won't say make love because love is not on the table yet; I'm scared to imagine how he'd run if he thought I was considering love at all. But it does come to mind when he stares at me like I am his world.

His salvation.

When he wrings a scream out of me that nearly splits me in two, I feel like I am being born and dying at the same time.

My emergence.

My oblivion.

It's as if heaven and earth collide when he moans my name. He's beautiful when he finally lets go, his eyes like a storm cloud and his muscles clenched until his veins are popping. I have never heard anything that moves me so much, that vulnerable raspy sound he makes when he explodes.

When we're both still, the magnitude of what we've just done settling over the room and our bodies like a giant down blanket, I close my eyes and wait for him to pull away.

I don't think I can bear it, but I brace myself.

Instead, his lips brush over my eyebrows, my hair, my ear, my nose, my chin, my lips…until I open my eyes to stare at the truth.

He looks at me with intent, his eyes stark but not apologetic. I feel a flutter of hope that he felt the magnitude of the night as much as I did. That this is not just a release of hormones but a revelation of sorts: I am his; he is mine.

"How am I ever going to leave this bed?" he asks, his nose burrowing into my neck. "This body of an angel…" He pulls out of me and I groan, my hands clasping together behind his neck.

"That's easy—don't."

He grins and climbs off of me, walking to the bathroom.

I stare at his backside as he walks away.

He walks back in with shorts on and I'm disappointed that I'm missing another good look at all of him. He smiles like he knows what I'm thinking and I reach for my shirt to cover up.

"Nuh-uh," he says, tossing my shirt.

I point to his shorts. "No fair, you totally bailed on the naked thing."

"I didn't want to scare you when I came in swinging."

"Swinging?" I laugh.

He shrugs. "It's what happens with long satisfied dicks; although it would've been short-lived once I saw you lying here again." He gets in bed beside me and runs his hands through his hair, sighing. "Are you okay?" he says, softer.

"I'm amazing," I tell him. "This night has been...beyond."

He turns and slides down so we're face-to-face. "You are a revelation," he whispers. "A song without meter, imperfect in its measures...color and sound colliding into me, and I am helpless to stand against it. I wouldn't want to...stand against it. I want to dive in, headlong, and feel the rush of loving you."

I stare at him, moved but trying to keep it light. "You make me sound far better than I am."

He smirks and I pause my strokes on his chest.

"Loving, you said..." I move closer, my lips drawn to his like a magnet.

He flushes and I grin wider.

"You're quite the poet." My words are punctuated with kisses between every space.

"Only with you. With everything and everyone else, I am ordinary. You are the only one who sees something more." His eyes are shining when I start laughing at him, his fingers digging into my sides with a tickle. "What? It's true…"

"First of all, you are full of *shite*," I overenunciate. "You have a mirror…not only is every female at school but Joand and Carma into you because you know, they're together and only into each other, but…Ms. Phoebe sees something more, let me tell you." I roll my eyes while his words "only with you" wash over me like a warm shower on the coldest day.

"Ms. Phoebe isn't allowed in this bed, even if it's just her name," he says, biting my shoulder.

I lean into the bite and moan and he flips me over until I'm on top. I slide the condom on him this time and ride him until we're both breathless.

CHAPTER TWENTY-ONE

GENTRY

I push on her chest and she lies back again, pulling me with her. When my lips touch hers again, we both gasp and start a fevered dance. Again.

I groan and feed the desire that has consumed me since the day I met her. My mouth covers every inch of her skin, saving the best for the long, tortured, last. When my tongue finally flicks across her tight little bud, she screams my name and begs me for more.

The guilt I have lessens with every touch. Everything about her feels right. If this is wrong, I've lost all touch with reality and every moral I've ever had has been meaningless, but it doesn't feel that way.

It feels like coming home.

It feels like truth.

It feels like I've found my missing piece.

I thrust into her with the next breath. She gasps and wraps her legs around me tighter, greedy for more. And I give it to her slowly, so slowly that it's painful, and still, she cries out for more. It's intoxicating, the way her fingers claw at my back and her eyes wind their way into my heart like roots that won't stop growing.

"I don't want to let you go," I tell her.

"Don't," she whispers. "This is everything I need right here. You are. Everything." Her head tilts back and she cries out, her body arching. "Gentry!" She falls apart in my arms and I feel like *this* is where I am king.

With her, I'm willing to risk it all.

When I kiss her goodbye, I should feel like the worst man alive and yet I only wish she could stay until morning so I could keep making her mine.

Even while feeling hopeful, deep down, I know a future with her is unlikely. She won't want me once she knows everything, so maybe there's even more to feel guilty about —having sex with her when I know there isn't a future— but for once, I lived in the moment. And it felt damn beautiful. I don't want to sully it with all the reasons why we shouldn't have been together. She felt too perfect writhing underneath me, too perfect riding on top of me, too perfect every single way I had her.

It will only feel wrong if she falls for me, but she's wiser than anyone gives her credit. Niaps is only a brief stopping point for the rest of her adventure. I am merely a signpost that she can look back on fondly as she goes to her next destination. At least that's what I'm telling myself when I crawl into bed without her, already missing her warm, soft skin against mine.

I won't regret it.

I won't.

During lunch the next day, I feel eyes on me when I leave the school to sit and look at the ocean. My thoughts are fighting with my face at school—it took all my willpower to set my features into nonchalance when I saw Ava in class this morning. I wanted to kiss those puffy lips, and my skin heated when I saw a mark I'd left on her neck. I wonder if she wore that shirt on purpose, so I'd see it and remember. It worked.

The hair on the back of my neck prickles in awareness and I turn around, seeing nothing but the sand for miles. There's not a soul in sight, but it doesn't change the wariness I feel. I get in the car and sit there for a few minutes, watching as cars pass before leaving myself. I haven't heard from Alex again. Jerome, the investigator I hired, proved that I am, without question, the firstborn son of the king of Yuman. What the fuck do I do with this information? It hits me in the face like a bullet every morning when I look in the mirror, and then I spend the rest of the day trying to forget. I want to squash it, pretend it doesn't exist, and live my idyllic life overlooking the water of Niaps. Something tells me that's not the way things will go.

It's part of why I gave in to my feelings for Ava last night. I needed something that grounded me before everything else falls apart. And as wrong as it might be, Ava is that for me. How she managed to do that in such a short time, I have no idea, but it doesn't change the fact that it's true.

I only hope that I got her out of my system.

I picture her as she rode me, her biteable lips parted as she moaned my name over and over again, and I slam my fist on the steering wheel.

What the fuck am I going to do?

My dad came to my house a few days ago, handing me a thick file.

"This should explain a lot," he said.

"Okay," I nodded, "finally, we're getting somewhere beyond these circles you're spinning. Why don't you just tell me everything first, and I'll look at the file later. It seems there was a good reason for keeping it a secret. I'm the bastard son—why would you even know who I am?"

"Victros and I were friends. And he hasn't kept his side of the bargain."

"What bargain is that? Me?" I scowled at my father, the beginning of a headache forcing its way into the edges of my mind. "I'm tired of the games, Dad. I had to hire someone— with money I don't really have right now, I might add—to get to the bottom of this. I don't trust anyone, and you're at the top of that list. So start talking. No more secrets. Please. You owe me that much."

He looks haggard as he sits down. "You're right. It's time." He touches the rim of the potted plant Ava gave me and stares absently at the leaves. "We grew up together in Yuman, Victros and me. I was the son of Victros's tutor. We did everything together and even though it disturbed our parents that we were best mates, no one saw too much harm in our friendship. I even followed him to Kings Passage— he went as a student and I went as his guard—and that's when he entrusted me with a secret...you. He met Shara, your biological mother, at a bar and they slept together only a few times before she told him she was pregnant. He paid her off and she disappeared once the baby was born—I still have not been able to find her—and I covered for him. I went home and married my sweetheart right away. Everyone assumed she was pregnant when we got married because you came eight months later. Victros promised he would tell you the truth when you were five and when that time came and went, neither of us wanted to mess anything up. I didn't want to give you up, and he didn't want to damage his king- dom. His father had passed in that time and he was well into ruling Yuman by then. We made a new arrangement… when you turned twenty-one or if he became sick…but when your birthday came and went, he managed to get out of that too, saying his alliance with the surrounding kingdoms was too shaky at the time to create more unwanted attention. And then there was the matter of his son, Alex, who naturally—along with everyone else—assumed the kingdom would be passed to him."

He put his head in his hand and took a few moments before speaking again. I was impatient to hear the rest and couldn't sit still. It was too much to process, all of it. I got up to pace the room, waiting for him to continue.

"I tried to force the issue when I was sick. I very nearly told you the truth then, but he promised." His voice quieter, he whispered, "He *promised*. And I wanted to believe my childhood friend was a man of his word, even then. But he's changed. So much has changed since we were kids. I still believe he's a good man in there, but his loyalty to his wife and kids is blinding him."

"I don't enter the equation of being his child. He wiped his hands of me, is that what you're saying?"

His shoulders bowed with the heaviness of what he'd carried, but I was still too upset to even look at him for very long. I didn't want to feel empathy for a man who had played into keeping my life a lie, no matter how good he'd been to me. I wasn't there yet and didn't know if I'd ever be. "Victros is sick, Gentry. He's sick and he has found a way to avoid telling the truth about you every other time. I'm not going to let you lose your birthright just because he's a coward. It's time the truth be told. The kingdom of Yuman is yours and you need to be there, learning from him while he's still alive, not here in Niaps, biding your time. This career of yours—I've always encouraged you to do what you want to do, thinking Victros would come through when the time was right, but your life as a teacher…it's going nowhere, son. It's not who you are."

The pain in my chest grew the longer he spoke, a lump gathering in my throat. Everything I thought I knew dwindled down to nothing.

When he was quiet for a few moments, I turned to face him again. "What if I don't want it?"

"There's no way for you to know whether you do or don't until you're there."

"Oh, I don't think that's true at all," I said, my voice hard. "If you think I'm cut out for that life, you don't know me at all. And it sounds like you've had firsthand experience with what it's like…what makes you think I could ever do that job and be happy?"

He sighed and leaned forward, his elbows on his knees. "It's not a job I envy anyone, but you're a good man. You chase peace and honor, you would lead with dignity and nobility…what more could we ask for in a king?"

"Who knew you were such a patriot?" I shook my head, amazed. It's like he was a complete stranger to me. My dad, my hero, the one I hoped I took after and strove to emulate, was not who I thought he was. "I never even knew you lived in Yuman…you didn't share with me your love for the country you thought I'd one day be leading, you didn't instill in me a love for the great King Forbrush. How were you hoping this would all transpire, and what did you stand to gain from all of it?"

His face flushed and he looked sad and maybe a bit angry. "It has been a daily struggle to let you go. You're mine in every way that matters. Your mother and I have loved you from the moment we knew we would be your parents, and if it were up to my selfish desires, I would've never revealed the truth to you. But I would be doing you such a huge disservice, a crime even. It would be a lie then, our love for you. Because in letting you go, I'm giving you your heritage, your calling, your rightful kingdom." He took a shuddering breath and added, "And with that, I'm hoping you will still find a place for me in your heart."

I ignored his last words because I honestly didn't know how I felt about him right then.

But I did know this:

"I don't want it. I don't want any of it."

I finish the rest of the day in a fog, my thoughts conflicted about what to do next about *everything*. Ava feels like the only bright spot in an otherwise dark existence and I can't even fully give in to her light. What will I do when that too is extinguished from my life for good?

CHAPTER TWENTY-TWO

AVA

Seeing Gentry the morning after is harder than I expected. I hate having to hide my feelings. I've never been good at that. My rebellious flair for saying how I really feel is at odds with squashing down how happy I am to see him. He's back to avoiding me and if he were texting me or giving me the slightest *anything* to show he's in the same lusty haze as I am in, it would make things a helluva lot easier.

But nope.

He's closed off and more distant than ever.

I'm also going to have to be more careful sneaking out because Harmi was waiting for me when I got home last night, and he was *not* happy with me.

"Next time you want to lose your guard, there will be a little family meeting with your sister and Luka," he said.

"I should be able to do homework at a friend's house without a guard," I told him with plenty of attitude, but inside I was shaking that I'd come so close to getting caught with Gentry.

I go the whole day without exchanging a single word with Gentry and am pretty pissy by the time I head to my locker. Linney tries to talk me into going to Fran's, but I'm just not in the mood.

How could I have imagined last night? There's no way I built up how amazing it was in my head, but in the light of day, is he really full of regret and remorse?

I want to bang my head against the locker, but instead, I lean on it and count to ten.

Breathe, Ava.

"Ava, can I see you for a moment?" His voice is stern and I lift my head up and stare at Gentry standing next to me, his face unreadable. For the first time today, I am able to take a deep breath that fully fills my lungs.

I look at Linney and wave back at her as she walks off, before looking at Gentry again.

"Uh, sure, yeah," I say, lifting my backpack higher. "Everything okay?"

"I just want to ask you about this assignment before I grade it," he says.

I wonder if he's saying that for everyone else's benefit or if I really did botch my essay on the social benefits of gleaning.

"Oh. Okay."

I pass Toph and Jacque, who heard the whole thing, and Toph gives me a scrunched funny face to try and ease my concern—at least that's how it seems. I hope he's not picking up the vibes I'm putting off about Gentry.

I follow Gentry to his classroom and before he shuts the door behind us, he looks down the hall to see if anyone is around. The halls have mostly cleared out.

"I've tried to talk myself out of this all day, but I just

had to see you," he says, leaning against the door. "Are you okay?"

I prop myself against his desk and fold my arms. "I'd be better if you'd look at me."

His eyes lift then and do a slow perusal up and down my body. I feel the heat burst through my cheeks and put my hands on my face to cool them down.

He takes a few steps toward me and stops a foot away. I make up the difference, stepping forward until our shoes touch. He smiles and my heart tumbles over itself.

"Remind me—what do you hate about being a princess?" he asks.

My head tilts as I study him. This isn't where I saw this conversation going, but I never know with him. "You are full of surprises. Okay, let's see…everything."

He tenses and then swipes his hand over his mouth. I watch, entranced. His *mouth*. God, I remember it all over me last night and can hardly think straight.

"Is it really *everything*?" he asks. "Or are you just saying an easy, quick answer?"

My brows come together in the middle as I stare at him, trying to figure out what this is about. Finally, I nod.

"Yes, I hate everything about it. Except I love my family… but I'd probably love them even more if I were not a princess."

"What about the financial security?"

"That part is nice, yes. But there's a price that comes with that. Expectations. It's cloying and makes me feel like I'm drowning. I want no part of it."

His face looks pinched when I say that, and I could swear he pales despite his usually tanned cheeks.

"What is this about?"

"Where are you going first when you leave here? Do

you know yet?" He changes the subject, walking around to the other side of his desk.

I take a deep breath, feeling the loss of him standing so close.

"I've never been to Yuman..."

His eyes are alarmed. "What?"

I put my hand on my hip and lean over the desk, my other hand on his papers. "What's wrong with that?"

"Nothing. I just expected you to say somewhere exotic."

"Well, it's a start. From there, I can go to all the other places I haven't been...I'd like to see The Sea of Caninsula... Buraties, Ephrome...but yeah, good old Yuman seems as good a place as any to start. It's close. It's more affordable than here."

"But you could afford to live anywhere."

"Just because I can doesn't mean I want to..."

His eyes narrow as he looks at me.

"What?"

"There's a lot to tell you. It'll just give you another reason to stay far, far away from me..."

I groan, the sound bouncing louder than I intended in the empty classroom. "Don't tell me we're back to that, Gentry." I step around the desk and stand next to him. I don't touch him because I'm not desperate, but God, he's driving me crazy with this emotional seesaw.

"You knew it was just the one night, right?" he asks. "I couldn't stand it if I thought I was hurting you."

I feel like the air is knocked out of me, like I shouldn't still be standing, but I don't show it. My game face has taken a long time to get just right, and it is switched *on* right now, no question.

"I hoped you would see how right we are together and

that it wouldn't just be a one-night thing," I admit. "But I'm a big girl. I can handle this too." I take a step back and he reaches out, grabbing my hand.

"It was the best night of my life," he whispers. "I can't stop thinking about it...you are...last night is something I will never forget," he finishes, his Adam's apple dropping as he opens and closes his mouth.

"So this was just you making sure I'm okay and letting me know it'll never happen again—do I have that right?"

He looks crushed with the tone in my voice, but I don't feel sorry for him.

"I was making sure to keep your future the way you want it—with as little drama as possible and as far from royalty as you can get."

The way he says that last part has me stumped. "What are you not saying?" I finally ask.

"It's best you don't know, Ava. At least not yet, trust me." He grabs his bag and adds a few more papers to it. "I'll see you tomorrow, okay?"

I turn and walk out, not able to look at him for another second. Once again, I'm put back in my place. A child who can't handle the truth. I'm over it.

I just wish I could be over *him* if that's his default.

But the more I think about it, the more something isn't adding up. My answer about hating being a royal swayed him. It doesn't make sense.

Jadon calls the next night.

"Are you ready for me this weekend? I can't wait to see you." He doesn't bother to say hello.

"So ready. Do you have to wait until Friday? Can't you come tomorrow?"

He laughs. "I wish. Unfortunately, I have back-to-back meetings for the next few days. Friday is the first chance I get, and I had to do major calisthenics to get that working…"

"Ugh. I hate your life."

He sighs into the phone and I can imagine his eyes getting that distant look in them when he makes that sound. "Most days I do too, little one. But…it'll make our time together this weekend all the better, right? *Right*?" he says, laughing again.

I snort. "You sound like you're threatening me to have a good time. I can't be bought, King Jadon," I say in my most proper Farrow accent.

"Nevah, nevah, good lady. I shan't resort to forcing anyone to do anything from henceforth."

"Oh, Lord, you need to get out more," I moan. "Hurry up and get here. You're losing your cool card fast."

He laughs and we hang up a few minutes later, after deciding where we'll go over the weekend. I promise to give Eden all the details and see what she can do with us.

Hopefully, it'll be just what I need to get my mind off of Gentry.

CHAPTER TWENTY-THREE

AVA

It's Thursday night before I realize that one of my bracelets is at Gentry's. I've looked all over my room and the entire mansion—even outside, and I've hardly been out there this week. I didn't think I wore it to his place, but when I've torn my room up for the third time, I vaguely remember taking it off and putting it on his side of the bed.

I could text him to bring it to school the next day, but that creates more problems. We've been safe at school so far, but I don't want to make it riskier than it needs to be. I wait until the house is quiet and then ride over there, managing to lose the guard just before the second to last turn. Harmi won't be pleased, but I don't care. I'm on a red scooter for crying out loud, how hard can it be to keep me in sight? Not that I'm complaining—I get off on the thrill of one-upping security.

I knock once and Gentry comes to the door wearing shorts and a T-shirt, his hair wet from a shower. He looks good enough to eat and I have to consciously remind myself that I'm not here for that.

He looks suspicious when he sees me and I lift my hands, already defensive before I've even said a word.

"I know you don't want me here. I just needed to see if my bracelet is here. I think I put it on your nightstand."

"Yeah, it's here," he says, letting me in.

He closes the door and I stand there, unsure if I should go get it or if he will.

"I liked having it here." He shrugs, his lips quirking up to the side.

"You are so confusing…" I sigh. "I thought I was pretty skilled at figuring people out, but you—" I point at him and shake my head, my hand falling down to my side when he laughs.

"Normally I'm an open book, but you've caught me in a weird time of my life. I don't blame you for wanting nothing to do with me."

"Who ever said I want nothing to do with you? You're the one who wants me out of the picture." I scowl at him as I say it and my face heats up. "It's like constant whiplash."

His head falls back against the wall and he tugs on his hair. "I'm so sorry, Ava." He steps forward and pulls me into a hug. I reluctantly put my hands on his waist. "There is no part of me that wants you to stay away. I *only* want you."

"Then why do you constantly push me away?"

"Why would you want a relationship where you have to be hidden for months? And you don't even know all that's going on with my family yet. It's not good, Ava. It won't be a life you want, either direction I decide to go."

"I wish you'd just talk to me. Give me the options. It's my choice to make," I whisper.

He puts his hands on my cheeks. "I don't want to make you choose a life of more misery. I care too much about you to let that happen. This is me putting you first."

"You're making no sense. And I don't know why we have to figure it all out now anyway. Let's have a nice, sweet fall into each other…"

"That would be so nice, wouldn't it?" he says. He leans his forehead against mine and the heat between us builds until it is physically painful.

His hands move down to my shoulders and down my back, my waist, and I can feel the taut way he's holding me now; he's being cautious, and yet, his body is hard against mine. The air is pulsating with desire and I'm so tired of fighting it.

I look up at him and he crashes into me, teeth and tongue and lips colliding.

"Ava," he moans. "Why can't I get enough?"

"Take all you want," I whisper between kisses. "I hope it's never enough."

He lifts me up and kisses me all the way to his room. When we get there, we don't even make it to the bed. He puts a condom on while he's standing, his lips never leaving mine. Once it's on, he nudges me into the wall and lifts me up until he can drive all the way in. I cry out, the rush of fullness exactly what I wanted.

"Don't stop," I cry. "Don't ever stop."

"Never," he whispers into my neck. "I won't push you away anymore, I swear it. I should, but I just can't…"

I clutch his face, staring at him as he thrusts hard into me. "No more, okay? Don't let me go."

He grits his teeth and presses his lips together before chanting. "Never. Letting. You. Go."

He turns us around and leans me back on the bed, still deep inside. His thrusts grow frantic and I meet him for each one, slamming my hand on the bed when I start to fall apart. He doesn't let up and I start to slow down, my body clenching around him, but he's relentless, and my body builds back up into a frenzy. Our bodies are both slick with sweat, the sounds we're making are pure filth, and I love everything about this. Everything about him.

When he yells my name, I lose it again, coming so hard my eyes roll back in my head. I shudder and buck and feel completely spent when our bodies finally still. He pulls back and touches my face, kissing me deeply. It heals all the hurt that has built up over the week, the hurt from him pushing me away, from not hearing from him. The hurt from knowing he could let me go that easily. This kiss speaks the truth, more than any words...but still when we break apart, I wait to see what he will say.

"I'm already falling for you," he says against my lips.

My eyes fill with tears. "I needed to hear that more than I thought," I say, my voice breaking.

He looks equal parts moved and guilty when I stare up at him and it makes my gut churn a little bit with nerves. But I don't ask him why. I'll regret it later, but I guess I'm too afraid he'll bolt again, even though he said he wouldn't.

"I have so much to tell you, but I just want to enjoy our time together, not bring it down with all my news," he says, kissing my brow and my nose. He keeps kissing down my body and then pulls me up, wrapping my legs around him. We walk to the bathroom and he turns on the shower, getting rid of the condom before we step in. He sets me down and his eyes roam leisurely down my body as the water sluices over my tired muscles.

"You're so beautiful." He tracks a stream of water down until his fingers are between my legs. He dips in and out, watching as my skin flushes. His teeth swipe over his

bottom lip and I watch transfixed. "Are we going to do this
—be something—together?" he asks, his thumb brushing
over my sweet spot.

I gasp and arch into his hand. "Yes," I whisper. "Yes,
yes, yes…"

He gets down on his knees and puts his mouth where
his fingers are still working their magic. When I feel his
tongue along with his fingers, I have to steady myself by
grabbing his hair hard and riding his face.

I want him to drown in me, just as I'm drowning
in him.

It's so hard to leave him. *So* hard.

I stay until just after midnight, after we dirty things up
again after our shower…on the couch. I was on my way out
and he put his hands around my waist, his chest against my
back, and he kissed my neck nice and slow…taking me
from behind. I was a goner…but I finally got some
willpower and told him goodnight.

I'm almost home when I remember my bracelet…still
sitting on his nightstand. I grin and pull into the Catano
driveway, my body tired but energized after our workout.
I'll just go get it later.

It feels good to know that he's not going to fight his
feelings for me anymore. He's not going to fight us being
together…maybe I'll leave my bracelet at his house
forever. A good luck token.

I chuckle out loud and cover my mouth, trying to
squash down some of my giddiness. The tall bush next to
me rustles in the breeze and I take my time strolling toward

the house. I'm almost to the pool when a hand clamps over my mouth and I'm pulled back into the bushes.

I kick and try to scream, my elbow hitting a hard gut and not doing a thing to stop me from getting pulled into the dark alcove.

"You try to scream again and this knife will go in your throat." The voice is cold and sends a chill straight to my bones.

"What do you want?"

"There are a lot of people you care about, aren't there, Ava Safrin? A lot of people who care about you...your sister, your brother-in-law the king...your *brother* the king...and Gentry Barrington—or is his name Barrington at all?" He chuckles and I shiver, still trying to shove his hands off of me.

"What do you want?" I repeat, going still when he grips me tighter.

He starts dragging me backward, moving deeper into the alcove, toward the beach and away from the house.

"There are just so many uses for you, I don't know where to start," he says, his lips brushing my ear.

I shake my head wildly and he curses when I knock my head into his.

"Fuck!" he says, loosening his grip just enough for me to head butt him again, while also trying again with the kicking. My boot hits a spot that causes him to cuss again and I'm able to turn and face him, this time aiming for his groin. I kick hard enough for him to bend down for a second and I don't hesitate. I run.

I have the advantage of knowing the alcove better than he does and I hear him on my tail until I make a quick turn, knowing another way out that I hope only confuses him. I can tell when I lose him and don't let it stop me. I run like my life is at stake because I think it just might be.

The bushes start to clear and I can see the house ahead.

I'm about to fall apart, my legs are screaming, but I keep going. I look behind me and can't see him anywhere. And then I hear the footsteps gaining on me. I try to push myself harder, but it's no use. He catches up and everything goes black.

CHAPTER TWENTY-FOUR

GENTRY

I get dressed with a lighter feeling in my chest than I've had in weeks. I can't wait to see Ava today. It's going to be hell as usual, not giving away how much I want to follow her with my eyes, see what she's thinking…touch her…but I can keep it together. She promised to come before Jadon arrives tonight, and I'm already looking forward to that.

There are police cars in the parking lot when I arrive at school and I try to see what could be the problem around the crowd that's gathering. I get out of the car, asking the first student I see what's going on.

"It's probably because Ava Safrin is missing," she says. "I heard it on the news on the way here."

"What?" I shout.

She flinches and stares at me before scurrying away.

I jog over to where a few policemen are gathered. "What's going on?" I ask.

"Are you on the faculty?" he asks.

I nod and hold out my ID card. "Yes, I'm a teacher here. Gentry Barrington."

"Detective Benson," he says. We shake hands and he flips through his notepad. "I'll be asking you a few questions in a while, if you don't mind. We're here to look into the disappearance of the king's sister-in-law. I see here that she's in your first-hour class. Ava."

I feel all the blood drain from my face and I stagger back, needing something to hold onto.

"Are you okay, sir?" the officer asks.

"She was here yesterday," I say, my voice sounding faint. *She was in my bed last night.* "I saw her," I finish lamely. I drag my hand through my hair and look around. "You've looked everywhere? Do you know how long she's been missing?"

"I'll be in to see you after your first class. Will that work? I'm not at liberty to discuss everything just yet and I'd like to ask as many questions as I can while I'm here... you understand we have a lot of ground to cover..."

I tune him out after he says he's not at liberty to discuss everything and wonder if I should tell him *my* everything. When he comes to my class, away from the ears and eyes, I need to tell him all of it.

The class goes by in a blur. Everyone is talking about Ava. Toph looks hollow and I wonder if that's how I look, like a shell walking around. It's how I feel. I give up trying to teach and tell everyone to quietly read a chapter from our textbook. It feels wrong to go on as normal when Ava's missing, and as soon as I've talked with Detective Benson, I'll be taking off. I don't know what to do or where to go first, but I can't think straight here. I have to do something.

I would hope she's just taken off somewhere—maybe her mom decided on a last-minute trip somewhere as it sounds she's prone to do—but Jadon is coming into town tonight and the two of us also had plans. Even if she had second thoughts about me after she left last night, she wouldn't skip town with him coming to see her.

Maybe she just needed space to think about everything. Maybe she regrets the boundaries we crossed last night. *Maybe* she's hiding out until Jadon shows up tonight and will have an explanation for everything.

I text Jerome that I need to see him. Another job possibility. He calls when the bell rings.

"I don't have much time to talk right now, but I need you to look into Ava Safrin's disappearance."

He whistles low and chuckles. "You don't think everyone is on that trail right now?"

"I hope they are, and I hope you find her first. She's in trouble." I wish I'd felt it when it happened—when whatever trouble she's in first occurred—so I could know the timeline we're dealing with, but now I know without a doubt that something is wrong. I feel it.

"You ready to face the fire that'll come out once people know about you and her?"

My breath catches and I clutch my chest just as the officer walks in the room. I hang up on Jerome, my mind swimming with questions about how he could know about Ava and me.

He's been digging into your life, you prick. Who else knows? Who else has been watching?

"Is now a good time for us to talk?" Detective Benson steps inside the room and looks slightly uncomfortable as he glances around the walls, studying the statistics hanging here and there.

"Sure," I say, holding out my hand for him to take a seat. "I'd rather not sit at a desk, if you don't mind." He chuckles.

"No," I laugh and it sounds forced, "here, take my chair."

I motion for him to sit down and he does. I sit down at one of the desks and feel like I've reverted back to high school in every way. Awkward guy in the dark who doesn't know what the fuck to do.

My nerves get the best of me and I jump in before he can. "Do you know how long she's been missing?"

"The last time anyone has reported seeing her was around nine o'clock last night. We're trying to get a solid timeline." He pulls a pen out of his pocket and I feel fevered, my forehead starting to sweat.

"You're positive she's not just visiting family somewhere? That she's truly missing?"

"All evidence points to signs that she's been taken."

"My God. There's evidence? What do you mean?" I lean over, my elbows on my knees, and try to catch my breath. All of my airways feel like they're closing on me.

"Mr. Barrington, are you okay?" He stands up and walks toward me, putting a hand on my shoulder.

I take a few more breaths, willing my heart rate to slow down, and nod. "I saw her last night," I tell him. "She left my house just after midnight. She was on her scooter wearing jeans, a white tank top, and a pink sweatshirt. She had on her black hightop boots, and she came to get her bracelet but left it again…" I trail off, my voice breaking. I swipe my hand across my mouth and look at him, pained.

He's staring at me like he's just seeing me for the first time. "You understand I'll need to take you in for questioning."

"I understand." I nod. "I know that I'll probably be considered a suspect now, but please don't waste time on me. Someone has been following me; they must have been following her too. I realize you might not believe me, but I did not hurt her. Ever. She means everything to me…I love her."

I stand up and he clears his throat. "I should cuff you, but I'm not going to…don't give me a reason to regret it. You will have to ride with me to the station, though."

I nod and we walk into the hall, the clatter of lockers slamming and kids talking over one another all fading into nothingness as I walk out with the detective. I pass Toph and Jacque and know they'll look at me differently when they see me again…*if* they see me again. I can't linger on the regret that tries to swallow me up. Too much is at stake to let guilt consume me now. All that matters is that Ava is found, and God, if she's not okay, there is no point in *anything*.

CHAPTER TWENTY-FIVE

AVA

I wake up disoriented, my head feeling like an anchor along the bottom of the ocean. The room I'm in is sterile and chilly. I nestle deeper into the covers and marvel at how weird it is that I'm apparently a prisoner with a bed and a nice comforter. I sit up and the room spins. I don't think I was hit on the head, but...he must have drugged me. My whole body feels heavy. I turn and slide my feet onto the floor then stare down at my feet; it's as if they don't belong to the rest of me.

Everything drags like a movie reel in reverse that's been slowed down to dissect one small part of a scene at a time. I turn to look around the room and nothing stands out. Nothing gives away where I am, who has me, how long I've been here. There are no windows, no pictures on the stark wall, no personal touches. I think back to the man's voice and wonder if I know him, and why he picked me. Something niggles the back of my mind, him mentioning all the reasons he had for taking me. And Gentry's face flashes before me. Why would he have mentioned Gentry?

What was it he said about him? I can't quite pull all the details back into focus.

He must have been the one following me.

God, Eden and Jadon must be frantic. I wonder if Gentry knows yet that I'm gone. I hope he doesn't think any of this is his fault. Or that I've had second thoughts about him.

And just like that, my mind is swirling, the thoughts spilling over one another like the coat pile of a party in Farrow.

I hope my family is okay. What if this has nothing to do with Gentry at all and my family is at risk? I try to stand and fall, my knees scraping the floor, my feet prickly from falling asleep.

"What do you want?" I call out, my voice hoarse and barely projecting. I cough and try again. "Hey, what do you want from me?"

I hear someone walking toward the door, heels clicking over the tile floor. The door opens and I meet my abductor. His hair is long and his eyes are shifty. His shoes are polished and they look crisp against the endless white.

"She is very pretty. Of what does she want from me?" His voice scrapes across my skin and I shiver, feeling a rush of fear. This doesn't sound or look like the guy who took me, but maybe my memory is playing tricks on me. It was late and I was distracted. *How many are there?*

I don't understand what he's saying, so I don't say anything.

He moves over me and holds out his hand. I take it and he helps lift me off of the floor. With a small nudge from him, I plop back on the bed and sit there waiting to see what he wants from *me*.

"When back to her senses, she will have a conversation," he says, studying me. His way of speaking confuses me—either that, or it's the drugs that are slowing down my brain. "While *here* she is, he will tell her this: Learn she shall do."

He bows his head, places his hands together, and backs out of the room.

I stare after him trying to make sense of what he said, but none of it computes. I have the strength to lie back and that is all, so I pull the blanket over me and fall asleep.

When I wake up the next time, things still don't make any sense.

I can't say how long I sleep, but I have horrific dreams about Jadon that feel so real. His face is distorted with anger and when he turns and looks at me with hateful eyes, a sword in his hand, I run until I can't any longer and then turn and slide my sword into his heart. I wake up sweating, my heart pounding out of my skin, and tears are running down my cheeks. I try to lift my hands to wipe the tears away, but my hands are restrained. My head feels strange, and when my consciousness fully registers, I realize I'm still in the same room, but now I'm hooked up to a machine with electrodes connected to my head.

My heartbeat makes a machine go off and a woman rushes into the room, turning off the alarm.

"What are you doing to me?" I rattle the thin chain that holds my hands in place.

She ignores my question and pulls off the electrodes one by one. She keeps the heart monitor and restraints on me even after she leaves the room and I stare at the machine, trying to figure out what's happening.

Shaken by the dream and yet so out of it—are they still drugging me?—I know I should care more about what they're doing to me, but I don't have the strength. It's like I'm being dragged by a horse underwater.

I'm almost certain the next person who comes in is the guy who kidnapped me. It was dark then, so I didn't get a good look at him, but his height is right and the way he looks at me sends a chill through me. His eyes slice right through me. He doesn't have to say a word for me to know he hates me. When I finally break away from his stare, I notice the food he's holding and my stomach growls in response.

"How long have I been here?" My voice is a hoarse croak.

He doesn't respond, just watches me. The woman who was in earlier steps into the room and she unlocks the chains holding my wrists in place. I rub the skin, the imprint from the metal creating latticework on my wrists. The man sets a bowl of rice on the bedside table and I look at it suspiciously.

"Eat up," the woman says. "Or next time your portion will be smaller."

"I don't see any utensils," I say, rubbing my throat. "Can I have some water, please?"

"Of course. And utensils must be earned." She motions for me to pick up the bowl of rice and I do, scooping my fingers in the white mush and sticking it in my mouth. It's lightly salted and tastes good. I close my eyes and try to imagine that it's filling every craving.

Now, instead of the sterile, somewhat chemical scent of the room and the machine, the warm, barely popcorn smell of the rice permeates the air. I open my eyes and see the guy staring at me and set the bowl down. His features morph into Jadon's and I scramble back in my bed like a crab on the sand.

He looks at the woman and I blink rapidly, wanting to ask Jadon what he's doing here, why is he tormenting me in my dreams? But somewhere deep inside I know I'm not thinking clearly.

You're hallucinating, I tell myself.

Eager to get them out of the room, I pick up the bowl of rice and don't look at the man again. When the woman starts to leave, I stop eating.

"When will the other man be back?" I ask. I feel more comfortable around him than these two.

"We will be in charge of you today. You need more rest and then we will begin your training," the woman says.

"The training?" I repeat, my voice hollow. "What is your name? What are you teaching me?" As one word leaves my lips, the next feels slower and more incomprehensible than the last. "Why...are...you...drugging—" I hear the bowl clatter to the floor, but I'm too far gone to pull back up from the water going back over my head.

The dreams start right up with Jadon chasing me again. I'm grateful that the stab marks from the earlier dream don't seem to be present, even though he's still looking at me with the same hateful stare.

"I'm dreaming," I tell him. "I know you will never hurt me."

Something tightens in my body and I cry out, feeling a sharp pain all the way to my marrow. It pierces through me and I feel Jadon closing in on me. I turn around to see how close he is and fall, covering my head to wait for the blow.

It never comes, but I still feel him watching, his breath heaving with exertion.

Stand up. Stand up, I hear the chant and look around to see who it is. We're in the woods behind the Safrin castle in Farrow. Jadon and I both know these woods like the back of our hand. He probably knows them better than I do by now, after all of his hunting excursions.

I see Gentry walk out of the woods and stay focused on him as he comes and takes my hand. I don't look for anyone else or turn around to see if Jadon is still there; Gentry is as real as Jadon was, his hand warm against mine, his smile hopeful as he leads me to an opening. Purple and yellow flowers are growing rampantly in the field and I inhale the scent and the sunshine air.

In the next second he's gone, but the peaceful feeling he left me with stays and I turn to the light, determined not to let this dream overpower me.

It isn't real, I chant. *That isn't Jadon. This isn't even really me.*

CHAPTER TWENTY-SIX

AVA

When I am calm, I'm released and taken to the bathroom. I still haven't had a shower by myself and I need one. My hair needs a shampoo. I try to bargain with the woman, but she ignores me, and when I fall asleep, she locks me back up.

I long for the skies of Niaps or the shocking cold of Farrow, anything to get me out of this unceasing stillness. The white walls and the beeping of my heart rate from the machine that hasn't left since they brought it in…it is at times soothing and at other times, like now, it feels if I hear one more stroke of the tick, I will lose all rational thought.

I sit up, shackled again and angry about it. I thrash against the covers as much as one can when in metal restraints.

"Let me out of here!" I scream until my voice is hoarse.

I try to rip the chain out of the wall when I notice that's what I'm attached to. It doesn't make any leeway, only resulting in bloody wrists. If this is a test I'm supposed to be passing, I'm failing. Whatever I'm supposed to be "learning" isn't working.

When hardly any sound comes out of me, I slam the bed into the wall. Again. And again. For what seems like hours. All day maybe. It's hard to tell. I eventually run out of energy and doze into a fitful sleep. I'm scared to fall asleep because I don't want to see the Jadon that has infiltrated my dreams. And when I wake up, I cry, shaken to the core that he won't let up. What is he trying to tell me? Or is he saying anything at all?

"I'm confused," I whisper. I see a dent in the wall that I've made in one of my slams with the bed. It restores some of my sanity. I stare at that and find comfort.

The man comes back. The one who spoke in riddles but somehow seemed to be in charge.

"Difficult she has been," he says.

"Are you talking about me?" I whisper, sitting up and leaning against the iron headboard.

"She has been wasting energy needlessly. Strength she needs for what is to come."

"And what is that?" I shake my chains and my eyes fill with tears. "Please let me out of these restraints. I won't do anything, I swear it."

"She forgets we know what she is capable of."

"How?" I spit. "And if I'm capable of all this shit, then you should be terrified for when I do get out of here."

He smiles then and his eyes are like a fed jaguar, satisfied and smug. "Endurance is a muscle that must be built up over time. It is not instant, as all things that have any real value are not. She is building muscle, and in turn, the endurance to finish the race."

I turn my face to the wall, wanting to shut him out along with the others. I don't know why I thought he would be any better. He's nothing but a man who speaks nonsense, and even more infuriating than the others because he acts like he has all the answers but refuses to speak clearly.

"If you knew me at all, you'd know that I'm shutting down with each day that I'm in here. You're killing me, and whatever purpose you have for me won't be accomplished if I'm dead."

Something flickers in his eyes then; and the change is crazy. He looks almost human like this. But it's over as quickly as it starts.

"She has a lot more fight left in her yet."

I slam the bed into the wall and get a sick pleasure out of the dent growing in the wall.

The man merely laughs and it makes my skin prickle in awareness. A twisted laugh that delights in my agony. I go still and silent and am relieved when he leaves, shutting the door behind him.

I think I will try cooperating and see what they expect of me.

Several days pass. Three, maybe four. There's no way to be certain. They feed me at random times, mostly I think, to confuse me. I feel lightheaded from forcing my eyes to stay open, sluggish from the restless sleep I'm getting when I give in. The only time I move is when I'm taken to the bathroom and when the woman lifts my limbs to give me a sponge bath. She washed my hair while I was sleeping and I wish I'd been awake to drown her in whatever she was using, but I wasn't so fortunate. I've been quiet, dutifully listening when the woman and the kidnapper come into the room to feed me, playing a part while my mind is wracked with guilt about my thoughts of my brother. I don't understand what's happening and I hope that when I get out of here, I'll never experience these feelings again.

Gentry comes and goes from my thoughts. I have to struggle to remember his face at times—that's how prevalent my torment is from Jadon. It's like a constant firework exploding in my brain over and over again. *He wants to kill me. He wants to kill me. He wants to kill me. I must kill him.*

When I wake up with those thoughts and am screaming, my voice restored from several days of silence, all three of my jailers rush in to see what I've done. The man with long hair seems relieved that I'm just waking up from a bad dream. The woman looks annoyed that I interrupted whatever she was doing. The guy who brought me here just stares his relentless stare.

I lie limply on the bed, worried that my arms and legs won't work if I don't get to move them more, and soon.

"She is ready to learn?" the man asks.

I nod. "She is ready."

He presses his hands together and gives a slight nod, his eyelids barely shutting in acknowledgment. He motions to the woman and she undoes my chains and helps me to a sitting position. She helps me stand and we shuffle to the bathroom. I use the toilet, more aware of her presence than usual because it's usually dark or I'm out of it.

When I flush the toilet, I wait for her to drag me back to

the bed, but she starts the water to the shower and hands me a new sponge with gel.

"Wash quickly. I will dry you when you're done. If you give me any trouble whatsoever, I'll have The Watcher dry you...you know, the one who only stares now that he has you here. You don't want to be alone with him, trust me. Not a pretty girl like you," she adds. "This pretty pale skin here," she skims her fingers over my neck, "will be as colorful as your tattoos."

"I understand."

I step into the water gratefully. I want to stand there forever, but I'm barely in a few seconds when she's reminding me to wash quickly. I scrub my skin and then tackle my hair, enjoying the feel of my fingernails on my scalp. She says something else about hurrying and I rinse my hair before I'm ready, afraid she'll stop the water before I'm done. It's hard to hurry when I'm so lethargic. I don't feel I've built any endurance. I'm weaker than I've ever been.

When I step out, she's waiting there with a towel and I let her dry me, modesty be damned. I stare at her, memorizing her face. The dark flecks in blue eyes, the dirty blond hair that hangs limply on either side, her thin lips with the dot of spittle on the bottom right side. She's taller than me and stronger and she likes wielding her power. I wonder why she's here.

She leads me back to the room where I have a new set of white pants and a white matching tunic, both loose and comfortable. My hair is in a turban that stays clasped with a button so it can't come loose. The man with the long hair is waiting and The Watcher is gone. I don't like that the woman didn't tell me his real name and decide I'll make more of an effort to figure out their names soon.

The man doesn't say anything, but he opens the door to the rest of the house or building—I'm not sure what this place is. The room I've been in almost looks like a hospital room. I don't know what I expected, but I didn't expect the couches and TV just outside my room. We pass that and enter a gym. I stop when I see the array of swords hanging on the wall. Some of them look like the ones from my dreams.

I'm so confused. My head doesn't feel right. What am I doing here?

CHAPTER TWENTY-SEVEN

GENTRY

I'm in deep shit. I knew it the minute I opened my mouth and I wouldn't take it back for anything. Not if it means bringing Ava home any faster.

The police aren't telling me anything. They ask me the same questions over and over and I've asked for a lawyer. I called Elias when I was allowed my phone call and he sent his lawyer, saying he'd come too as soon as he could. I don't know if there's much Elias can do, but I'm counting on his lawyer to get me out of here.

Still, the things I said at the school are now out in the open and it's not making me look good.

Montgomery Hughes looks the high-profile lawyer part and I would've done everything to avoid him on a normal day. But when we shake hands and he tells me with a confident smirk, "Don't worry, I'll get you out of here," I believe him and have never been more grateful for an arrogant lawyer. We go over the timeline again, and I tell him everything I told the officer. I also tell him that Jerome has been doing some work for me, and maybe he'd know more about who has been tailing me and most likely, Ava. I even tell him about Alex and my dad's claims that I'm the rightful heir to King Forbrush. When I've spilled every-thing out and laid it before him, I realize the weight of what I've confessed.

"I will trust you because I trust Elias, and I need your help. Otherwise, I wouldn't repeat any of this until it's common knowledge—the part about my biological father." I tug on my hair and stare Montgomery down. "Please swear to me that you're worthy of my trust. I don't care about any of the extenuating circumstances—I want to find Ava. I want to find who's responsible for this. I'll do what-ever it takes to get her back."

"You're risking a lot for this girl. Are you sure there's nothing to gain politically for you if you claim you're in love with her?" He assesses me shrewdly and I have to hold myself back from slamming my fist into the table.

"I can't see what I'd be gaining. I think all I'm gaining is a bad reputation and I probably lost my job the moment I got in the back of that squad car today."

He nods, looking over his notes. "Fair enough."

"You said you could get me out of here. Is that the truth or are you feeding me a line?"

"Do you agree to the police searching your dwelling and property?" My question slides off his back like water on a duck.

"Yes. They'll find a bracelet of Ava's on my nightstand."

"Did you give her the bracelet?"

"No, she left it there when she came over."

"Did you ever coerce her into coming to your house, force her to have intercourse…did you ever use force in any way, physically or mentally?"

"Never."

"Then I should have no trouble getting you out of here. My guess is they're already checking your property and will now enter your house. If there's nothing suspicious there, we should be good."

I start worrying that someone has set me up. What if they planted something to make it look suspicious? *You're the one who started this when you confessed to your relationship,* I remind myself.

"Please tell me there's word about Ava...I'm losing my mind, not knowing. Has she been found?"

"So far, I haven't heard any news about her being found, no. I'll let you know when I do." He stands up and I look at him, feeling like a trapped dog and I'm not even in the cell yet.

"Will I stay in here overnight, you think?"

"My goal is to get you out tonight...but they need to search your house first."

"Okay, right. Yeah, okay." I put my head in my hands and want to lose it.

Cry.

Yell.

Hit something.

Everything from the past few weeks is coming to a head and I'm going to fucking lose it right here in a police station. *Ava is missing, goddammit, what the fuck is happening?*

"Hey, man, breathe," Montgomery says, putting his hand on my shoulder. "I know it should've never happened

—Ava being abducted...if that's what even happened—but if she was, she's got the top investigators all over the world who will search for her. It needs to be ruled out that she wasn't in an accident. Nothing is concrete yet, which is why I have an even better chance of getting you out." He grins and knocks on the door for the guard to let him out.

I sit and wait and when he comes back forty-five minutes later, he is accompanied by Detective Benson and a woman.

"We'd like to ask you a few more questions," Detective Benson says.

"Okay." I fold my hands together on the table and try to calm my breathing.

"Where did you meet Princess Safrin for the first time, and how long after you met did your relationship start?"

I close my eyes and grind my teeth together before speaking. "As I said the other three times you asked me this...we met at Princess Mara Catano's wedding to Elias Lancaster..." I repeat everything I've already said and hope that I haven't done anything to postpone the search for Ava.

I'm in a cell, sitting on a metal bench, when Montgomery steps inside. "You are free to go; as soon as they come to get you, you can walk out of those doors a free man. You are still a suspect. Everyone is until Princess Ava is found."

I nod and shake his hand. "Thank you."

He leaves the cell and I wait another twenty or thirty minutes before the guard comes to let me out. I sign a document and collect the things they kept for me while I was inside. I feel like a shell of myself, all hollowed out inside and foggy eyes that can't focus on anything.

Ava

Ava

Ava

Where are you?

As I leave the main building and walk down the hall-way, Elias and Luka step out and flank me on either side. I look at Elias with concern and he's impossible to read. I turn to Luka then and I'm shoved into a bathroom. Elias guards the door as Luka leans into my face and points his finger. I would imagine Luka's guards are making sure no one comes into the bathroom, so if the king kills me, no one will be the wiser.

My body is on edge, my skin crawling in awareness, but I'm still blindsided when he sends his fist into my jaw with a loud *THWACK*. It's quickly followed with a one-two punch in my gut that knocks the breath out of me.

I take the beating like the man I am. I deserve this. If someone fucked my too-young sister-in-law, I would be feeling the same rage as Luka right now.

"If you know where Ava is, you tell me, you *mother-fucker*. I can't *believe* you put your hands on her." His voice is a low rumble of thunder. He clutches my shirt in his fists, tightening the pressure against my throat.

"I don't blame you for wanting to kill me," I respond, my voice guttural with him still tightening around my neck. "This isn't how it seems. I don't know where she is. I'm trying to help, I swear it. I won't rest until we find her."

"There is no *we* in this. We are going to find her and then you will stay the fuck away from her," he yells this time, looking like a king in war. "I will kill you myself, if I hear you laid a hand on her without her permission."

"Never," I say, my voice breaking. "She'll tell you herself when we find her. I will tell you everything now, if you want, but I understand you might not believe me. Elias knows I had no idea she was seventeen when we met. We hit it off immediately and I didn't touch her…until after she turned eighteen."

"What difference does that make? She's your student. She's off-limits." He lets go of my shirt and steps back, folding his arms across his chest.

Elias stands with his hands clasped in front of him. "I know you don't want to hear it right now, Luka, but Gentry really cares about Ava. He—"

Luka holds up his hand and Elias silences. "You're right, I don't want to hear this. We can't afford to waste another second. We *have* to find her. You tell me everything you know and don't leave anything out this time."

CHAPTER TWENTY-EIGHT

AVA

He's very good. The way my captor wields a sword is staggering. I've never seen anyone better than Jadon. I like to tease Jadon that I'm better, but we both know he's going a little bit easy on me when we spar.

I haven't been able to stop thinking of Jadon since I got here and now is no different. I compare the way the man moves with Jadon, the way Jadon chases me in my dreams, which haven't stopped haunting me. I stumble and my sword clatters to the floor. The man waits for me to pick it up and I do, brandishing it in front of me.

During my third training with him, the woman rushes into the gym, yelling, "Samson!"

His long hair flies as he turns abruptly, which allows me full access to his chest with my sword. He comes to a dead stop when he feels the tip of my sword against him, his eyes tracking back to mine while he stays completely still.

I could plunge it into his heart right this minute, watch

his blood spill out across the floor, the red looking almost black against the dark floor...

But I don't.

I acquiesce, gently pulling back the blade and taking a step back.

The woman stares back and forth at the two of us, her chest rising and falling. Her eyes are frantic and the man I finally have a name for—Samson...is that his real name? I'm doubtful—moves quickly toward her. They speak in hushed tones and I can't catch any of it, save one word: compromised.

Things move rapidly then. Samson hurries me out of the gym, as the woman runs ahead. Instead of leading me back to my room, I'm taken down a dark hallway that I've never been in. This is the first time Samson has seemed anything but collected and controlled. His movements are quick and jerky; he reaches out to stop me suddenly and then pushes a lever that opens the door to another hallway. We go down a few sets of stairs and I have the urge to scream. I hold onto Samson like he's my savior and keep up, even as his steps quicken again.

We go down another set of stairs and there are five doors at the bottom. He opens the door in the middle and it's another room that looks similar to the one I've been in. I'm disappointed. I'd hoped we were leaving this prison, but instead, it feels like I've been driven deeper into the pit.

The air smells like apple air freshener mixed with dampness and I turn on him suddenly. If he's alarmed, he doesn't show it. His calm is back and I feel anything but.

"I need air," I tell him. I pace the small sterile white room and he folds his arms across his chest. "I can't breathe. I need to go outside. This is crazy. I haven't tried anything and I won't. Please, just let me get some air."

I stop when he doesn't respond or even show a change in expression. I throw my hands in the air and yell, wishing I could strangle him but scared that I wouldn't be able to find my way out of here if I did.

"Rest," he says simply...as if I didn't just have a meltdown in front of him. "Time for lessons must wait. Rest now you must do."

His way of speaking is beginning to sound normal to me and it makes me want to scream.

"I don't want to rest. What's going on?" My voice bounces across the room with its concrete floor and metal bed doing nothing to cushion it.

He turns and walks out, shutting the door with a resounding thud. I slump down on the bed and feel utterly alone. I scrunch my knees up and drop my head on them, defeated. I'll have to do better than this if I'm going to get away. I don't entertain the thoughts that he's leaving me down here to die...beyond the first few minutes. And then I feel the claustrophobia threatening to take me under again.

You have control over your mind, I repeat the words over and over again in my head...until my breathing calms and I am able to close my eyes.

When I finally sleep, it is without dreams, and I rest for the first time since I've been here. I wake up feeling hopeful again.

Stay strong, Ava. You can't let them win.

Samson is the one to bring meals. Based on the meals, I'm assuming I'm down here for five days. It's still as bland as ever, but I eat it like a woman consumed. We forego the training and I exercise in my room, jogging and pacing around the room and in place, crunches, squats, push-ups, anything to keep my muscles from atrophying down here in this hellhole. The boredom is sometimes unbearable, but I tell myself it's better than being abused in any way. *Things could be much worse.*

When The Watcher comes to get me on the sixth morning, I remember why I despise being near him. He looks at me as if he'd love nothing more than to rip my head from my neck. We make the climb back up the steep stairs and all the squats I've done make the burn that much more intense. My ears pop as we climb and I'm anxious to get to the top. I don't trust The Watcher down here alone. He makes my skin crawl.

We reach the last step and I have never been more relieved when the door opens and Samson is standing there, holding the door open for us. The light is behind him and he feels like safety in comparison to The Watcher.

I'm led back to my original room and it's strange that now it feels like a luxury to be in this one instead of the one deep under the ground. The air is crisper and I don't smell that strange combination of odors. My head feels clearer and part of me wonders if that time down there was actually good for me, despite how much I hated it. I slept so well. Not having the dreams tormenting me—

What are they doing to me?

I get up and search the room, the vents, the bathroom. I look for cameras and find nothing.

The woman brings rice and I wait until she leaves to lift the spoon to my lips. I pause and sniff the food—why haven't I thought about it before now?

Because you were too hungry to care...

I dump all but a few bites of rice into the sink and eat

what's left, hoping it will sustain me for now. Maybe it isn't the food, but I'm almost certain whatever they'd been doing to me stopped when I was below.

I do my exercises and add two reps to each one, sweating by the time I'm done. When the next meal comes in, I do the same and again at dinner.

This time, when they wheel the machine in, I'm not half-asleep. I pretend to be though, and unlike the other nights, I'm wide awake when the electrodes are attached to me, earbuds placed in my ears—this is the first time I've been aware of earbuds.

The woman stands next to me for a few minutes—I assume she's watching the monitor—and once satisfied, she leaves the room. The chanting in my ears begins then.

Kill Jadon.

Kill Jadon.

Kill Jadon.

My eyes pop open and I cover my mouth to hold the scream in. I want my screams to override this voice in my head, but I don't want them to know I'm onto them. I close my eyes and imagine that I'm in Gentry's house. The beautiful tile he created from my drawing, the colors so rich and vivid. I curl into a ball in the corner of his bathroom and chant inside:

I am free.

I am free.

I am free.

By morning, I've imagined myself all over Gentry's house and overlooking the water in his back yard. I've twirled in the grass with the cloudless sky overhead and I've heard his laughter warming my scarred soul. I've imagined Jadon too, and Eden, all the times we had together before our father died. Snow fights and birthday cakes and hugs that were healing. I live in that bubble until morning comes, and then exhausted, I open my eyes when the electrodes are removed and begin a new day in this prison.

But I still can faintly hear the words echoing through my mind and nearly driving me to the edge of insanity: *Kill Jadon.*

CHAPTER TWENTY-NINE

AVA

I'm hungry, but my mind is sharp. During the day when I'm not training with Samson, I sleep. Each night is a test of my willpower and sanity, but I'm no longer tormented with dreams of Jadon. And the times I do fall asleep, it's as if I'm hovering overhead, on the look-out for any danger that might attack. They're trying to turn me against my brother and I want to know why. Who are they and why am I here?

When I make Samson stumble, my sword ready to plunge and he steps back, sword up, I see a flicker of pride and fear in his expression. I go back to my room, memorizing every part of it, seeing if anything is out of place. Throughout the past week, I've taken note of the fan in the right corner, the wooden chair that looks easy to lift, the door that the woman goes in and out of, the number of steps it takes to get from the gym to my room.

I stay awake all night, nerves edgy that it won't work, but I'd rather die than not try. This time when I'm hooked up to the electrodes, I'm calmed by the feel of Gentry's hair against my fingers, his lips across my skin, the way it feels when he moans my name. I feel closer to him than I have since I've been here and I know by that alone that the drugs are nearly out of my system. I've had to eat enough to sustain me, but only just.

I wait long enough for everyone else to settle, for them to do whatever tasks they do after they lock me away for the night. The second I start to get too relaxed, I yank off the electrodes, plucking them off of my skin as fast as I can. When the last one is off, I get up and run to the door, ready for someone to come.

Samson rushes in and I nearly falter when I see it's him instead of the woman, but when he sees the bed is empty, he turns and I kick him in the groin and then elbow him in the face on his way down. He pulls me down as he goes and we struggle, his hands clasping my neck. I have the element of surprise, but he's quick and skilled and I feel myself weakening under his grasp.

I tremble and shudder, trying to catch my breath as he squeezes, and then just as soon as I feel like I'm about to go under, he lets go and I clutch my throat, chest heaving.

He tips my chin and studies my eyes. "Trained you have been. Go and do what is meant to be done. We will be watching."

His fingers drop and he steps back. I look around like someone is about to jump out, but he raises a hand when The Watcher comes into the room, and I scuttle past him like a rat scrambling out of a hole. I run into the main room and hear them behind me, but I don't turn around to see if they're following. I hear a woman screaming in the background and stop, my blood running cold. Is someone else being held prisoner here? I turn then and see Samson watching to see what I will do. The woman's screams turn into whimpers and it feels so familiar I nearly run to see how I can help.

"Run, Ava!" the woman yells.

"Mother?" I move in the direction of the sound and Samson blocks my path.

"She cannot help you now. Go do what you must and return to tell me when it is finished."

"That's my mother!" I say quietly, unsure if I should pretend to be as coherent as I feel or if I should be in the scattered state he expects me to be.

His next move makes my decision for me, when he pulls a gun from the back of his pants and quietly points it at me. It's the only time I've felt threatened by him—the woman and the Watcher, yes, but not him.

"Please don't hurt her." My voice bounces off of the room in quiet staccato. My pulse quickens as I wait to see what he will do.

"There is but one purpose for you. Fulfill it and your mother will live."

Kill Jadon.

Kill Jadon.

Kill Jadon.

I school my features into obedience and nod vacantly.

He stares me down and I make my choice, turning and going in the opposite direction, away from the gym and past the couches, away from my mother.

I'm too relieved when one of the doors I try opens that I don't let my guilt over leaving Mother here stop me. If I tell someone where I was, I can get help and have backup with capturing Samson and the other two. The problem is, I step out into a dark alleyway and am so disoriented, I don't even know if I'm still in Niaps or another kingdom.

I wake up in an alley, faint and disoriented. I wonder how many drugs they've been pumping into me.

The next time I wake up, I expect to see one of my three jailers standing over me, but I open my eyes and a beam of light is shining through the crack in the buildings, a shaft shining across my hand. I hold it up and watch the light and shadow shift, depending on how I turn my hand. It feels like an eternity since I've been outside. How long has it really been? I sit up and look around; there are no signs of life, not even my jailers are around. I think I would feel them if they were. But why let me go? Why now?

I stand up, a little wobbly from moving too quickly, but I hold onto the ledge on the window of the building and walk toward the end of the alley. I'm tempted to look until I find someone, but who can I trust? What would I say? Who would believe me? I need to get as far from here as possible and not let anyone know where I am. It feels like the longer I walk, the clearer my jumbled head becomes. My steps feel like brooms sweeping out the cobwebs, but then it feels so literal—my mind's eye seeing the brooms swishing through my brain—that I hold my head and bend over with a wave of dizziness again.

Don't go down, I tell myself. I don't want to pass out again—it's too dangerous. But my stomach is queasy and my head is a mess. I turn on my side and throw up on the street. Is that the last of the drugs in my system? I've always stayed far from narcotics, the lure of experimenting not ever a temptation for me. They tried to control my mind in there. What kind of madness is that?

And more importantly, how much of it worked?

When my stomach feels better, I get to my feet and stand a few moments before trying to move on. No one has come around...maybe it's too early in the morning for anyone to be out yet. I still don't sense the eyes on me, but I won't get so confident that I become stupid.

The first stirrings of life are closer to the water. If I'm in Niaps, it's on the outskirts and a part I haven't seen. The wharf is waking up and fishermen are coming and going, some already with a full net of fish; others are just heading out for the day.

I walk along the water under the shade of the trees and through a few rock formations as much as possible. I don't want the sun to burn me, not when I'm already so weak. There are houses scattered here and there, but soon there are fewer and I give up on asking anyone for help. I just keep going, taking breaks along the way. I find a long pliable twig and pull my hair back, wrapping the ends around the twig until it's all off of my neck. The heat is oppressive and when it gets too unbearable, I find a hollowed rock and lie down, letting sleep pull me under again. It's too tempting to sleep the day away now that I don't have the voice constantly commanding me to kill my brother.

CHAPTER THIRTY

GENTRY

She's been gone for two weeks. Two weeks that have been absolute hell. Two weeks where I've imagined all of the worst possible scenarios.

I've been terminated from my job—that was another hellish day in its own right. When I was called into the office and had to pass Lindsey and Phoebe to get there, I could tell by the accusation in their eyes that they already knew and had made their own list of assumptions. I don't blame them—I know I violated the most fundamental principle of a teacher by falling in love with a student...even if I know it happened before I ever met her at school...those particulars are meaningless in the code of ethics.

My dad has been coming to the house to check on me regularly. I've shut down all conversation about Yuman and the Forbrush family, of which I *do not* consider myself a part of, and have told him in no uncertain terms that I refuse to do anything about my birthright. I'm perfectly willing to let the secrets of my biological father's indiscretions die with the both of us.

I pull up to the Catano mansion and am glad to see Elias's car here already. Luka hasn't budged on letting me be part of the investigation, but I can't stop trying. I have to know she's okay. I wish the whole country would stop everything and search for her. I bet she's here somewhere, in some obscure place, but close.

At least I pray she's close and…alive.

I knock on the door and Elias opens it.

"I should've talked you out of this," he says, looking me over. "Dammit, man, you can't just stop eating. You look like shit."

"Good to see you too." It's our normal lighthearted banter without any of the lightheartedness. It feels forced, but I'd rather this than the yelling I'll probably encounter with Luka. "Did you tell him I was coming?"

We walk toward the office.

"Yes. He doesn't like it, but he's desperate to find her."

We get to the door and Elias raps on it twice before opening it. Luka is standing by the window and he looks like shit too.

"I still don't like this," he says, still looking out the window, "but I believe you when you said you have nothing to do with her disappearance. I've had you thoroughly investigated, even before all of this."

My ears are on full alert, unsure of where he's going with all of this. "What did you find out?"

"That contrary to what Alex Forbrush would like to admit, you are the rightful king to Yuman once Victros passes. Did you know his health has not been good?" He turns and looks at me then and I flinch with the anger that's still directed at me.

"I've heard a little bit, yes."

"So you should be there, getting ready…not here in my home, sniffing after my wife's little sister."

"I want to help find her. I won't rest until she's brought back and I know for myself she's okay."

"You think I care about your rest?" He rubs his hands across his eyes and looks so tired.

He's younger than I am and I can feel the weight of his responsibilities pressing down on him from across the room. What must it be like to carry the weight of a country on your shoulders? Maybe it's just all about Ava right now. I'd like to think it is, that he loves her that much…because then it means *he* will never rest either, until she's brought back safely.

"Let's work together. Are you making any progress? Do you know who took her?"

By the dull look in his eyes, I know he hasn't.

"Did anyone know about you and Ava?" His jaw ticks.

"I think my investigator Jerome knew; it's possible Alex knew or whoever he was having watch me."

"Alex claims he didn't know about your proclivity for young girls—" Luka's eyes take on an angry glint.

"I don't have a proclivity for young girls at all," I insist and hate how guilty I sound. "Have you seen Ava? Had a conversation with her? I met her and she's more mature than the teachers that hit on me at school."

"Speaking of the teachers who hit on you—"

Someone knocks on the door and comes in without waiting to be acknowledged. King Jadon…I only met him once at Elias's wedding. I didn't get to know him well, but I liked the guy.

He looks at me and his blue eyes are like steel, both in color and in hardness.

"Gentry," is all he says.

I bow my head slightly to acknowledge and respect his greeting.

"I'd like to help." I grip the chair in front of me and don't back down when they all turn to stare at me.

"I should kill you, you know," Jadon says. "For now, I'll allow this because we need a fresh set of eyes and Elias has fought relentlessly for your integrity." He glances at Elias. "Everyone should have such a friend." He turns those eyes on me again and it's like he can see through my soul. I stand taller and don't back down from his glare. "But know this: if we find my sister and she has one negative thing to say about you, consider yourself warned. Whether you're Gentry Barrington, former schoolteacher, or Gentry Forbrush, king of Yuman, it means nothing, you will be dead."

"Noted."

For a moment, I wonder how they all got to the truth of my identity so quickly when Alex seemed to still be in the dark. I wonder if that's changed too.

It doesn't matter.

Until we find Ava, nothing does.

"You mentioned teachers hitting on you—any reason one would suspect you had a relationship with Ava? Anyone who would have reason to want to see Ava hurt?"

"There's one—Phoebe—who was interested in me, and she's the type who stays on high alert looking for gossip, but I still don't think she suspected anything, no. And I don't really believe she's capable of hurting anyone."

We look at the footage of Ava running the night she was taken, the tall man who knew exactly where the cameras were and rushed past, leaving so little to go on. They've looked at it countless times and are only doing it for my benefit, to see if anything about him is familiar. I've bugged Elias until he got through to Luka and Jadon and I'm glad they're finally letting me be involved. Even though I feel more helpless than ever with so little to go on. We know he's tall and that's about it. There are no distinguishing features that stand out, other than his shiny shoes. He's wearing a mask but never shows more than a profile, leaving his eyes a mystery.

"The footprints have been tested and we know the brand of shoe—Draymen, size twelve. The mask is most likely a Ray or Capelli brand ski mask, unusual for around here."

"We have them everywhere in Farrow, so we're exploring all of my enemies, as well as the enemies who don't appreciate our alliance with Niaps," Jadon says. "And now this Phoebe—"

"I really don't think Phoebe is a thr—"

"You should have told us about her when we first asked for every detail," Luka throws in.

I glare at him, unable to hold back any longer. "Go ahead, look into her. I don't think you'll find anything more than a nosy teacher." I take a steadying breath. "You know what? Tensions are going to be high, but we don't have to be complete assholes to each other."

"Until we hear from Ava, you're on the shit list with them," Elias says, pounding me on the back and grinning. "You're here, aren't you? That says something about how much they trust me. You're going to have to earn theirs."

Luka lifts an eyebrow. "Or that saying about keeping

your friends close and your enemies closer…let's just say we probably should've been breathing down your throat the past two weeks and have been too distracted." He puts his hands on the wall and his head sags. "We have to find her. The longer this goes—"

And any anger I feel toward him dissolves. The torment in his voice—I wouldn't wish that on anyone.

When I see Eden's face, Luka's heartache pales in comparison. She looks gaunt, with dark circles around her eyes. I don't know Eden well at all, but I know Ava would be heartbroken to see her sister in such agony.

God, help us. I put my head in my hands and pray for a miracle.

CHAPTER THIRTY-ONE

AVA

I end up near another wharf. I can't tell if I'm getting closer to Niaps or going in the opposite direction. I find a wall to lean against and fall asleep there, waking to money being thrown my way. I look around to see who dropped it, but I can't tell from the people walking by. No one is paying attention to me, which helps salvage some of my pride.

I buy a loaf of bread and eat a chunk of it slowly as I walk and try to get my bearings. My head is a bit clearer and I know I should decide now whether I'll keep walking or if I'll find a place for the night around here. A strip of shops in pastel shades stands out against the white sand and blue sea behind. Happy people stroll in and out of the shops while I stare at them, feeling more lost than ever. I look down at my filthy clothes and turn toward the mountain near the ocean. The wind whistles through my clothes, while I shiver and decide I'd rather keep moving. The thought of trying to hide from strangers in the dark while also trying to stay warm feels more daunting than walking as far as I can before I drop.

It's not a smart move. I know that about a mile in. My energy level is low and the need to sleep and eat is gnawing at me. Whatever my body is missing from being medicated for the past few weeks has me feeling antsy yet exhausted. I take breaks, huddling near rocks by the ocean, careful not to run into someone else doing the same.

The last thing I need is for someone to figure out who I am, so as soon as I hit another small town with a scattering of shops, I look for a place to get a few necessities. There's a little shop at the end of a row of shops that's closed and it looks like the best choice for what I'm about to do. The town is probably sleepy even in the daytime, at least that's my hope, as I grab a rock and throw it in the window by the door. I also hope it's not up-to-date on alarms.

Nothing goes off as the glass shatters or when I reach in and unlock the door to Nina's Beach Stop. I make it quick in case it's a silent one, grabbing a jug of water, toothpaste, a three-pack of soap, dried meats, a box of granola bars, a sweatshirt, and scissors. Touristy canvas bags are for sale near the check-out counter and I stuff everything but the jug inside. At the last minute I see a watch in a box and toss it in too. It looks like the kind where the numbers light up that my mother would never let me get because she said they were too tacky for a princess.

I feel a new rush of panic about leaving my mother behind and it speeds me up. I can't waste time. I need to help her before it's too late. There's an office in the back and I grab the first phone I see, punching numbers as fast as I can.

Eden picks up on the second ring, her voice muffled on her first hello.

"I don't have much time. I've escaped and they have Mother. I don't know where I was, but I'm in a town that has a shop called Nina's Beach Stop now. I think I'm going in the direction of Yuman, but I'm not sure. Just saw a sign —" I hear commotion in the shop and drop the phone. I run out the back door and hear someone yelling behind me, but I don't look back until I'm huffing and puffing by the beach a few blocks away.

I kick a rock and regret it, my anger spewing out in a long stream of curses—I didn't even tell her about Jadon. What is wrong with me? I fall on the sand and clutch my foot, cursing myself again for being so stupid. I repeat Nina's Beach Stop in my head multiple times so I won't forget who I have to pay back later, and it reminds me of the words that are constantly just under the surface of my memory: *Kill Jadon.* It's become a game to see how long I can go without thinking it now.

I get up again, my body resisting to move another inch, but I make it to the public restroom on the beach and make sure it's empty. The tunic comes off and the sweatshirt is almost comforting. The night air is cooling down and I want to wash the tunic so it'll have time to be somewhat dry before morning. I eat a granola bar, slowly savoring each tiny bite and allow myself two swigs of water.

As I stare into the mirror, contemplating my next move, I lift the scissors and start cutting. My hair falls to the ground in thick black and blue ropes of satin and when my lip trembles, I bite down hard on it and keep going.

Jadon has to be safe. If they're counting on me to kill him, I need to get to him quickly and let him know. I don't know why I didn't call *him* when I had the chance. I needed to hear my sister, but also…maybe part of me is still confused about the whole brainwashing I've been enduring.

What did they do to me besides invade my mind and

teach me how to fight better? I picture Samson's hands around my neck and the way I was able to skirt around him the last time we practiced sparring. I put my hands on my neck. I'd forgotten that we didn't just use swords.

What else have I forgotten?

After I wash the tunic and wring it out, exhaustion has attached itself to me like another body part. My eyes blur and I hold onto the sink, not wanting to pass out again. The longer I'm awake and coherent, the more aware I am of chunks of time missing from the time I was taken. If they thought they could hypnotize me into killing my brother, what else did they tell me to do—or worse—what have I already done?

I shake my head and study my face in the mirror, already missing the way my hair would feel swishing around my arms. I look rough. There are circles around my eyes and my skin is sallow. I don't take time to contemplate my new look, it's too depressing. I scoop up the hair from the floor and throw it in the garbage, keeping one thin strand and tying it around my wrist a few times, like a bracelet wrap. To remind me of who I am, of what I am and am *not* capable of.

I am capable of taking care of myself. In a strange place, with no money, and no weapons.

I am not capable of murdering the brother I adore.

No. *No.*

And I never will be.

My hands tremble and I trip over a stone in the sand.

I find a rock that must be ten feet tall and test it out to see if it blocks some of the wind. I pull my arms out of the sleeves and wrap them around my stomach tighter, trying to get warmer. I wish I could've called Gentry too. I don't know what I would've said...maybe something like *I'm sorry we can never be*...no, that's dumb. *I'm sorry you're probably worried about me right now, but don't be. It's best that we don't see each other anyway*...or I could just tell him I love him and will never forget him. Yeah, that's what I wish I could say.

CHAPTER THIRTY-TWO

AVA

Tiny needles stab, stab, stab down my throat when I swallow. So dry. My eyes are glued shut. I feel around for the water jug and rub my eyes, sitting up enough to lean my head onto my knees. It's hot and when my forehead touches my knees, I flinch.

The sun.

I'm baked.

I groan when I hold out my hand to study the damage.

Like a crab claw.

"Shit." It comes out as a croak.

I lean over and throw up violently in the sand.

When my eyes are as wide open as they'll go, I take in my surroundings. I scoot back from where I threw up, nearly gagging when I see the vomit, but there's a small round black object in the middle of it. I want to study it closer, but I don't want to touch it. I wonder—surely it's too small—if it's a tracking device. It would explain why Samson was willing to let me go so easily.

I back away quickly, my heart rate tripling, and I move

down the beach, my steps picking up as my stomach settles more. There's a couple on the beach not too far away, but not close enough to see their features, so I'm hoping they haven't noticed me either. The ocean is calmer than it sounded during the night, the wind has died, and the sun is only going to get more aggressive with zero clouds in the sky.

I don't have a clear plan—nothing about me is clear. I feel worse than I did locked up.

Withdrawal.

Hunger.

I don't know which is worse. My head is jumbled and the only thought that consistently sticks is that I need to get to Jadon. Make sure I get to him first. I shake my head to clear the fogginess and picture him slamming a knife into my throat. I touch my throat to remind myself that nothing could be further from the truth.

I take a few bites of the dried meat and it lands in my stomach like a hard melon. Still, the protein helps. I hear tires squealing and run to a boulder. I wait, not sure if I'm losing my mind or if I should be hiding. No one could be here that fast. I didn't give Eden enough to go on and Samson let me go. I'm just being paranoid.

Movement from the corner of my eye catches my attention and I pause, shrinking back further and ducking into the curved out hollowed place. I scuttle back and stay as still as I can, hoping I'm as hidden as I feel. I can still see where I've been through a few cracks in the rock.

And when I see him, I put my hand across my mouth and start shaking.

The Watcher looks around wildly, his arms flailing as he turns around in the sand. He sees the couple and walks toward them, but before he reaches them, a van of kids pulls up and they pile out onto the sand, their buckets and shovels ready for a day of sandcastles. He turns in circles and kicks at the sand before turning and stalking back to the car. It's too far to see inside, black and sleek with tinted windows. I wonder if Samson is driving, but The Watcher gets behind the wheel and his tires squeal again as he speeds away.

So that *was* a tracker. I study my body for any lumps in my skin or weird patches where they could've inserted something. Was there only one?

And why didn't The Watcher look harder for me?

It takes a while for the shakes to subside and when I have strength again, I get up, gather my things, and keep walking.

I reach Yuman in the wee hours of the morning. The streetlights are still shining and the water looks like a shimmering light in the distance. I go to the wharf and watch a few boats going in and out. A dog wanders over to me and I pet him for a few minutes before his owner whistles and he runs to meet him.

Now that I'm here, I don't know what to do. I try to remember what Eden and Luka have said about Yuman. Mara has been here a lot; her best friend, Nadia, lives here and Mara comes for work, but I can't remember any of the details. Thinking of Nadia reminds me of her brother Alex, the guy who behaved so crazy with Gentry. I wonder if he's here or still in Niaps.

I just need to get to Farrow and I don't know the best way to go about it.

I stand huddling under a tree and try to get warm. It's not cold in Yuman, but by the water this early, I could use a light jacket or blanket. The dog barks out by the water and I jump. I don't hear anyone come up behind me until he has his hands on my throat.

"What's a little treat like you doing out here so early?" He pulls what he can of my short strands of hair and my head jerks back. "A boy as pretty as you shouldn't be alone."

The dog and his owner get on the boat and move out into the water while I suppress a scream. The man tightens his grip—one hand holding my neck and the other pulling my waist back against his groin. My eyes blur with tears and I shake as my anger builds. I wait for the right moment, that brief second when he loosens his grip, and I turn, kneeing him as I punch, and when he lands on his knees, I get behind him and put my hands on his neck. Squeezing. My hands work of their own accord, knowing the exact spot to inflict damage. I hear him gasping for breath and trembling underneath me, but my mind is attuned to his pulse as it slows down to a complete stop.

When he gives one final shake, I stand up and look around, my mind blank. I look at him again and then fall to my knees, trying to find a pulse and give him CPR when I realize what I've done.

How did I know how to do that? I do compressions and count, panic setting in. He's much bigger than me and could have easily overtaken me in a fight if I hadn't known exactly how to kill him.

When I am certain he's dead, my hands fall to the sand, defeated. I touch his throat softly where I squeezed the life out of him and bow my head, asking God for mercy on both of us. This man might have done a lot of damage to me if given the chance, but I don't want to be the one doling out justice.

I don't want to be whoever this person is now... someone capable of taking a life.

I stand and stagger back, feeling that dizziness again that's becoming a normal occurrence. Hands steady me at my elbows, holding me in place.

"Clean up we will do, worry not," Samson says, his voice like a torch and a caress, exposing my sin like a proud papa.

I jerk away from him and start scrubbing my hands together furiously. "What have you done to me?" I shake my head and back further away. "I just killed a stranger!" I whimper and cover my mouth with my hand. I turn and start running away from him.

"Wait," he calls. He catches up with me in no time, reaching out and grabbing the sleeve of my sweatshirt. "You're meant to go home." He takes my hand and puts money in my palm. "Head down, no unnecessary attention. Mission only."

"How did you find me? I threw up and saw a tracker. The Watcher came and—" I put the money in my pocket and wipe my face, my nose, my eyes. I don't know what else to say and stand there waiting.

"We will know when you've completed your mission and freedom will be yours."

"You're making no sense. How can I be free when I've just killed someone?"

"Complete your mission and freedom will be yours," he repeats and I consider making the same move on him as I did to the stranger who's now lying dead on the sand. But I don't have the same fury running in my veins; I feel as if I've run a thousand miles and have no fight left within me.

I should be a mess, beyond hope, but I'm absolutely *numb*. I keep reminding myself that I've killed a man and expect the guilt to settle in me, but it never fully comes.

All that has been proven today is that if I carry out the mission Samson keeps talking about, there will be more bloodshed...by my hands.

CHAPTER THIRTY-THREE

GENTRY

When Eden ran into the office last night and said that Ava had called, the office filled with the investigators on the case and the Catano security team. Eden played the recording of Ava again and again, and I imagined a new horror of what she must be going through every time it played.

Half of the team has gone to Nina's Beach Stop, which was located in a small town called Hargrove, not too far from Yuman. Jadon returned to Farrow earlier this morning, unsettled about not being able to reach his stepmother. I have a feeling he'll return as soon as he's talked with her and gotten a few matters settled there.

"I'm going to Yuman today," I announce. "I can't sit here and wait. If there's a chance she went there, I want to find her."

"I'll go with you," Elias says.

"I'll send three guys from my team with you," Luka adds. "I'm tempted to go myself, but I need to ensure

Eden's protection too…and someone should be here if Ava returns."

"She'll return." Elias massages his temples and looks grave, but when he sees us looking at him, he lifts his shoulders. "She *will*." He turns to me then. "And you need to fill me in on a few things…"

I nod, even though I have no intention of telling Elias more about my family saga…*or* details about Ava.

After being briefed on what is expected of us by the security team—stay together, report anything suspicious, my phone would be tracked, etc.—I go home to pack a bag and wait at the house until Elias and the three men who will be going with us show up. I put in a quick call to Jerome to update him on the situation and to see if he's found out anything, but he doesn't have any new information. I've actually found out more being at the Catano mansion after Ava called than all the investigators put together.

It's shocking how she'd been taken to begin with; Luka has been at odds with his surveillance and security team and I don't blame him. To think you have an airtight system working, only to find out his sister-in-law was not only kidnapped but has been sneaking out to see me…I'm ashamed I didn't think of what the implications of that meant before now. And I'm filled with guilt that she was out late at night when she should have been safe in her own bed…because she had come to see me.

I ignore a call from my dad and when he calls a second time, I switch my phone to vibrate, throwing my toothbrush and toothpaste in my overnight bag. I haven't talked to him since all of this began and I know he's going crazy thinking I'm angry with him, but that seems so meaningless now. I don't have room in my brain for one more traumatic event beyond Ava.

I should probably be concerned about going to Yuman, with Alex gunning for my throat, but I can't be worried about that either.

Elias knocks and steps inside, the three guys filing in behind him.

I hold my hand out and shake their hands, introducing myself. They each tell me their names: Frederick, Seb, and Malak. So far Frederick is the friendliest; the other two assess me coldly and then take in their surroundings as they wait for me to grab my bag.

"This should be fun," Elias says drily, clapping me on the back.

Once I have everything and we're outside, I lock the door and then remember the plant Ava gave me. I go back inside quickly and tuck the plant in my arm, avoiding the guys as I walk out.

"Didn't take you for a gardener." Elias smirks as I put the plant in the back of the SUV next to our bags.

"Ava gave me this plant."

I don't know why I bothered to admit this, but it feels good to say her name in something other than the kidnapping. It feels good to say her name out loud, period, and to know that I'm not hiding anything anymore. Keeping my feelings a secret was weighing heavily on me—I had no idea how much. My guilt about the whole thing is still like a noose around my neck, but I've at least owned up to my shit. When we find Ava, I will happily work through the rest of it. I wouldn't blame her for wanting nothing to do with me when she gets back, especially when she knows who I am, but we have a few less obstacles to work through since I've lost my job...and since I don't intend on ever being a king.

The drive to Yuman is beautiful, but I don't think any of us particularly take note of it. Frederick goes through a list of places she could be in Yuman. The Forbrush estate is brought up because she knows Nadia and I tell them that she's met Alex too. They didn't seem to be aware of that fact and I don't tell them how I know. I'd like to look in the beach areas and shelters first, and mostly the solitary places —if she's running from someone, she might be staying away from areas where innocent bystanders could get hurt. At least that's the way I believe she thinks, and Elias agrees.

"Ava is tough and underneath all that bravado she puts out, she's got a heart of gold. She has Mara wrapped around her little finger and that doesn't happen easily with my wife," he says. "I think she'll try to handle things on her own...otherwise she would've come back to Niaps."

That's bothered me since the moment I heard her mention Yuman. Why isn't she coming back? I hope it doesn't have anything to do with me. The last thing I want is for her to try to protect me.

We pull into Yuman in the late afternoon, the sun blinding as we drive through traffic. Yuman is much smaller than Niaps, but it has a resort vibe to it. People come here to get away from their everyday lives and to live it up by the beach. Money practically oozes from the land-scaped trop- ical yards and elaborate beachfront properties. The buildings aren't as historical as Niaps, the feel decid-edly more modern. The turnover of people must be constant, which could make it so much easier to stay hidden than someplace where the regulars saw something or someone suspicious and immediately investigated.

I wondered how I would handle driving into the kingdom where my supposed family rules, but I feel nothing but a chill as I think about how disconnected I am even from the family who raised me.

No time to figure it out today, I think, and get out of the car when we stop in front of the beachfront house we've rented. I put my bag in the free bedroom and look at the paperwork Frederick has already set up on the desk. There are maps and I look up all the coffee shops. It's wishful thinking that Ava could be free and sipping coffee on the beach right now, but I like to think she is.

I point to a place on the map that's near the beach and has three coffee shops in the nearby vicinity.

"I'd like to take a look here and can also grab coffee for everyone," I offer without looking around.

There's silence and I look up, taking in the serious expressions. They're all facing the TV and I can only see their profiles, but it's an immediate sombering. Elias turns the TV up and Ava's face flashes on the screen. It's a beautiful picture of her at Mara and Elias's wedding and I'm taken back immediately to that day and the first time I saw her.

"We have reason to believe Princess Safrin has been seen in Hargrove and could be in Yuman now. If you see or hear anything related to the search, please report to the nearest constable."

"How has word gotten out that she's close?" I ask. "Is that wise? What if the people following her had no idea and now they do?"

"I think there's more of a chance of others spotting her

and us getting to her faster with more people on the lookout than whoever is tracking her seeing this on TV," Frederick says.

I swallow my quick retort, biting my tongue. I don't know all the ins and outs of investigative work, but I'm itching to get out here and see for myself if I can find her. I'll go crazy if I have to stay in this house very long. Or anywhere closed up, for that matter. I'm losing my mind. She's been missing too long.

"We're wasting time watching this," I say. "We know what she looks like. I'm going out there."

Elias picks up his phone and nods. "I'll go with you."

"Malak, why don't you go with them," Frederick says.

"Seb and I will separate and look in this area." He points to two different places on the map.

"If we all split up, we could cover more ground," I say when I reach the door.

"We don't know what these people are capable of. The king hired us to look out for you guys and we're required to do exactly that," Frederick advises. "Just act like Malak isn't there if he's getting on your nerves." He grins and I roll my eyes, turning to open the door.

Elias follows me to the car and Malak gets in the backseat, at least letting me feel like I'm somewhat in control. I start the SUV and head to the nearest coffee shop, my eyes pealing the streets for any sign of her. I park near the two that are closest and we hit the shops, asking every shop owner between the locations if they've seen anyone with Ava's description. We've printed flyers and pass them out, pin them on bulletin boards and street posts, and look in every nook and cranny along the way. When it feels too hopeless to breathe, I take a side walkway to the beach and stand looking at the water for a few minutes.

I've never felt more alone, more helpless.

A breeze drifts over me and I close my eyes, as I plead for whatever force out there that could bring Ava back to me. The water laps up against my shoes and I'm surprised —I didn't think I was close enough to the water for it to reach me. I turn around and walk back toward the buildings, feeling a little better than I did when I stepped out here.

I hear a commotion down the beach and follow the sound. A crowd has gathered and the sound of an ambulance gets closer. I jog to the crowd, my heart pounding with each step. I can hear Elias next to me, but I run faster, the panic building.

I maneuver through the crowd and see a body on the sand. At first just a foot and then the rest of the body. When I see it's a man, I want to fall to the sand in relief, but I keep pressing forward.

"Does anyone know what happened?" I ask.

"I think he was murdered," a girl says. She pushes her hair back and her eyes widen as she looks at me. She grins a flirty smile and I glare at her, causing her smile to drop. "I mean, I don't know that. But either that or he killed himself." She shrugs.

What happened to general decency toward human life? I look around and make sure Ava isn't in the crowd. Elias finds the officers on the scene and talks to one who will answer a few questions once he tells him why we're in town.

"I haven't seen anyone who fits her description," he says. "And I doubt the two are related at all, but it was a young woman who called in about this man. She said she'd seen someone kill him, but she wasn't here when we arrived."

That opens up an endless round of questions…to which I feel we find even fewer answers to, but I have this feeling in my gut that it was Ava. She was here.

The question is: where is she now?

CHAPTER THIRTY-FOUR

AVA

I realize the money Samson gave me is gone a few hours later. It must've fallen out of my too-small pockets somewhere on the beach. I go back to look for it and it's a lost cause. Finally, I clean up in a beach bathroom and head toward the wharf, asking around for odd jobs I can do. I have to keep busy and I have to figure out a way to get to Farrow without putting anyone else in danger because 1) in the quiet, still times, I have too much time to think and my mind goes to unthinkable places, and 2) I killed a man with my bare hands and I am terrified of what else I'm capable of doing.

When I'm still, it encapsulates every thought, every action, every memory and foreboding of the present...when I'm busy, it merely rings in my ears like a faulty speaker.

I'm losing it.

I've tried every way of rationalizing what's happening to me, every way to defend myself against the horrific act I committed, but the quiet, cold, hard truth is I'm scared shitless and think I should have killed myself instead of that man. That would've been safer for humanity, for me to not be a part of it anymore.

He might've been attacking me, but I didn't have to kill him. Once I'm far from Samson, I call and ask for help and then go back long enough to see the fire trucks and ambulances arriving. It's only then that I make my escape.

I don't like the way Samson and the Watcher come and go, as if they have complete access to me at all times. When I'm able to finally find a man who says yes to me selling fish at a little kiosk near the wharf, I work through the dinner rush and sneak bites of the fish on the side. In the lulls, I check my body for any bumps that I might've missed…any tell-tale signs of a tracking device buried underneath my skin.

I see the three men just before the sun goes down. Elias is front and center and I'm floored when I see Gentry next to him, and another guy I don't recognize with them. They look out of place among all the tourists, dressed a little nicer than beach attire, and standing taller and better looking than everyone. I get stuck on Gentry and stare openly, feeling safe in my little smelly kiosk.

My heart does insane leaps while I stare at him. It's so good to see him. I want to cry and scream and run to him, jump in his arms, and beg him to never let me go.

Until he starts walking toward me. All three of them. I scramble to get down on the floor, and the owner, Jer, I'm working with looks at me like I'm crazy when I hide under the table we're using to filet the fish. He's frying a batch and I was supposed to be doing the gross part of fileting.

I hear Gentry's voice and I shake my head frantically at Jer.

I can't let him see me. I don't want to bring him into whatever mess this is that I don't even understand myself. There are too many unknowns and a dead man on a beach because of me. And this never-ending nagging sense that I have to get to Jadon before I see anyone else...knowing Samson is just waiting for me to go to Jadon.

"We're asking around—have you seen this girl? About five foot seven, these tattoos on her arm and leg..." His voice drops off as he waits and the anguish I feel for his pain is acute.

I hold my breath waiting to see what Jer will do.

Jer looks at whatever Gentry holds up and studies it a moment. Then he shakes his head. "No, I'm afraid not. I'll watch for her, though," he says. "Someone who looks like that would be hard to forget," he adds. He smirks and glances down at me and I cringe. "She actually looks familiar..."

They don't say anything about who I am and I feel my skin crawl when Jer looks at me again. His eyes are practically swimming with dollar signs now. I clutch the knife I'm still holding and when Gentry walks away, I crawl out from under the table.

"You didn't tell me you had a price on your head," Jer says, grinning.

I hold the knife up and study it before looking at him.

His smile drops when he sees the look in my eyes.

"I'm kidding," he says, holding his hands up. "I need the help and the peace. I'll keep my mouth shut." He throws a few filets on the griddle and the sizzle of the grease sounds loud all of a sudden. "We can come up with some kind of arrangement..."

"I'm going to need some money," I tell him. "This is the arrangement: you give me money and let me go without telling them you saw me and I will let you live."

He jerks back like he's been hit. "What are you talking about? No." He shakes his head and laughs. "I'm not getting robbed by a fucking girl. What are you, twenty at the most?"

I laugh and it sounds unhinged. He blinks rapidly and presses his lips together. He takes a step back, closer to the door, and reaches behind him for the knob. I hold up the knife and point to the cashbox.

"Empty it." I stand to my full height and he stares at me, unsure if I'm really doing this. I'm not sure myself, but I don't know what else to do.

Jer groans and his shoulders sag as he opens the cashbox. He pulls out all the shartrovs and I suppress the excitement when I see how much he has.

He holds it out to me and I snatch it.

"Thank you." I point to the other side of the kiosk. "Move over there, please. Let me go without telling anyone you've seen me, and I will find a way to repay you." I wave the money. "Do we have a deal?"

"Yes," he says with one nod. "I should've known better than to hire a stray. At least you're one with connections," he says, grinning.

I smile back. "Thank you, Jer. Maybe you're halfway decent."

He shrugs and tilts his head toward the door. "You better go before I change my mind."

I put the money in my pocket and look around before I walk out. I see Gentry at a shop on the other end of the strip of food trucks and touristy shops and walk in the other direction. When I turn around again, he's walking toward me and looks up. It's too far away to know for sure if he sees me, but I turn and duck in the first alleyway I see and run.

He wouldn't recognize me anyway, not from far away, I remind myself when I see my reflection in a window. He doesn't know I chopped off all of my hair. I don't even recognize myself.

I count the shartrovs before I get to the train station. I have enough for a ticket. I'm not sure if I have enough for the fast track or not. Maybe. I only need enough to get to Farrow, the sooner, the better.

My skin is crawling. I'm glad I ate and have kept it down, but I still don't feel right.

Because you killed a man.

How is it possible for me to keep putting that out of my mind? It makes no sense. I rub my temples and feel dizzy. I'm tired of feeling this way. I try to shake it and stay focused, to keep moving until I get to the train station.

I do have just enough for the fast track to Farrow. I buy the ticket and keep my head down until it's time for me to board. I watch the doors, making sure I don't spot Gentry, or worse, Samson or the *Watcher* boarding the train. I don't think I have to worry about Jer telling him...it's the way Gentry knows me. It won't take him long to find me if we're both in Yuman.

I board the train, breathing just a bit easier than I was when I stepped into the station. One step closer to home, one step closer to Jadon.

I don't fully relax until we're moving and then I close my eyes while we fly across the track at record speed.

CHAPTER THIRTY-FIVE

AVA

I haven't taken a train since I was a little girl and my father took me on a day trip just so I could have the experience. I was fascinated by the idea of the train and once I was on it, I stared out the windows and was happy…for about an hour. Then I wanted to get there and we still had a long way to go.

This train goes faster than I want. I lose the little food I've had in the bathroom, my eyes looking hollow and dark as I wash up afterward. I sit down again and can't wait to get off of the train. I need to sleep and eat…get my bearings before I figure out what's next.

I fall asleep a few minutes before we're scheduled to arrive, so when I start dreaming about Jadon and then hear over the muffled speaker that we've arrived in Farrow, I feel more disoriented than I did before I slept.

I get off the train and follow the cattle walk up above ground. The chill of Farrow feels like home and foreign at once; I'm not dressed for the snow and my blood has thinned considerably since I was here last. I take a bus as far as I can and then walk the rest of the way, shivering the whole way. It's a long walk, and just when I think I can't go another inch, I see the first signs of home.

I'll have to be smart about this. It suddenly seems very important that no one can know I'm here...so I walk the perimeter of the woods toward the back of the property. I know these woods well, but I'd prefer to be inside when the creepy crawlies start coming out later tonight. And it's getting colder. I pick up my steps and rub my hands together, imagining how warm I'll feel when I crawl under my covers tonight and when I take a bath in my tub...it propels me to walk faster and faster until, before I know it, I'm looking around and putting the code into the door of the staff entrance.

The house is as quiet as a tomb when I walk inside. I walk down the back hallway and pass the offices, tiptoeing to keep my shoes from clicking on the floor. The kitchen is even empty and I pause, making sure I'm not missing someone in the shadows.

When I get to the parlor, I finally hear hints of someone speaking, but it's not loud enough to make out the words. I follow the sound and it ends in Jadon's office, which he moved to be next to the dining room. I listen for a few seconds and hear Jadon talking to someone I don't recognize and my heart starts its rapid freefall into the floor. My hand grips the table to steady myself and I try to hear what they're talking about. They mention my mother and me, but I only hear our names and everything else is muffled. When the sound gets a little closer, I run to the back staircase and am up the stairs before the office door downstairs opens.

I rush to close the door and look around my room, feeling warmth spread throughout my chilled body just by the familiarity. Everything has been kept the same and it makes me miss my mother more than I have in all the time I've been away. I'm jolted by a flashback of hearing her call me as I was escaping. How did I manage to put that out of my mind? I've been looking for her around every corner since stepping inside this house! I slide to the floor and sit there, huddled up, my head in my hands. My head begins the dizzy wash of blur, like a filter in my brain that clouds everything over.

No! Focus! I tell myself, but the pounding starts, and I lie down with my hands covering my eyes, willing the pain to stop. It's some time later that I pull the comforter off of my bed and cover myself. The effort it would take to get in the bed feels daunting and I fall asleep on the floor, dreaming the crazy dreams I dreamed when I was locked up.

My room is pitch black when I wake up and I'm sweating from being under the blanket so long. I get up and feel my way into the bathroom, where I turn on the light and run a bath. It's two in the morning and I should probably be quieter, but my room is on the opposite wing from Jadon's, so I should be fine. I lock the bathroom door and hope for the best. I want a bath more than anything right now, consequences be damned.

When I look at myself in the mirror, I'm taken aback by the bruises and cuts that I didn't know were there. It's as if seeing them has made me suddenly feel them and I wince when I get in the steamy water. My body sinks under and the cuts burn, but everything else feels too good for it to bother me much. Something niggles my mind about a tracker, but I close my eyes and let my thoughts drift to how good this hot water feels.

Something isn't right. It's not that I'm ignoring it or don't know it; I just can't pinpoint what it is. Just out of reach, like I've known at one point but lost it. How could that be possible?

I wash my hair; it feels so strange to barely have any hair to work with, so the job is done much faster than usual. I lean my head against the back of the tub, closing my eyes and nearly drifting off, until the water gets cool and I force myself to get out.

I half-expect a guard to be in my room when I open the bathroom door into my bedroom, but it's quiet. The night is still and calm despite the waves of erratic thought in my mind. I'm glad that I'm unbothered and was able to sneak in without any repercussions, but it's also troubling that my family castle is so easy to infiltrate. Who else has come and gone so freely over the generations?

I crawl into bed, dropping the towel at the last minute and enjoying the feel of the cool covers against my bare skin. I fall asleep thinking about Gentry and how I loved the weight of his body on mine. My dreams are fragmented; I want to dream of Gentry, but instead, I keep jerking out of dreams that I'm falling or on the verge of being caught by a faceless man who is on my heels, chasing me.

When I wake up, I feel better than I have in a while. My head feels clearer once again. I stretch my arms and they feel stronger, less weighed down by whatever intangible binds keep dragging me to the ground. I feel more myself and I don't try to overthink why that feeling comes and goes. I walk to my closet, checking to see what is still here. I thought I'd done a better job of clearing it out, but there are still dozens of cute blouses and jeans, short skirts, and leather jackets. I opt for a black sweater and ripped jeans, my black boots sliding on like faithful friends.

The house is still quiet when I leave my room, too quiet. The loneliness is throbbing throughout the house and I feel a wave of sorrow for Jadon, that he's been stuck in this dark house for all this time without everyone but guards and my mother...who has never liked him. He must be going crazy here without Eden and me keeping him company, placating our mother and distracting both of them from having to deal with one another.

I need to find him.

That becomes the drilling thought in my head, so much so that I have to bend over and clutch my head with my hands when the thought becomes too loud. I hear something outside and stand up, going to the window to peer out the curtains. A crowd has gathered on the west lawn, the green buds popping out on the trees despite there still being snow on the ground. Jadon stands on a small stage in the center of them and he's raising his arm and shouting something while they cheer.

I grab a hat and jacket and bundle up before going outside to see what's going on. I'm almost to the door when I remember I need a gun. I go to Jadon's office and push several codes on the locked cabinet before I get it right. The lock clicks and I stare at the array of weapons—swords and knives and guns—before settling on something small that I can handle.

I lock it back up, pull my collar up so my neck won't be exposed, and go outside like a woman on a mission.

CHAPTER THIRTY-SIX

GENTRY

We get our first lead from the guy at the fish stand who initially said he hadn't seen Ava. About an hour after we questioned him, we circle around again and he changes his story. Maybe he was lying then, maybe he's lying now, but he says he's seen her. She looks different though—short hair, much thinner than the picture we showed him—but he's sure it's her. We give him money when he tells us the direction he saw her going…and we end up at the train station where an employee says he sold her a ticket to Farrow.

That's all we need to know.

It's her.

I have a million questions, but first and foremost, I have to know if she's okay. It's what's driving me, despite the fear and lack of sleep and uncertainty. I need to see for myself. I don't understand why she hasn't gone to the authorities or called me or her family again…but I just hope and pray that she's safe now and that all the questions will be answered.

Luka's jet picks us up in Yuman and we get to Farrow in the early hours of the morning. We search the train station, but there's no sign of her there or in the surrounding areas. I think I'm too wired to sleep, but after Elias talks to Jadon and he says to come stay in the castle and get some rest before we figure out what to do next, I collapse in one of the guest rooms and sleep for an hour like a guy drugged.

It doesn't take much sleep for me to feel a little better. I'm already hopeful knowing she was on her way here and maybe being in her home is helping too. I feel her everywhere. I get up and shower, then make my way outside where Jadon has a crowd gathered. He's talking to them about his missing mother and sister and they listen attentively, ready to do whatever he asks.

"My mother went missing a week and a half after my sister and it's been confirmed that the two abductions are related. We don't know who has them yet or where they've been kept, but we got word that my sister has escaped. At least we think she has—she was seen alone in Yuman yesterday and at a train station later where we heard she's on her way here. We don't know what she's been through, how fragile she is, or what she's seen. I ask you to treat her with care and the utmost respect. Bring her to me safe and sound and I will offer a reward of two million shartrovs."

The crowd cheers and there's a heady mix of anger and outrage in the air. There are signs with Ava's face everywhere and the fervor of the people for their princess is a sight to behold. I know it's not what she wants and I understand that more than ever, but this time, their obsession with her and her family could help.

"Unfortunately, we know nothing about my mother, or even when she was last seen…I was in Niaps searching for my sister, and as far as I know, our mother left of her own free will while I was gone. It's not been proven yet when she was taken or if she's been freed, but I know what my gut is telling me. We need to find her immediately...I believe she's in danger."

The crowd cheers again and the sound is deafening this time. Jadon has a way of pulling out the passion in his people and I can't help but be in awe of him. What must that feel like, to have everyone ready to do your bidding? I shudder and think for the umpteenth time since finding out my lineage: *I will do whatever it takes to* not *be king.*

The crowd disperses and Jadon sees us standing there. His eyes narrow when he sees me, but he doesn't look as angry as he did the first time we met. His guards surround him as he walks toward us and several women try to get through his protectors, wanting to offer their condolences by way of hugs and offers of fancy meals to help out at this horrendous time. Jadon's jaw clenches when the last woman is led away and he shakes his head at Elias and me, his eyes stormy. He looks like he hasn't slept in weeks and I feel another pang of pity for the guy, that this is his life. I'm feeling all of my own shit about Ava, and it's fucking hell, but I'm not having to run a country while my sister is missing like he is.

"I'm glad you guys are here," Jadon says. He looks at me. "Yes, even you. I might not like you, but we need all the help we can get."

I nod. I wouldn't like me if I were in his shoes either.

"I think we're close to finding her," Elias says, putting

his arm around Jadon's shoulder. "She's here." We walk toward the house and he looks over at me, smiling. "I have a good feeling about this and I'm not just saying that. Luka will be here tonight and hopefully we can get you and Eden reunited with your sister soon."

A shot rings out and I watch as it plays out in front of me in slow motion. Jadon goes down and I run to him while the guards run toward the shooter. Jadon is holding his shoulder and looks up at me for a few seconds before holding his hand out for me to help him up.

"I'm fine. It was just a graze." He wipes the blood from his shoulder and rubs his fingertips together, smearing it.

"Stay down," one of the guards yells.

Near the house, two figures are locked in a struggle. I squint to try to make out who it is, but we're still quite a distance away and it's hard to tell...but the one...is that Ava? She has her arms around another woman's neck and appears to be choking her.

I help Jadon up and take off toward the women. I get within thirty feet or so and there's no question, it's Ava... and it looks like...what the hell?

"Mother," Jadon yells, still clutching his shoulder.

Ava and her mother turn and there's the strangest expression on Ava's face. She staggers back and her mother stumbles with the sudden release. Ava walks toward Jadon as if in a trance, her eyes wide. I stare at her, transfixed, but then her mother rushes forward and points a gun at Jadon.

When she gets ahead of Ava, it seems to shake Ava and her eyes veer from Jadon and to her mother. All the color rushes from her face and she yells, "Mother, no!"

She jumps on her mother's back and the gun goes off again.

CHAPTER THIRTY-SEVEN

AVA

I wish I could undo everything.

I was almost to the door when she stepped out of the shadows, her eyes and smile forced.

"Ava, darling. I see you've beaten me here." Mother stood tall and held out her hand for the gun.

I shook my head and tried to reach the door before she did.

I wish I had run the other direction, locked the gun back up, and restrained my mother until I could talk sense into her.

Because the minute I saw her, it all rushed back over me, the electrodes plugged into my head, the dreams of Jadon trying to kill me, the words repetitively drilled into my mind—*Kill Jadon*—my mother calling out to me from the compound where we were kept.

What did she suffer at Samson's hand?

By the deranged look in her eyes, I don't think she had the reprieve I had, and I've still been messed up.

We fought over the gun. And she screamed and opened

the door when she finally got her hands on the weapon. I kicked and hit and scrambled to reach the gun, something I never imagined doing with my own mother, but I know how lost I've been...and she doesn't seem to have that same consciousness...

"We're on the same side," she whimpered when I punched her in the nose.

"We are not on the same side if you want to kill Jadon."

Her face crinkled and she blinked rapidly, shaking her head. "We have to. You have to. Once you do, we will both be free."

"That's a lie. It's not you talking, Mother."

She screamed again, knocking me down, and we fell down the steps and onto the lawn. She lost focus on me when she heard Jadon and she stood up and aimed...fired.

And now I feel the rush of that foreign feeling. *I should've run. I should've never come here.*

Something strange happens to me when I see Jadon too. It's like he's all I see and I must put an end to him.

No, no, no, my brain yells.

I picture a sword and the sword shattering those thoughts as I shake my head.

"No," I yell out loud.

I pull my mother down and kick the gun away from both of us.

When I do, I see Gentry helping Jadon stand up and I feel like I'm going to pass out. My hair is yanked back and I see stars when the wind is knocked out of me. I go down and stare at the sky before everything goes dark.

I try to fight it. I need to make sure Jadon is okay. I want to see Gentry. Someone has to stop my mother. But it's too much. I go under and when my body finally gives in, I feel an overwhelming sense of relief.

.   .   .

I wake up with a roomful of eyes on me. I'm on the living room couch with an IV attached to my arm. I try to sit up and Jadon's hand steadies me.

"Easy there, little one. We need to get some liquids in you. You're severely dehydrated. The doctor wants to run tests on you and we're just waiting for some of the machines to be moved here." He leans in and whispers, "It's best if we keep all of this under wraps until we can figure things out. How are you feeling?"

"Like I got hit over the head a dozen times with a baseball bat."

"Mother's aim was good, but not *that* good." He tries to sound lighthearted, but I can tell he's shaken.

Gentry stands just behind him and his worried expression makes me almost lose it. "Gentry," I whisper.

I grab his hand and squeeze it and when Jadon turns to look up at Gentry, I take his hand too. "I have a lot to tell you."

"Yes, you do," he says pointedly. "Some of it is out already…" He points his thumb back toward Gentry. "Settle something for me, if you're up to it—should I kill this bastard?"

My mouth drops and my eyes grow huge. "No! What are you talking about? I love him. Don't you dare hurt him!"

He nods slowly like he's contemplating it all. "I had a feeling you would say that. I don't know how I feel about this guy yet, but the one thing he's done right is telling us everything so we could try to get to the bottom of who the last person was to see you. Lost his job and has done every-thing he could to help us find you…"

I look at Gentry, biting the inside of my jaw. "I'm sorry. I know how much your job means to you."

"Nothing compared to what I feel for you," he says, taking a step closer.

Jadon takes a deep breath and shakes his head. "Not ready for these declarations." He pats my hand. "What happened to you?" His eyes fill with tears and mine do too.

I try to sit up again and my head hurts too much. "Jadon, where is Mother? You shouldn't trust her *or* me. We —" I look around frantically and when I don't see her, I try to pull the IV out.

"Hey, hold on, stop—" Jadon bats my hand away and Gentry holds my shoulders down.

"What's wrong, Ava?" Gentry studies my face, the groove deepening between his eyebrows.

The trembling takes over my entire body and I shake my head back and forth. The voice in my head, the need to hold onto reality, always feeling like it's drifting…I put my hands on my head and yell, the sound haunted even to myself.

"Tell us what to do," Gentry pleads.

Jadon moves and I vaguely hear him talking to the doctor. The doctor comes over with a syringe and I scream, "No, no, no, don't drug me. Jadon, stay away from Mother. Stay away from me!"

And that's the last thing I remember before the drugs fill my system.

I'm in my room the next time I wake up. I'm hooked up to more machines and it reminds me of being hooked up to the other machines with the woman and Samson and the Watcher…but my mind feels sharper.

I saw Jadon and I didn't kill him.

If I hadn't seen my mother trying to kill him, would I have done it myself?

It's a question I don't want to think about too long… I'm afraid I won't like the answer.

Is it gone? Are the thoughts gone?

I try to get out of bed and hear footsteps.

"Whoa, hey, easy there, love. Don't try to go anywhere just yet. What can I do for you?" It's Gentry and he looks like a drink of water in the desert.

"I missed you." I sound like a croaking frog, but he smiles and I feel that butterfly explosion in my chest.

"I missed you too," he says.

"I need to get out of here." I grab his hand and squeeze it hard. "Listen, the best thing you can do for me is to help me leave. I can't stay here. I can't see Jadon. I can't be around anyone. I have to get well. My head—what they did to me…Gentry, do you hear what I'm saying?"

He runs his fingers over my face and grips my chin. I close my eyes and he taps my lips until I open my eyes. "I do hear you, and I want you to tell me everything, but first…we have to take care of you right here. Your blood pressure is scary low, you've lost too much weight, and you're going to keep passing out if we don't get liquids in you."

"You don't understand." I turn my face from him and bring my legs up to my chest, my head leaning against the headboard.

"Exp—" he starts, but Jadon comes in then with the

doctor and I stare at him, terrified of where my mind will take me.

"It's so good to see you awake. Are you feeling any better?" he asks.

The doctor wraps a blood pressure cuff around my arm and sticks a thermometer in my mouth, while also attaching a thing to my finger that shows percentages of my airflow. I'm at 92% and he frowns. He bends down and brings a nebulizer mask to my face while turning the machine on. I give up trying to talk and let the medicine do the work to my lungs.

I stare at Jadon and Gentry and try to make sense of all that has happened. I don't even know how long I've been gone. It's all jumbled. And as much as I want to find it all out now and make a run for it, I feel so, so tired. My eyes drift shut and I fall asleep to the sounds of the men I love talking about me.

CHAPTER THIRTY-EIGHT

AVA

Jadon is asleep in a chair next to the bed, and Gentry is staring at me from across the room. He stands up when he sees that I'm awake. The door opens and we both turn as Eden rushes into the room and to the bed to hug me, tears running down her face.

"Are you okay?" she says into my neck.

I pat her and wipe her face when she leans up. "I'm feeling much better."

Jadon wakes up and stretches. Gentry sits back down and I can tell he isn't comfortable around my siblings, but he's hanging in there.

"I'm not the one who was shot," I say quietly, looking at Jadon.

He takes a deep breath and Eden turns to him, holding onto his arm tightly.

"I'm fine. I was just grazed," he says. He looks at me and his eyes narrow. "Quit stirring up trouble. Our focus is on *you*, which is where it should be. How are you feeling?"

"I'm feeling better." I touch my head. "I haven't felt dizzy in a while. I haven't—" *felt like killing you lately either*, I want to add, but I keep that to myself. I look at Gentry and will him to get me out of here. I don't trust myself. Not yet.

"Why would Mother do that? She would never—" Eden starts. She blows her nose and looks between Jadon and me. "I mean, I know she has her issues with you, but she still cares about you…" Her voice trails off.

"Where is she?" I haven't seen her since it happened.

"She's being watched closely." Jadon leans forward, his elbows on his knees.

"She's here, in this house? Jadon, you can't let her near you."

"She's close and there are guards on her nonstop. I haven't talked to her yet, I've been too worried about you. We need to get to the bottom of this, but only when you're feeling up to talking…"

"Three people were involved. I believe a man named Samson was the one calling the shots, but another man took me from our property and a woman was there too…and they found me even after I escaped. I threw up and saw a device…but there must be something else or they were following closer than I knew because they found me again after that. I believe we were brainwashed." I regret letting the words come out of my mouth as soon as I say them. It sounds too far-fetched. Too unbelievable. "I've lost time, I've lost memories…half of the time, I haven't known what was real and what they were putting in my mind as they drugged me and had me hooked up to machines. Every night I'd dream you were trying to kill me, Jadon."

"What?" His face pales and he clasps my knee over the covers.

"One time, I didn't take all of the meds and I faked being asleep. They attached electrodes to my head and I could hear the words *Kill Jadon* being chanted over and over, a thousand times, more…I don't know. I tried to keep it out, but…as I was escaping, Mother called out to me. She knew I was there. I didn't see her and I don't know if she was there the whole time, but that vacant look in her eyes… that's how I've felt. I came here to—I don't even know…I just knew I had to get here. Samson said I had a mission and I think it was to kill you. I don't know what I would've done if Mother hadn't been here. It was like seeing her made me remember everything and I was able to pull myself out of the trance."

The shock on everyone's faces is almost comical…if I wasn't telling them something so horrific and unbelievable, I think we'd have a good laugh over the crazy story. But they stare at me in horror and I swallow hard, waiting for them to say the whole thing is ridiculous.

"Do you think you can describe these people to our security team? We can have something drawn up as soon as you're able to tell them."

"Yes. Their faces are one thing that hasn't come and gone. My memory has been strange."

"Do you still want to kill me?" Jadon asks finally, attempting a smile.

"I haven't had the overwhelming thought since I saw Mother shoot you. That changed something in me. But I don't trust it, Jadon. I need to get out of here. Get far, far away…just in case. And until I'm sure it's gone."

"I don't believe you'd ever hurt me." He takes my hand and is careful not to mess up the IV.

"I never would've thought Mother could. And I never would've thought I'd have the overwhelming thought that I had to come here and get rid of you…but I did."

"That's why you asked me to get you out of here?" Gentry asks.

I give him a pointed glare. "I was still hoping you'd get me out of here." I lean my head back on the pillow and groan. "Way to ruin our escape."

"I can't do any more secrets," he says, grinning. "Thinking I'd lost you only drove one point home: I want to do things right from here on out."

"Oh, so you're breaking up with my little sister?" Jadon rubs his hands together. "Great. Glad we've got this all sorted out—"

"No," Gentry interrupts. "I want everyone to know I love her. I don't want to hide us ever again. I want to show her the world, if she'll have me."

Jadon rolls his eyes and when I smile, biting my lip to keep from getting a dumb lump in my throat, he groans. "You're falling for this crap?"

I nod, my eyes on Gentry's. "You really want me after I almost killed my brother, you lost your job over me, and we've never even been on a proper date?"

He moves closer, taking my hand and kissing it. "More than ever. You're a survivor and there is no one I'd rather explore life with than you, Ava."

Eden sighs and Jadon groans again. I ignore them and stare at Gentry. "I think I need to sleep more. This has to be another hallucination."

He kisses my hand again. "Go back to sleep. I'll be here when you wake up."

"First, can you get one of the guards in here and I can describe—"

"On it," Jadon says, rushing out the door.

I'm questioned for what feels like hours, but I get a second wind while talking to the team of officers and feel hopeful that we can get somewhere with this. I'm concerned about my mother and wonder what her state of mind is, where she's staying, what her plans are for Jadon. My mother is a good person. She's struggled with her feelings with Jadon and it's been the only contention between us...beyond the normal mother/daughter tensions...but she's not a murderer. She was determined when she saw him though—she was willing to take me down to get to him. The whole mission bullshit—what nonsense is that? And I don't know if she's even aware that it's happened to her, this brain-washing, to try and fight it.

I eat something and feel more like myself after another bath and a hot cup of tea. Eden makes sure I'm in the comfiest pair of pajamas before I crawl back into my bed, and Gentry comes in after I'm situated, looking shy.

"Can I trust you not to whisk her out of here?" Eden asks Gentry, hands on her hip but smirking.

"If any whisking is done, you will be fully appraised of the situation," he says with a wide grin.

I pretend to be annoyed but am secretly overjoyed that my sister and boyfriend—it feels so weird to be able to call him that—are getting along.

Later, Elias comes in to check on me and Luka flies in even later and it's like a party in my room. Nothing is resolved—there are still people out there who wish my family harm...

even our mother...but I'm alive and getting healthier the longer I'm around my loved ones. And Gentry is in the center of it all, looking at me like he's never going to let me out of his sight again.

CHAPTER THIRTY-NINE

GENTRY

It's been an epic time of chaos. I'm not sure I would've believed any of this was real a year ago, if I didn't know this family for myself...if I didn't know Ava Safrin and the kind of person she is.

"I'm so angry," I tell her when we're finally alone.

"Why?" She looks alarmed. I have my fingers looped with hers and her grip tightens.

"You don't take any bullshit, you aim straight, speak your truth...you know who you are, I think you are loyal to a fault..." I shake my head and lean over to touch her cheek. "The fact that you were taken from your own yard and these monsters tried to condition you to kill your brother—it makes me so fucking angry. Who would do that to someone like you? It's not even like you're in the political scene...you're so far from it, it's not even funny. I wonder if the people who did this even know you have no desire to be a princess...how you love your family more than anything and would risk everything for them..."

"Maybe that's exactly why they chose me. Because I

seem like the last person who would take my brother's life."

"This Samson guy…he sounds awfully confident that you'll fulfill his demands."

She flinches and I move to sit next to her on the bed, putting my arm around her and pulling her close. "Is this okay? Are you still sore?"

"Not too bad. Don't move," she says when I try to make her more comfortable. "I missed you so much. Exactly how long was I gone?"

"Three weeks and four days."

"I can't believe it. I have fragments of my time there, but a lot of it is a blur. To be honest, there are times now that I feel I've completely wiped out."

"Do you think they did something to make you forget once a certain amount of time passed?"

"It would make sense why they'd stay on me until I completed my task." She sits up and looks at me, her eyes wide. "What if they're watching now?"

"This place has triple the guards it had when you arrived. I think you're safe here."

She leans back and closes her eyes, taking a deep breath. I stare at her, thinking she's never looked more beautiful, bruises and dark circles under her eyes and all.

"Your hair fits you. I loved it before too, you know that, but…this makes all of your features jump out and grab me."

She laughs and peeks at me out of the corner of her eye. "You sound like you're finally giving in to being whipped by me, Gentry Barrington."

"That's Mr. Barrington to you," I say against her lips.

She leans back slightly. "You kind of confessed your

love for me in front of my brother and sister...did you mean all that?"

I kiss each side of her lips and her nose. "I do love you. And yes, I meant all of it. Probably more than you're even ready to hear at this point...I need to take you out on a date first. You'll probably ditch me when you realize I'm not as cool as you are, and I'll have to move to Farrow to live where it's winter most of the year...the summer of Niaps and Yuman would be far too happy for me."

She smiles and grabs my cheeks, her lips fed up with my teasing. Our kiss is sweet and unrushed, a steady stoking to the fire we always ignite when we touch. My love for her is so real it hurts, but I don't tell her that either. I just got her back; I don't want to scare her off with my grandiose declarations, but I feel it more than I've ever felt anything in my life.

I'm in love with her. And I don't want to run from it ever again.

"I love you too," she says when we finally break away. "I'm saying it now and I will say it again after you fill me in on all the secrets you were keeping from me before I was taken."

"Like I said, you don't take any bullshit and you speak the truth..." I laugh and she smiles, but she also waits for me to tell her everything. "I've been avoiding even thinking about all of my mess," I admit.

She turns to face me a little better, as much as she can while still being hooked up.

"Are you feeling okay?"

"You're not getting out of this by distracting me with questions about how I'm doing." She laughs. "I've felt a lot worse the past few days than I do right now in this warm bed cozied up to you."

"When you put it that way…"

"Stop stalling."

I laugh and run my hand along my jaw and start from the beginning. "So my dad was close to Victros Forbrush growing up…you know, the king of Yuman…"

I start and stop several times: the doctor comes in and out and I wait until he leaves before starting again, and Ava interjects comments here and there…especially when I get to the part about Alex.

"What an asshole! I can't believe he didn't look into it more thoroughly before coming to see you. Do you think he knows the truth now?"

"Honestly, looking back, I think he probably knew the truth when he saw me and just didn't want to admit it. Have you ever seen King Forbrush? It's weird how much I look like him…and even a little bit like Alex."

She studies my face. "Yeah, I do see it. I just thought he looked familiar, but now I know why. You're much hotter though." She grins, leaning her forehead on mine.

"Pretty sure you're the only female in the world who would think that."

"False humility will get you nowhere, Mr. Barrington. Have we not discussed this already, how you're the hottest thing Niaps has ever seen?"

"If you think so, that's all that matters."

"Well, you're a prince, so that ups your sex appeal to the world even more. I won't stand a chance when you're announced as the next heir to the throne."

"Oh, I'm not going to rule Yuman…ever."

"Don't you think you should go meet your family and see how you feel?"

"I already have a family and the family member I met didn't exactly give me warm fuzzies."

She scowls. "Alex will come around. You should meet your father at least…and Nadia is really nice. Did you meet her at Mara and Elias's wedding?"

"I only remember one person from that wedding," I say against her skin, my lips lifting as I remember dancing with her on the beach.

She nuzzles into my neck with a contented sigh. "It's your call, but I think you might regret it if you don't at least meet them."

"I'll think about it."

But I already know I want no part of the Forbrush family. No part of anyone else knowing I'm connected to the monarchy.

I will need to figure out what I'm doing now that I'm not teaching anymore, but it can all wait until Ava gets better.

We talk until her eyes are drooping. She wants to hear about how I was fired, what I did when I found out she was missing…and when she jerks in her sleep but then tries to shake herself awake, I kiss her and tell her to give in to the sleep.

"I love you," I whisper in her hair. "We have plenty of time to catch up on everything."

"I'm scared to sleep," she says groggily. "Scared of my dreams…"

When she's sleeping soundly, I find Jadon in his office talking with his security team. The guys Luka sent are in there too, Frederick taking copious notes on his device.

"Any idea where they were holding her?" I ask.

"We know it's not far from Yuman since Ava was able to walk there after she got out, so we've got troops covering the territory there and around the surrounding areas of Niaps." Jadon clears his throat. "I got a concerning call from Delilah Farthing. I don't know whether to believe her or not. She hasn't exactly been truthful to me yet…"

"What did she say?" Luka interrupts.

"She said Caulder is out for blood and to watch my back."

"Well, shit, that's a pretty huge threat right there," I mutter under my breath.

"I know. And then she asked if my sister had been found yet…"

"Fuck," Luka says. "If they're a part of this, that means we're talking *war*."

"I don't want to go there yet…but yeah, it's really troubling."

I stare at Jadon with his calm demeanor, talking about someone trying to kill him like it's nothing and wonder where these people came from…nope, I am not cut out for this life and now I want to get Ava as far from it as I can.

Before I go back to Ava's room, I grab the plant she gave me from the guest room and set it on her nightstand so she'll see it when she wakes up. I crawl into bed with her and hold her so if the dreams come again, I'll be right here.

CHAPTER FORTY

AVA

I'm still being treated with kid gloves even though I'm feeling so much better. I still have waves of dizziness come over me at times…which I keep to myself…but other than that, I'm beginning to feel more normal every day. Gentry and I take walks through the trees behind the property and each day we're able to go a little deeper into the woods. The trees are so beautiful right now and the cliffs just beyond are spectacular when the sun is setting. I'm proud of my country and it's been fun to show Gentry where I've grown up. I'm still pinching myself that he's here and seems all in with me—I guess if I had to pick one positive, that's the only good thing that has come out of me being kidnapped.

He argues that we were already working our way to one another, it just would've taken more time to be out in the open, but I think we both would've found excuses for why it wouldn't work if I hadn't been taken.

I guess we'll never know.

We stop at the edge of the cliff and I close my eyes

when I feel my eyes blur. I stay as still as I possibly can and when Gentry calls my name, I take a deep breath before turning to face him.

"Are you okay?"

"Just enjoying this fresh air." It's true, I am enjoying the air and being with him outside, but sometimes I worry that the effects of the drugs they pumped me with…and even more troubling, the hypnosis will stay with me forever.

"I love these mountains. I could imagine living here…"

"If it weren't dark so much of the time, and remember, you're not seeing it with as much snow," I remind him. "It's a different place then."

"We can visit Farrow every spring and summer…and for the holidays," he says. "Or whenever we're in the mood."

I grin, wrapping my arms around his neck and gazing up at him. "Are you getting attached to me?"

"Oh, that happened from day one, I'm just now giving in to how attached I am." He leans down and kisses me but stops when it gets a little too good.

I groan. "Quit treating me like I'm sick. Yesterday the doctor said I was cleared for *everything*." I wiggle my eyebrows when I say *everything* and he laughs.

"Your family would break the door down if they heard us having sex. They're already reluctant to even let you leave for a walk."

"There's a thing called silent sex…you should try it."

He tickles my side and I jerk out of the way, laughing.

"You talk like you know how to be silent when I'm loving you." He tries to tickle me with each word and I hop out of the way, holding my hands up.

"It's been so long, I don't know how you'd remember… and I'd consider it a challenge to be silent—one I am willing to work very, *very* hard on." I have to fight to get the words out, I'm laughing so hard when he gets too close.

"I like to think we have all the time in the world," he says, his expression getting serious. "I hesitate saying things like that because you're too young to settle down… too young to be in a committed relationship…but I'm here for as long as you want me."

"Hey, you don't get to decide what I'm too young for, okay? I'm here for as long as you want *me,* but I've also learned that life has a way of stealing from us sometimes, so I want to live every moment to the fullest. Which means *sex,*" I add, lightening the mood again.

Gentry laughs, swiping his hand across his face and looking sheepishly at me, his cheeks pink with the crisp air and his happiness. God, I love him. And I hope he's right… I hope we have all the time in the world.

Life takes over in that way I was talking about, stealing away our blissfully slow days and leisurely healing time when Alex Forbrush comes to the Safrin castle. He's never been here before and it's all very formal when he's introduced to the household and staff who haven't had the pleasure of meeting him yet. He gives his greetings to Jadon and Eden, asking about Luka, who has just returned to Niaps with Elias, all before he turns to Gentry and me.

I scowl at him and he looks more serious than the last time I saw him, even though he was furious at Gentry then. I clutch Gentry's hand and stare at Alex defiantly.

"Ava, I'm so sorry to hear about all you've been through since I last saw you," he says.

I nod and wait to hear why he's here.

"On behalf of the Forbrush family, we'd like to offer our support in helping find who's responsible for this."

"Thank you."

Eden and Jadon repeat their thanks after me.

And then Alex turns to Gentry. "I'd like a word with you," he says, his words clipped.

"You tried to beat Gentry to a pulp the last time you had a word with him." I drop Gentry's hand and take a step closer to Alex, hand on my hips. "I think you should say whatever you have to say right here, so we can all make sure you know your place."

Alex's eyes flash and he barely holds back a smirk, so I know he's not too angry with me. He holds up a hand and nods. "Fair enough." He looks at Gentry and his jaw clenches. "We seem to like the hotheads...must be a family trait."

Gentry looks surprised and swallows hard. "I know I like *this* hothead," he says quietly.

"I owe you an apology for not talking to Father before I came to see you. I thought I was protecting him, but in truth, I was terrified of what he would tell me. I'm sure you already know you are the biological son of my father—first son, so the heir to the throne—and also my half-brother." He takes a huge breath before continuing, and I almost feel sorry for him, the weight on his shoulders seems so heavy. "Our father is desperately sick and he wants to meet you. I want him to have what he wants, and I hope you'll consider coming. He doesn't have much time, and I will never forgive myself for the part I played in keeping the two of you apart."

"I'm sorry he's ill," Gentry clears his throat, "but I don't think you're to blame. He made the decision not to keep me all those years ago and hasn't tried once to meet me. I really don't see why we should meet now."

"I think he was afraid of what my mother, Nadia, and I would think of him if we knew the truth...afraid he'd lose us. And he knew you were in good hands with...your parents."

"Who you basically called the devil when I last saw you," Gentry's voice is cold.

"I didn't trust your father. Now I know how wrong I was," he says, head bowed. His eyes are bleak when he looks up again. "Please consider it. Bring Ava if you like. We will make sure you're both very comfortable and I promise you'll feel welcomed from all of us."

Gentry clasps his hands together and stares at Alex. I wish I knew what he's thinking, but he's harder to read than ever. The silence grows heavier the longer no one speaks, and Jadon finally steps forward and claps Alex on the shoulder.

"I'm so sorry to hear about King Forbrush's health. What can we do to help during this time?"

My brother, always the one who knows just what to do and say. I smile at him gratefully and take Gentry's hand again. He doesn't look at me right away and I lean into him until his arm wraps around me. I feel the stiffness fall off of him.

"Would you go with me?" he asks softly.

"Absolutely."

He wraps both arms around me then and I lean my head against his chest. "As soon as Ava is ready to travel, we will make a trip to Yuman...with your blessing, Jadon."

Jadon looks terrified, but he glances at me and knows the look in my eyes. He sighs and gives a slight nod. "If you'll take guards with you, I'll feel a lot better about it."

"Done," Gentry agrees. "Frederick, can your team be ready to go?"

Frederick stands a little taller. "Of course, gladly."

"I can be ready by tomorrow," I add, grinning. "You know I've been stir-crazy for a while now."

"Let's not rush this," Jadon argues.

"The doctor cleared me for *everything*," I remind him. "And we'll be so careful, right, Gentry?"

"I won't let her out of my sight," he promises.

Alex looks relieved and we head into the dining room for a delicious lunch. I eat better than I've eaten in a long time and when I feel that dizziness and nausea as I stand up, I blame it on my stomach not being used to overeating anymore.

CHAPTER FORTY-ONE

AVA

We travel to Yuman on Alex's family jet—I guess I could say Gentry's family jet, but he looks the most out of place of all of us, eyeing the gaudy interior and sitting carefully on the plush seat.

"Relax," I whisper. "You look like you're ready to split the leather with a knife."

"This is just all so weird. I miss my little house overlooking the water," he says wistfully.

"I miss your little house overlooking the water too, but I'm glad we're not taking the train back to Yuman. My stomach wasn't prepared for the fast track."

"Yeah, give me a good old-fashioned train any day... the fast track makes me queasy." He crinkles his nose when he looks at me and buckles his seat belt.

"Same."

I feel Alex's eyes on both of us and when he catches my eye, he offers a wary smile.

"Does your father know I'm coming?" Gentry asks Alex once we're in the air.

"Yes."

It seems like he's not going to offer any more information than that, but he looks down at his hands before speaking again.

"He has maxeltonia and has stopped all treatments."

Gentry looks at him with alarm. "Oh, I didn't know. I'm so sorry."

Alex nods. "I don't blame him for not wanting to continue treatment—it's made him so much weaker—but it's hard to see him not trying every option. I want every day I can have with him, you know?" He realizes how that sounds and looks apologetic. "I'm sorry, that was—"

"No, I get it. I felt that way when my father was going through chemo. I'm ashamed to say I've neglected him at times since he recovered. At first, I spent every chance I could get and then…life got in the way."

Alex nods. "I've been guilty of that too."

I watch the two of them and take note of the way their face structure is alike from the eyes down. I think about Nadia and remember the shape of her eyes and lips, realizing she might look even more like Gentry than Alex does. This is so strange.

"How does Nadia feel about all of this?" Gentry asks.

"She doesn't know yet," Alex looks ashamed, and he quickly adds, "but we'll tell her as soon as we get there. Everything has been upside down since Father got worse. She'll be kinder to you than I've been." He smiles and all the hard feelings I've had toward Gentry's brother fade with the genuine look in his eyes.

The rest of the flight is quiet or at least the part I'm awake for. I snooze on Gentry's shoulder and wake up when we're landing.

"How are you feeling?" Gentry asks the moment my eyes open.

"We're not going to worry about me, okay?" I yawn. "This trip is about you."

"This trip is about getting you out of your siblings' line of hearing," he teases.

"Oh right, like you're not going to be nervous now in *your* siblings' line of hearing?" I say it just low enough so Alex can't hear me, but Gentry's cheeks still flush when he laughs.

"I don't give a fuck what they hear," he whispers in my ear.

And it's my turn to blush.

The Forbrush castle is not as large as the Catano castle or as foreboding as the Safrin castle. It is a little on the flashy side for my taste, but I can appreciate the beauty in the tall ceilings and crystal chandeliers. The view overlooking the water is spectacular, and it reminds me a little bit of Gentry's view from his charming cottage in Niaps. His love for the water must have been instilled in him since birth.

Our guards are shown to their rooms and Frederick follows us as Alex takes us to a guest suite on the second floor.

"We will take turns guarding this door at all times," Frederick says.

"Is that really necessary?" I ask, looking at Gentry with my hands on my hips. "I'm sorry, Alex. I don't want your family thinking we don't trust them."

"Don't worry about what anyone thinks here. We all

understand the dangers of being part of a royal family and while we will also be doing our best to protect you, we want you to have the guards you're comfortable with too. It's no offense to us whatsoever."

I sigh. He really is a nice guy underneath all that swagger. "Thank you." I look at Frederick and widen my eyes, hoping he'll settle down with the bulldog routine. "Make yourself inconspicuous while we're here, got it?"

"Yes, Princess," he says, smiling.

I roll my eyes. "It's Ava, for the zillionth time...*A-va*."

He gives a slight bow and steps outside the room after he's thoroughly checked everything. I groan and Alex and Gentry both chuckle.

"We will be serving dinner in a few hours. If you need to rest, feel free to do whatever you'd like. I will be speaking with Nadia before dinner and you can either be part of that or wait to see her at dinner. I'll leave it up to you."

"I'll let the two of you have that conversation. It's going to be awkward enough, springing myself on her like this." Gentry picks up a book and studies it, then looks at Alex with a tentative expression. "When should I see your father?"

"How about after dinner?" Alex clasps his hands together and the grief he's feeling is palpable.

Gentry nods and Alex closes the door behind him as he walks out.

Gentry and I haven't even made out since I returned, so when we're alone in this beautiful suite, the air crackles with nerves and tension. I know his shoulders are taut with stress over meeting his family, and my nerves are all over the place from being alone with him after so long...and also from the weirdness I'm still feeling from time to time. I want to put his mind at ease and not do anything to make him more uncomfortable, so I lie on the bed and hold my hand out to him.

"Want a nap before dinner?" I ask.

"Do you need a nap?" he asks, sitting on the bed next to me and smiling sweetly.

"I already napped on the plane." I grin then press my lips together.

"Oh..." He leans down and puts his hands on my cheeks. "What if we don't nap at all?"

"I'm here to be your stress reliever," I say, laughing into his mouth when he bends down to nibble my lip. "We could also take a shower or go for a swim...or stare at that view out there."

"I want to stare at this view right here," he says, pulling my shirt over my head. "Are you sure you're feeling okay?"

"I think if you ask that one more time, I will lose my mind."

He laughs. "So dramatic."

"You know you love my drama." I pull his face down to mine until our noses touch.

"I love everything about you."

It feels like a lifetime has passed since we were together like this, and when he pulls my jeans down my legs and kisses his way up to my lacy panties, I know I never want this much time to pass between us again. The thought of losing him or getting taken again flashes in my mind and I tremble, the lump in my throat growing. I push those fears away and get lost in the feeling of his tongue tracing lazy circles over my lace until he gets desperate for skin and rips them off.

I try to be quiet and mostly am, putting a pillow over my mouth. It's later, when he's thrusting into me faster and faster and I see the love pouring out of his eyes, that I lose it and cry out with him when all of the touches and thrusts and feelings culminate at the perfect moment.

CHAPTER FORTY-TWO

GENTRY

To say I am a wreck is an understatement. I have no idea what to expect when Ava and I walk down to dinner, hand in hand.

"You look so beautiful, I'm going to have a hard time keeping my hands off of you," I tell her before we walk in.

"Good thing you sullied me up earlier." She grins and smoothes my tie before the door opens for us. Alex and Nadia are the only ones standing by the dining room table and Nadia looks flushed.

She tries to smile when she sees me and it doesn't quite reach her eyes, but she holds out her hand and grasps mine tightly.

"I can't believe this," she says. "And we've even met before...how did we not see the resemblance?"

"We weren't looking for it, I guess," I reply.

She takes my other hand and stares at me. "Right. I apologize for everything Alex has put you through. He told me about his behavior and I want to let you know, even though I'm a hundred percent shocked, I will not treat you like that." She smiles then and I appreciate her attempt at humor.

"Easy, I'm right here," Alex says. He steps forward and kisses Ava's hand and I hear her sigh, which makes me bristle.

She glances at me then and giggles, like she can hear every thought I'm thinking.

"Hello, Ava." Nadia turns to Ava and they hug.

Ava filled me in a little bit before dinner on the history with Nadia and Luka and Eden and I'm glad to see there's no animosity between Nadia and Ava. She claims there's none between Eden and Nadia either, but I'll have to see it to believe it. Some women can carry grudges forever.

"Our father isn't well, as I know Alex told you. I'm really grateful you came as soon as you did," Nadia says as we sit at the table. "I don't know what I'd do in your situation, and we're just glad you're here."

"You're taking this remarkably well. I have to say, it helps a lot..." I look at Ava and she takes my hand. "I don't really know how to feel about all of this, to be honest." I look at Alex then and watch as wine is poured into our glasses. "I should tell you now, and hopefully this will put your minds at ease...I have no intention of being king. I don't know if I will continue to be kept a secret or announced far and wide for the kingdoms to know, but the throne is rightfully yours and I will do nothing to stand in the way of that."

Alex's mouth opens and closes, his face a compilation of disbelief and maybe a little respect. "I don't know what to say."

"You don't have to say anything. I'll make sure your father knows this as well."

"Our father," Nadia adds.

"Our father," I echo.

It sounds too strange to say it again, though, or to even think of their father as mine. I picture my dad and his firm belief that I'm due the throne. I don't know when I'll get used to the fact that he's not my biological father, and I think we're going to have many arguments over my choice, but he's still my dad and the one I will do anything to keep.

"How is he feeling today?" I ask as we start eating.

It's a strange dish—something that tastes like meat but isn't quite...with lentils, tomatoes, peppers, and a spice I don't recognize. I like it, but it's just another reminder that I don't even eat the same food as these people who are supposed to be my family. Why didn't my parents instill any of the Yuman culture into me?

"He's had a good day." Nadia's voice breaks and she takes a long swig of wine. "Our mother is sitting with him and has told him you're here."

I nod.

"Any word on your captors, Ava?" Alex asks.

"None that I know of," she says. "I don't think they'll be easy to find, but I'm hoping I'm wrong."

"Why would they take you? Is it all about money?" Nadia asks.

"They want Jadon dead," Ava says bluntly. "So we're going to need all the allies we can get to help bring them and whoever they're working for, *down*."

"We'll do whatever we can do, I swear it," Alex says.

Nadia nods. "Absolutely." She holds her glass up and we all follow suit. "To our new family, new connections, and new allies. Welcome to the Forbrush family!"

We all clink glasses and take long swigs of the wine. I'm still tense, but not as much. Maybe I could get used to these people after all; they're not so bad.

. . .

Ava and I are led down the hall after dinner.

"We've moved his room to the first floor this month, it's just easier," Nadia whispers outside his door. "I'll check on him and see if he's awake and then we can go in if he is."

I don't say anything. This is the most awkward experience of my life. I'm shocked that Nadia and Alex are handling it with such grace. I don't think I'd be so calm and accepting if I was on their side of this.

She steps into the room for a few minutes and Ava reaches out and hugs me, gripping my cheeks in her hands when she pulls back.

"Just be you. Don't make any apologies, even to yourself, for being exactly who you are. You are brilliant, the best-looking man I've *ever* seen"—she winks—"and the kindest. Any family is lucky to have you and don't you forget it."

"I love you," I whisper, skating a kiss across her lips.

Nadia opens the door and waves us in. Alex is already in there and he's standing next to Victros's bed. Victros is sitting up, propped on a bunch of pillows, and he looks like a shrunken version of the man I've seen in pictures.

"Gentry," he says, his voice hoarse and weak. "You sure are a handsome young man...and I've heard you're much more than that. The fact that you're here simply because Alex asked you to come says a lot...especially after he says he was pretty rough on you."

"I'm glad to come," I tell him, and to my surprise, I

almost completely mean it. "I'm sorry to hear about your health, sir."

He waves his hand and beckons me to come closer. "Your father was a dear friend of mine," he says.

"So I've been told."

"I did the wrong thing by him, the wrong thing by you... we should've never kept you a secret. I hope one day you'll find it somewhere in your heart to forgive me. I've lived in fear of losing my wife and children, and they have shown me such compassion, I feel like the biggest fool. I *am* the biggest fool—so much wasted time."

A woman steps into the room then and Victros holds out his hand. She comes to stand by him and grips his hand tightly.

"My wife, Anais," Victros says.

"Nice to meet you," I tell her and she nods, smiling faintly.

"You too," she says.

"And this is Ava Safrin." I hold out my hand toward Ava and she steps closer.

"Beautiful," Victros says. "You look like an actress who was popular in my day with those violet eyes."

Ava smiles and Victros turns to me again.

"You've come at the right time," Victros says. "I don't have much time left, and we need to make things right for our country. I don't know if you realize the fortune you're about to inherit, but that's always been coming to you, whether you ever realized it was coming from me or not."

I clear my throat and try to speak, but the words get tangled in my throat. Ava squeezes my hand and I take a deep breath.

"I assure you, I didn't come for an inheritance, and in fact, once you hear what I have to say about my future here in Yuman, you probably won't want to give me anything...I would expect that and am completely fine with it. Really."

His eyes narrow on me. "Nonsense," he says.

"I don't want anything to do with running this country," I tell him. "I'm glad I was able to meet you. This family seems loving and warm and welcoming, and I'm honored you've invited me here...but I expect nothing from you, and, more to the point, I *want* nothing from you."

"Well, whether you decide to spend time with us and get to know us better is entirely up to you...although I will say, I'd enjoy nothing more than to get to know *you*. I'd like to discuss your role in the kingdom a little more before you make your final decision, but as for your inheritance, that's a done deal. Your adopted father made sure of that before he signed the—" He starts coughing and it's a devastating sound. Wet and croupy, his whole body is wracked violently as he coughs.

Anais helps him with a drink and looks at me somewhat apologetically. "I'm afraid that will have to be all for tonight. He's worked himself up over this and needs to reserve his strength."

"Of course, I'm sorry," I add.

"Don't be sorry," Victros says, his voice a rumble as he tries to hold back another cough. "This conversation should've happened long ago. I've been a coward and I will never forgive myself for it."

I step closer to him and meet his stare. "Never apologize for wanting to protect your family. You put me in very capable hands. I couldn't have had a better upbringing. It's a bonus that I get to meet all of you now, but I expect nothing." When I'm done, I feel almost weak with all the apprehension that's leaving my body.

"You won't get rid of us that easily, even if I'm in the

grave." Victros laughs before going into a coughing fit again.

I take Ava's hand and we walk to the door, stopping to look back at him before turning around.

"I hope to see you tomorrow," Victros says, wiping his brow with a handkerchief.

"I'll be here," I say with a nod.

When we leave, I'm shaking and feel such a combination of emotions. I consider sticking around to talk with Nadia and Alex longer, but I'm maxed out right now.

Ava puts her arm around my waist. "Why don't we get some rest? You can face all of this again tomorrow."

"You are exactly what I need."

CHAPTER FORTY-THREE

AVA

Victros dies in his sleep during the night, and Gentry feels the loss more than he expected to. I hold him as the tears run down his face.

"I thought I was protecting my heart from this," he says. "I didn't want another family, didn't need one…why am I crying for someone I never knew?"

"I think it only took a minute in his presence to know he cared about you and wanted to make things right. And that matters," I tell him, wishing I could take every ounce of his pain from him.

"Thank you for talking me into coming. You're right—I would've regretted it if I hadn't…and now that I got to meet him, I only wish I'd come sooner."

It's a long day of feeling a bit out of place. Alex and Nadia include Gentry, even when he asks for his identity to be kept quiet and to be out of the picture, they still make sure he's part of the conversation regarding the funeral and the reading of the will. It could've gone such a different way, yet it seems his brother and sister don't want to do anything to jeopardize their father's wishes. The family lawyer knows Gentry's identity, but beyond that, it will hopefully go no further than a rumor here and there that Victros had an illegitimate son.

I stay in the suite as the will is read and when Gentry comes back a few hours later, he looks shaken.

I sit up in bed. "What's wrong?"

He shakes his head. "This is all so crazy."

"What happened?"

"Alex asked again if I was sure about denouncing my title. I assured him I was, and the will was opened. It was just the lawyer, Anais, Alex, Nadia, and me in the room..."

He sits on the bed and puts his arm around my shoulder as we lean back against the headboard.

"I have more money than I know what to do with, and an invitation to be here as much as I want. They're willing to respect my wishes of keeping my identity a secret, but they both assured me they'd rather be open about it all. I do want them in my life. It's weird that I could get attached so quickly, but, well, you saw how easy it was with us...even Alex, once he got over his suspicions about me."

"The three of you are strangely similar. It's very weird and very cool." I grin, thinking of the way they'd finished each other's sentences at lunch.

"I'd like to stay for the funeral and then let's figure out where we're going next. You need to finish school..."

"You can tutor me...or if you don't want to, I can call one of my former tutors. Honestly, I have all my credits already and was mostly in Niaps for the experience. I could probably walk with everyone to get my diploma if I want."

"If that's what you want to do, let's go back for graduation...I don't know if I'll be allowed on the premises, but I'll be cheering you on from afar."

I make a face. "Actually, I think I just need to have a long video chat with my friends and catch up. I didn't expect to get attached to any of them either and I miss them."

"Well, that's easy enough, and if there's a time you want to go see them, we can do that. I'll want to eventually check on my house there, even though Elias promised he would."

We have dinner with Alex, Nadia, and Anais, and even though the air is thick with sadness, the mood shifts when stories are shared about Victros. Gentry takes it all in and I'm glad he has this time to find out more about himself. It makes me miss my family and wish that I could see my father again. He'd know what to do about Mother—he was the only one who could ever soften her about Jadon.

The funeral is a beautiful, somber affair with a lot of music and rituals that I've never seen. When they put his body on the float made of wood and flowers and send him into the water before the whole thing erupts in flames, I'm bawling along with the entire kingdom. It's the saddest and most captivating sight I've ever seen.

Gentry and I stay with the crowd, not the family, and it's fascinating and heartbreaking to see the devotion

Victros's people have for him. Alex will have big shoes to fill.

And I've tried my best not to sway Gentry in any way regarding his future, but I'm glad he doesn't have any desire to fill those shoes himself.

Gentry calls his parents and hangs up with watery eyes, but there's peace in his expression that wasn't there before. I think they'll be okay with a little time.

When we leave Yuman, our hearts are full. There are many hugs and tears between Gentry and his family, and we leave feeling like we both have a new family to come back to whenever we want. It hasn't even been a week since we arrived, but with some people, time is nothing; a connection sparks with one common thread and is unbreakable.

We drive to the Sea of Caninsula and I fall asleep on the way, exhausted from the trip and all the emotion that came with it. When we pull up to a two-story house by the sea, I squeal.

"Is this where we're staying? It's perfect!"

"I thought we could both use a quiet place with no one else around…well, except for the guards who watch over us nonstop," he adds, laughing.

"Yeah, where are they going to sleep?" I laugh.

He points to the cottage in the back. "I'm hoping in there, although Frederick will probably make sure someone is in the house with us at all times."

I sigh. "Yeah, I guess our loud days are over for a while. It was fun while it lasted."

"You've gotten better at being quiet," he says, leaning over to kiss me before we get out of the car.

"Thank you, Prince Gentry. I'm trying to be dignified now that I know you're a freaking prince."

He laughs and pulls me out of the car, and we walk to the door. Before he opens it, he picks me up and carries me inside. I squeal again when I see how pretty it is.

"Think you'll be happy here until we go to the next place?"

"Oh yes." I wiggle until he puts me down and we explore the house, getting stuck in the bedroom. I practice being quiet once again as he throws me back on the bed and strips my clothes off.

I have a hard time waking up the next morning. I got up during the night and thought I might pass out again. It scared me and I stayed awake for a few hours, tossing and turning. Why am I still feeling like this?

When I wake up, there's a note from Gentry on the pillow with a flower.

I went to get a few groceries for us, Sleeping Beauty.

The guards are here. Rest and then decide what you'd like to do today.

This is (sort of) the first day of our adventure... ;)

I love you,

Gentry

I stretch in the bed, smelling the flower and smiling wide, as I read the note again. I hear something downstairs and jump up. I thought he'd be at the store a little longer than that, but I guess I don't know how long he's been gone. I hurry into the bathroom to brush my teeth before he comes upstairs. I'm humming when I wipe my mouth with the towel and it sounds ominous when I look up and see the Watcher standing in my bedroom. I drop the towel and edge toward the door, seeing if I can make it to the staircase before he catches me. He watches me come out of the bathroom and waits to see what I'll do, grinning like the wolf who's caught his supper.

I take off and run down the stairs with him on my heels. At the bottom of the stairs, Malak lies on the floor, dead. I bend down to grab his gun and am hit on the back of my neck. I fall next to Malak and stare at his open eyes, counting a few breaths before I turn and fire my first shot at the man who loves to torment me.

I knick him in the arm and he looks down, momentarily caught off guard. I shoot again and this time, I aim at his heart. He clutches his chest and stumbles toward me, falling forward and gripping my neck in his fists, squeezing, squeezing...I gasp when he falls back, his pain apparently taking effect, and I shove him off of me. That's when I see the other guard, Seb, and the woman both lying dead by the door.

Shit, how did all that happen without me hearing a thing? Now, I'm on the lookout for Samson...he wouldn't send the other two to do all of his dirty work. He's got to be close...

The brilliant and stupid things that collide in our minds when our life is hanging in the balance...

God, please help Gentry stay safe. Keep him away from this until it's over.

Please let Frederick still be alive.

What a shame this beautiful house is now marked by death.

*I should've gone to Farrow instead of this adventure...
at least until we knew the risk was over.*

*I wish I'd die in something other than this bra and
panties; even a color other than white would've been
cooler.*

A hard blow on my back takes me down again and I
turn to see the Watcher looming over me.

"Die already," I yell.

"Not until you die first," he says under his breath.

I shoot him again and he goes down, this time for
keeps. I take his sword and slide his gun across the room.
Why, I don't know, but I guess on the off-chance he's not as
dead as he looks.

I go through every room of the house and don't run into
any more dead bodies, but I'm unsettled. Samson is here, I
can feel it.

I don't want to go back upstairs even though I need
clothes. I don't want to get stuck up there. I inch toward the
front door and throw it open and there he stands. He sees
me holding the Watcher's sword and he grins, pulling his
sword out. He moves so I can step all the way outside, and
when I do, we begin our dance.

This time I won't go easy on him and I suspect he
won't go easy on me either.

The gun is still in my hand and it's like I'm so condi-
tioned to train with him with my sword, I don't even realize
I'm holding it. We clash swords several times and the
sound jars me enough to remind me there's another way. I
hear the car pulling up and don't look. If I draw attention to
it, I'll take Samson's attention off of me and onto Gentry
and that's the last thing I want. I up my swordplay, getting
faster and a little bit reckless. I hear the car stop and
Samson glances behind me, smirking. And when I hear

Gentry's voice, saying, "Let her go," I remember that I have a gun in my hand.

Memory is weird sometimes. So is shock. I've killed two men now and it's barely registered, but I hear my lover's voice and all of my sins come rocking back into my body full-force, along with the will to do anything at all costs to protect him. Samson's expression changes and he lunges for me, catching me by surprise. I lift the gun and fire one, two, three times, and then drop it like it's an open flame.

Samson smiles at me as I look down at him.

"Who are you working for?" I ask.

"The mission will have to be fulfilled another way," he says.

"Who are you working for?" I yell. "Stop speaking in riddles and answer my fucking question!"

He just smiles that knowing smile that has haunted my dreams for far too long and takes his last breath.

CHAPTER FORTY-FOUR

AVA

"I have to go home, I have to go home." I rock back and forth, my hands flying over Samson as I try to revive him.

Gentry pulls me back and holds me as I fight against him. I'm glad Samson can't hurt me, but I don't want him to be dead. I feel a strange attachment to him and I put my hands on my head, still rocking.

"Something is wrong with me, I have to go home," I repeat over and over.

"I'll take you home, Ava. Come here, let's get you inside. I'll call Jadon. We'll fly home."

"I can't go in there. There are dead people in there. I don't know where Frederick is—where is Frederick?" I turn to him, panicked and shaking.

"He went with me and is now making sure no one else is here. He'll take care of the bodies in the house. I should've made sure he was the one to stay behind."

"No, he's my favorite and he'd be dead if he'd been here."

Gentry wraps his arms around me and I finally let him, stilling under him. "I can't believe I nearly lost you again. How did you survive this?"

"I was taught by the best...Jadon and—" I point to Samson. I shudder and he holds me closer. I let him for a moment and then pull away. "Call Jadon. I need the doctor to check me out again."

"What's going on, Ava?" He puts his hands on my shoulders, looking into my eyes and trying to gauge the level of crazy.

"How was he able to find us? There's something still inside me that is leading them straight to us and I don't believe Samson is working alone. I'm not the one they want to kill...they just want to keep controlling me so I'll kill Jadon." I pull at my skin, my eyes filling with tears. "I've still had dizzy spells and the nausea. Last night I couldn't sleep, I was so dizzy. Get it out," I yell at him.

"Okay, love," he says, his hand on my face. "Let's get out of here and Jadon can send a jet to another location. You don't need to be around this any longer."

I nod and Gentry makes a few phone calls. Frederick comes around the back of the house with our luggage. Gentry pulls clothes out for me and helps me get dressed, and we get into the car without saying another word.

Gentry drives to an open field about ten miles from the house and we wait for an hour before a jet lands in front of us. We get on the jet and fly back to Farrow. I feel like I want to crawl out of my skin and set it on fire.

I'm fevered and talking nonsense by the time we get home. I hear myself and know that I sound crazy, but I can't stop myself. It pours out of me and I only wish I could shut up so Gentry wouldn't look so afraid.

I hear him talking to Jadon and the doctor and explaining that he thinks there are more devices in me. I don't even bother to rationalize the situation to myself. It's too much. I don't understand how it's all happening, I just know it is, and if anything is left in my body for another day, either I'll combust or I'll make sure someone else does.

I barely hear the doctor as he tells me he's going to put me under. He's seen something in the scan that looks unusual and is going to blah-blah-blah. My eyes blur together and I can't make out another word. It all jumbles together and my eyes roll back.

When I wake up, I'm still hot, but I don't feel as desperate. In fact, I wonder what had me so worked up. I can barely remember what I was ranting about, and chalk it up to being traumatized over seeing Samson and the Watcher again.

I remember feeling sad that Samson was dead, but I don't feel that way now. I blink rapidly, my eyes clearing, and I see Gentry and the doctor huddled in the corner with Jadon.

"What's going on?" I croak.

"I was able to get all of the devices out," the doctor says. He holds up a bowl and shakes it and the rattle of little plastic trackers or whatever they are makes a racket.

"There were six of them. It's a wonder you haven't rejected them before now. I believe your body was starting to more and more. It's why you had such a high fever. Most of them were tracking devices, but one was administering small doses of a hallucinogen."

That hits me like a jolt...and also makes sense. "Are you sure you got all of them?" I ask.

"Yes. I've checked multiple times. We didn't do a full-body scan when you first got home and we should have. Now we've done two and the second time, there was nothing left."

I close my eyes and let my mind drift over everything that's happened. It feels like it happened to another person.

"How do you feel?" Gentry asks, taking my hand.

"Like my mind is finally one hundred percent my own," I admit. "I didn't realize how foggy I still was until I woke up just now and felt free of it." My voice breaks and I squeeze his hand harder. "I'm sorry I led all of that danger straight to us—I should've said exactly how I felt, I just didn't know...I had times of feeling normal and it was just all so confusing."

"Don't you dare apologize. You are the strongest woman I know. You singlehandedly saved yourself out there in that house. I don't know anyone I'd feel safer with than you," he says, his voice light and teasing.

I open my eyes and grin at him. "Damn straight you're safe with me. Anyone dare mess with you and I will take him *down*." My tone sobers when I think about the lives I've taken. I never dreamed I would be responsible for ending a life, and now I've ended three. "As soon as I'm better, I want to get out of here and live the simplest life we can live. Somewhere we can get home quickly if we need to, but where no one knows our names or cares about who we are… someplace safe and free and where I won't ever take anyone's life again."

"You saved yourself. You'd never take a life if your life or someone you loved wasn't in danger."

I press my lips together and look between Gentry and Jadon. "I would do anything for the two of you…and Eden. Anything." I clasp Jadon's hand. "I don't think this is over — someone is coming after you. Their plan didn't work with me, but it's not over."

Jadon's eyes pierce me as he grips my hand tighter and nods. "Don't worry about me anymore, little one. You get better and I'll be okay. I'll watch my back. And I know I'd be safe with you around—you're better than my three best men, for goodness' sake," he teases. "But I know you want to be free of this, and I want that for you more than anything. I've been talking to Gentry about a place you could go. Heal, rest, take as long as you want…you guys can talk it over, but I've sent a security team to check it out in case it sounds tempting. It's a little island off of Zegue, not as far from here as it sounds. I'd feel better if you were far from here for whatever is about to go down…with your mother… with this threat on my life…it would give me peace if you're safe elsewhere."

"I like the sound of this place, but I don't like the thought of leaving you."

"You know I'll drive you crazy with video chats every chance I get." Jadon laughs. "And I've more than tripled the security here. I'll be fine. You know I can handle myself."

"I'll think about it," I promise him.

When I've regained some of my strength, I pay a visit to my mother. She has been scanned now and is free of the devices that were in her; however, her brainwashing went further than mine ever did, so I want to see for myself how she's doing.

"You look well," I say when I see her. Her hair is down and curly, and she looks as beautiful as Eden sitting in the bright blue chair.

"You do too, dear," she says, hugging me. "Although this hair is dreadful on you. You'll grow it out, won't you?"

"I don't know. Gentry says it makes me look more badass than ever. You know I've always been a sucker for that." I grin when she wrinkles her nose.

"When will I get out of here?" she asks. "Why are you walking around freely and I'm still like a bird in a cage?"

"Because I didn't attempt to kill Jadon and you did."

"But you thought about it," she says, her eyes lighting with a fervor that makes me uncomfortable.

"Yes, I did, but I gained my wits and blocked those thoughts out. You embraced them and fired a gun at him; there's a difference."

"The difference is minimal at best."

"I didn't come to argue with you, Mother. I came to tell you I'm leaving for a while. Please get well and take the therapy seriously. It's important. We need to have you back to yourself. I miss you."

"I miss you too, and I assure you I'm myself. I don't need therapy...I need to get out of here...where is Eden?"

"Eden is in Niaps with her husband."

"It's like you've both deserted me." She puts her head in her hands and sobs. "I don't understand how you could turn your back on me like this."

I back away from her and put my hand on the doorknob. "I'll be back to visit you when I return. Please get better. I'm worried about you."

She starts yelling about Jadon keeping her locked in a cage and I get out of there, my heart heavy.

Later that night, I tell Jadon not to let her go…no matter what she says. It's not safe for him if she's free.

GENTRY

The morning we leave for Zegue is a crystal clear, sunny day. It's been two weeks since Ava's surgery and she has been stir-crazy since day three. She wanted to leave a week ago and we talked her into one more week of recovery in Farrow. She's had video chats with all of her friends in Niaps and I've even talked with some of them, the conversation with Toph definitely being the most awkward.

"So you and Mr. Barrington," I heard him saying as I walked past.

"We met before school started and didn't start going out right away," Ava insisted. "Although I wanted to more than anything…he was trying to do the right thing."

"So why didn't he wait until you graduated to get in your pants?"

"Hey!" I said, walking over and sticking my head next to hers. "Watch how you talk to her, yeah?"

Toph looked repentant but also indignant and I sighed.

"I should've handled things better than I did, but I love this girl and did from the moment I met her. Waiting until she was legal was the best I could do and I won't apologize for it anymore."

"Yeah, right, you waited until she was legal," he said with a smirk. "Now that I think about it, you did eye me like you were jealous half the time."

"I did wait, and yeah, I did eye you like I was jealous. You could openly flaunt your crush for the whole world to see and I had to hide my feelings every day. Fuck yeah, I was envious of that."

Toph flushed but also backed down.

"Are you guys done with your pissing contest?" Ava asked and Toph and I both laughed.

The last few times they've talked, he's asked to talk to me too and I'm glad that it makes Ava happy to have her friends back in her life, albeit long-distance.

I grab the last bag and check the bathroom to make sure we're not forgetting anything. When I walk downstairs, Ava is hugging Jadon, and Eden has come to see us off.

"The minute you see anything suspicious or miss home or just need a change of scenery, you come to Niaps or Farrow or Yuman...or call...or I don't know..." Eden sighs. "Are you sure you want to leave?"

Ava hugs her and laughs. "I need this. I don't know how long we'll be gone, but I've had the itch to travel for as long as I can remember. I'll make sure to come and see you guys as much as I can, I swear it. Especially if you give me a niece or nephew," she says, pinching Eden's cheek.

"Well, that's not happening anytime soon, so I better be enough to draw you back," Eden sasses back.

When we've said all the goodbyes we can take, we all walk outside to where the jet is waiting. Frederick and Jerome are on the plane already, the guard and my former investigator glaring at each other like they've already had time to know they hate one another. They sit on opposite sides of the plane and I lead Ava to the seats in the back, as far as we can get from their foul juju.

"One day there will be no guards, no need for security, just the two of us out on the open road…or the open sky," she says, smiling out the window.

"Let's pretend like it's just us now," I say, buckling my seat belt.

"I can do that. I'd rather do that in the bedroom, though." She lifts an eyebrow and tilts her head back.

"Are you suggesting we christen the bedroom?" I ask. "I thought maybe we should still take it easy on you…your body has been through so—"

She covers my mouth with her hand. "If you take it any easier on my body, I'm going to die of sex starvation. Honestly, Barrington, I know that you're older than me, but you cannot start acting like an old man before the age of twenty-six. Dude, live it up. I know I'm the emotionally mature one in this relationship, but you need to find your inner child and get a little dangerous."

I undo her seat belt and pull her onto my lap, holding her ass in my hands and grinding into her, wishing we were naked. "Dangerous, huh?"

"If that's what you heard out of all that, I am one happy girl," she says, pressing her body closer to mine.

Ava

Zegue is exactly what we needed. We get off the plane so starved from teasing one another that we don't even make it to the bed before ripping each other's clothes off. I don't know the first thing about what Zegue looks like yet, or this house we're staying in, but I know Gentry has claimed me three times before we even see a bed.

"This is going to be the best adventure I've ever been on," I tell him, rolling my hips as I ride him.

We're on the floor in the—I look around...what is this, the laundry room? How did we get here?

"We should let your family know we've made it," Gentry pants, a bead of sweat rolling back into his hair.

"I hardly think they want to know we've made it this many times...or at all, for that matter. TMI."

"I meant that we made it to Zegue," he says, laughing. He flips us over and gets serious about things. "Let me hear you scream. I don't think you were loud enough the last few times."

"You're not working hard enough, you're still talking," I tease and start meeting him thrust for thrust, harder and harder.

He groans and neither of us can talk for a long time. My eyes roll back in my head and I let out incoherent screams that turn Gentry into a machine. I'll have to be careful about calling him an old man. He's about to wear me out and it's only the first day of the rest of our lives.

"Where do you think you'll want to go next?" he asks when we've been in Zegue for a couple of months.

"How about we try a big city next? Go between isolation and civilization so we're fully cultured when all is said and done. How does that sound?"

"As long as we're together, I'm there." He leans over and kisses me and I bask in the feeling.

He is where I want to always be. The locations can change and I won't really care, just as long as he's there.

We drive with the stars casting shimmery light over the ocean until we find a place for a picnic. It's our last night in Zegue. Gentry hasn't told me where we're heading next—it's a surprise. He pulls out a blanket and the basket we packed, and together, we find the perfect spot. There are a million stars out tonight; they almost look fake, they're so bright, and the full moon gives us the perfect moody light.

We stare at the sky for a while and sip champagne. I lean back against Gentry's chest and feel total peace.

I gasp and Gentry laughs as we both sit up straighter.

"Did you see that?" I tap his chest, hoping he saw the shooting star.

"Hard to miss, I thought it was going to fall right on us."

"Did you make a wish?" My hand finds his.

"I wished for a lifetime of starry nights like this one, a lifetime of sunny or snowy days, it doesn't matter…just as long as they're next to you."

I sigh, my heart pounding over his sweet words.

"I wished for a dog," I say it with my most serious voice but can't hold in the laugh. "I'm kidding…my wish was just as romantic as yours—I wished that this would never end, me and you."

"Well, that's easy."

"Do you ever wish you were in Niaps teaching sociology…or living up your title as prince?" I twist around to look at him.

He grins. "And miss this here with you? Not even a little bit. This is a dream I didn't even know I had, this life we're creating together. You're it for me, Princess Ava."

"Ava, just Ava," I whisper. "You're it for me too, Gentry. I'll love you from kingdom to kingdom…for an eternity."

"From this eternity to the next."

He kisses me and we forget about the food and stars and wishes until much later.

This adventure just keeps getting better.

Want more Kingdoms of Sin? The final book, Pride, is Jadon's story.

Read on for a sneak peek and get Pride here!
https://geni.us/prideWA

PRIDE PROLOGUE

JADON, AGE SIX

I bundle under the fur, as close as I can get to Mum while she sleeps. She's been sleeping a long time now and her body is cold. Usually we get warm when we cuddle, and sometimes we chat under the blanket, but she's quiet and I'm tired of lying here. I'm tired of being cold too.

Miss Lang raps on the door and I poke my head out of the blanket when she yells out, "Hurry, boy, it's cold out here."

I scramble to the door and fling it open, letting Lang come inside.

She comes to a quick stop when she sees Mum lying under the fur and puts her hand to her mouth as it opens in a silent scream. Her expression is confusing and I put my hand on her arm.

"What's the matter, Miss Lang?"

She clutches my shoulders and looks in my eyes. "You poor boy. When did she pass?"

"What...do you mean?" My face crumbles when tears start running down her face. I hate it when Mum or Miss Lang cries. "What's the matter?"

She wails louder and holds me to her chest, and I start

sniffling too. I'm cold and tired and it's been quiet too long. The last thing I want is a wailing Miss Lang.

"You poor, poor boy," she repeats and I sigh, wiping my nose.

"You're going to wake Mother if you're not careful," I finally say.

"Your mother is dead, child. She's gone and I'm so, so sorry that she won't be coming back."

I take a deep breath and stare at my mother for a few moments, willing her to open her eyes.

"She's not gone! She's right there!" I run to my mother and hold her hand up. It feels strange and flops back down by her side. My eyes widen as I try to shake her awake. "Mum, wake up! Wake up!"

She lies there as still as can be and I lean into her neck and cry until I can't cry any more.

***

Miss Lang takes me to her house, dragging me out of mine, kicking and screaming.

"I can't leave Mum! She said we stick together, no matter what." I've said it in every way possible and still, Miss Lang insists that I cannot stay with Mum in our cottage any longer.

"It's time for Mum to go to heaven. We will have a funeral for her and say goodbye then," she says. "I need to get in touch with your family, you poor boy."

I want to tell her to stop calling me that, but it doesn't matter, Mum will make her stop when I see her again. Mum *is* my family, the only family I've got.

"I want to see Mum," I repeat, as we walk into her dark place. I step over things on the floor and rub my arms as I try to get warm.

"You won't be seeing her again, child. I know you don't understand it now, but your mum is gone."

***

A few nights later, I meet a man whose hand trembles when he reaches out to shake mine.

"I'm Neil," he says.

His eyes are kind. When I shake his hand, I feel safer than I've felt since leaving Mum in our house.

"I'm so sorry I didn't know." His head bows and he presses his fingers to his eyes. When he lifts his eyes again, his eyes are wet and he looks sad. I frown at him and he pats my shoulder. "I didn't know about you until now or I would've been here sooner," he says. "Jadon, I'm your father, and I will take good care of you, I promise."

I swallow hard. I feel like crying. I miss Mum more than anything, but I've always wanted a dad. She told me it was just us though. I don't understand how I have a dad now, but I really want to go with him, so I don't say anything. He pats my shoulder again and takes a steadying breath.

"Are you ready to go to your new home? Your sisters will be excited to have a big brother."

"I've always asked Mum for a sister," I say excitedly. "How many are there?"

"There are two. One is a few years younger than you and the other is just a baby, but you'll like her too. Even though all she does is cry and smile." He laughs and I do too.

I can't believe I have a family. I run and get the bear I have and the little bag Miss Lang put my clothes in and rush to my father.

I still can't believe I have one.

***

It takes a long time to get to my father's house. I fall asleep against his shoulder a few times on the way. And when we arrive, it's the biggest house I've ever seen. A *castle*.

I feel so nervous as I walk inside, holding Father's hand. A little girl runs up to me and holds out her doll. I smile and when I don't take the doll from her, she waves it in my face until I do. When it's in my hand, she snatches it back and runs circles around me.

"This is Eden. Someone is sure happy to meet you," Father says.

A woman walks in, holding a baby and I stare at her. She's beautiful and tall and the baby is so cute. I smile and the woman doesn't smile back, looking at my father. She stares at him for a few moments but doesn't say anything, instead turning around and walking out of the room with the baby.

"Katherine and Ava," Father says. "She'll come around. It'll just…take time," he says under his breath.

Eden waves her doll in my face again and I start a game of peekaboo behind the doll, forgetting all about the woman and baby.

During the night, I hear the baby crying and leave my room to find her. I'm a little scared because Father tucked me in and I shouldn't be out of bed, but I find baby Ava's room not far from mine. I go inside and she's in her crib wailing. I look around, but no one else comes, so I reach over and hold onto her little hand with mine. She stares up at me, eyes wide, and I sing a little song Mum always sang to me. She quietens and even smiles a little smile before eventually drifting off to sleep.

I fall asleep lying on the floor by her crib, just in case

she cries again. I don't want her to feel like she's alone, the way I do without Mum.

PRIDE CHAPTER 1

JADON

Chapter One

I go visit Katherine. She's being watched in the cottage to the east side of our property. She claims to be a bird in a cage, that I'm locking her up to torture her and to put her in her place. If I was that kind of person, I would've done it as soon as I became king.

Katherine Safrin has hated me since the day I came to live in her house. I'm the illegitimate son of her husband, and as much as she loved him, she never forgave him for the affair he had while he was away at war for two years. Apparently my mother never forgave him either, because he went back to his wife once the war was over. She never told him about me, and until the day he died, he did everything in his power to make sure I knew how much he loved me, to make up for those formative years in my life when I didn't have a father.

Katherine isn't locked up because I hate her. I've never hated her—I've been *hurt* by her...there's a big difference—but I don't trust her right now. It's been a month since she tried to kill me and while I know it wasn't strictly her fault —she was kidnapped, given heavy hallucinogens, and hypnotized nightly with orders to kill me. My sister, Ava, also underwent the same brain- washing and she tried to *save* me when Katherine shot me.

To me the difference is clear and profound: Ava loves me and could never really hurt me, and my stepmother would love nothing more than to see me dead.

So yes, I do feel the need to supervise her recovery process a little longer, despite her manipulative attempts for freedom. The whole ordeal has been exhausting, not to mention an emotional lapse into the insecurity I felt growing up with Katherine as my stepmother. It also feels like a distraction from what I should be focusing on: who was behind her kidnapping? And who is still out there waiting for the right moment to kill me?

There are probably too many to count, but one was brave enough to kidnap my mother and my sister…both not in Farrow at the time, although that does little to ease my concerns over security since both Ava and our mother snuck back into the house without detection.

I'm walking along the path to the door, bracing myself for whatever mood Katherine will be in when my phone rings.

It's a number I don't recognize and I'm tempted to ignore it, but with my sister having been kidnapped before, I'm on the paranoid side and rarely avoid calls. Not many get past my team anyway, so if my phone rings, it's usually important.

There's always a small amount of fear that Ava will be taken again and that would put me in the ground. If anything happened to either of my sisters, I may as well take my sword to my gut and be done with it.

Enough morbidity, answer the damn phone.

"Jadon Safrin speaking."

"As in King Jadon?" An amused raspy feminine voice that sounds like feathers mixed with claws catches me by surprise.

"Who's asking?"

"This is Delilah Farthing."

"Delilah," my voice lilts at the end, "I was beginning to think you were merely a signature at the end of your family's endless emails getting *out* of meetings."

"Touché. I assure you, I'm more than a signature."

She sounds playful and I have to say, it surprises me. Her family has been an endless headache to my peace of mind.

"To what do I owe this surprise?"

"I think it's time we meet…somewhere neutral. Perhaps Ivalis or Grawlan?"

"What makes this time different? Forgive my bluntness, but I don't have time for another no-show." Every nerve in my body is on alert as I wait to hear her response. What are the Farthings up to now?

"My father is in remission, so I am freer than I've been in some time. However, I'd like to keep our meeting between us, if that's okay with you. Tensions are still… shall we say, to the ceiling? I don't know about you, but I love my kingdom and want to keep it in one piece. Something tells me you feel the same about yours."

"Is this a trick, Delilah? Because it seems to me, nothing would explode negotiations between our kingdoms more than your father finding out about us meeting behind his back."

"I'll put it this way: you don't *want* my father or my

cousin, Caulder, knowing about our meeting. What I have to say is between me and you. Can you be discreet?"

I squeeze my forehead with my thumb and forefinger and look up at the blue sky. This could be a death trap I'm walking into, but it's a risk I'll have to take.

"Full of intrigue, Princess Delilah. Yes, I can be discreet. Question is, can you?"

"Ivalis day after tomorrow, noon, at the Cave of Stars. I'll be alone. Don't make me regret this…oh, and King?"

"Yes?"

"Watch your back."

Shit. What kind of game is this?

"Always do," I respond, my tone chilly. "I'll see you in Ivalis."

***

I walk into my stepmother's room already in a suspicious mood after that troubling conversation with Delilah. I'm distracted but on guard and when she glares at me as I enter, I try to tamp down the resentment that has steadily grown toward Katherine. I've tried to be kind to her, tried to understand why she hated me when I became old enough to know how my father's infidelity must have hurt what seemed to be a flawless relationship…I've even tried to not care. But it all comes down to the simple fact that I have longed for a mother since the day my own died, and Katherine will never want to fill that role.

Today when her upper lip sneers as I sit down across from her, starting our chess game where we last left off, I brace my heart for the rejection. You'd think I'd be a stone-cold wall of defense by now, but that doesn't seem to be my way.

"Hello, Mother. You're looking especially lovely today."

"I look dreadful and you know it. Now is not the time for false praise."

"I assure you, when it comes to your beauty, there is no such thing as false praise. Your attitude, however, is another thing altogether." I attempt a light tone, but when I make a move she doesn't like on the chessboard, she growls and I groan. It's hard work, being around her. Some days I wonder why I try.

"Let me out of here and I will be sweet as pie," she says, her lips curling into more of a grin than a sneer. It still rings fake.

"Still feel like killing me?" I cross my arms as I wait for her move. One of the guards in the room clears his throat and sounds like he's trying to cover a laugh. I shoot him a look. "Glad I can be your comic relief," I say dryly.

He bows his head, pinching his lips together. "The days are long, King Jadon." His voice is apologetic, but I hear his desperation.

Her doctors think she's been clear of the effects of the hallucinogens for a while, but the hypnosis she went through is another matter. Her hatred of me makes it even harder to determine. My guards are ready for more exciting work spent somewhere other than these four walls watching the Queen Mother every day, but I don't know what to tell them.

I stand abruptly, shoving the chair back and then righting it when it almost falls backward. "I'll be seeing you, Mother."

"Jadon?" She stands too and one of the guards moves closer to her, so she can't make a move toward me without running into him.

"Yes?"

"Let me out of here and I will feel less like killing you."

I smile and her eyes flash. "As always, it's been an experience. Good day, everyone."

I step out of the cottage and it's like a thousand pounds immediately lift.

Duty #4,528 of a king's day completed.

***

I'm almost to the door of the castle, my guards a nice distance away. They knew by my mood when I left Mother to let me have extra space. A pitiful whine stops me in my tracks and I turn around, looking everywhere for the source. I don't see anything right away but move toward the sound. Under a tree sits a beautiful white dog, its large paw caught in a trap.

I get closer and she whimpers. "What have you gotten yourself into?" I ask, bending down. I carefully work on the trap, taking care to not hurt her in the process. When it finally releases, she licks my hand and face. "Oh my. Okay, that's enough. You're welcome." I laugh. Her paw is a bloody mess and I slowly pick her up. "You're quite heavy," I groan and it looks like she's smiling when she licks my face again.

I step out of the clearing and walk toward the house. "See that she's taken to the vet right away, please," I tell Quincie, one of the guards. "I'll take her to my office while you make arrangements."

"Sir, the dog is bleeding," Quincie says.

"Yes, I'm aware of that." I laugh. "My hands are covered in said blood."

"I just mean…do you really want to mess your office?"

"Let me worry about that. Just please move quickly. I don't want this pup to suffer more than she already has."

I hurry to the office and pull a blanket off of the chair, setting it on the floor before carefully laying the dog on it.

She looks up at me eagerly, her tail thumping loudly on the floor.

"I'm not getting attached until you get a clean bill of health," I tell her, rolling my eyes at how cute she is, even a complete mess.

When Quincie comes in a few minutes later and carries the dog out, I already miss her.

A sure sign that life as a king is not all it's cracked up to be. From death threats and meetings with future queens and murderous stepmothers to a gaping hole in my chest where the loneliness constantly resides…this is my reality.

ACKNOWLEDGMENTS

Huge thanks to Christine Estevez, my assistant and beta and life coach and dear friend that I never want to live without!

Thank you to Brower Literary for believing in me.

Thank you to my spectacular betas for keeping me on track: Jennifer Mirabelli, Tosha Khoury, Christine Bowden, Darla Williams, and Vicki Cuic.

Thank you to my friends and family for keeping me sane.

Thank you to the bloggers out there who tirelessly share my work. I'm so grateful for you!

And thank you to every reader who gives my books a chance.

I love you all!

ABOUT THE AUTHOR .

Willow Aster is a USA Today Bestselling author and lover of anything book-related. She lives in St. Paul, MN with her husband, kids, rescue dog, and grandcat.

For ARCs, please join my master list: https://bit.ly/3CMKz5y

For behind-the-scenes of my books and freebies every month, sign up for my newsletter: http://www.willowaster.com/newsletter

www.willowaster.com

ALSO BY WILLOW ASTER

Standalones

True Love Story

Fade to Red

In the Fields

Maybe Maby (also available on all retailer sites)

Lilith (also available on all retailer sites)

Miles Apart (also available on all retailer sites)

Falling in Eden

Standalones with Interconnected Characters

Summertime

Autumn Nights

Landmark Mountain Series

Unforgettable

Someday

Irresistible

Falling

Stay

Kingdoms of Sin Series

Downfall

Exposed

Ruin

Pride

FOLLOW ME